Scholar-Ship-Bound

A novel by K.S. Riggin

Book 1 of the Shaarvan Series

Table of Contents

Main Characters & Places in the Shaarvan Series

Altar: Original home of the Shapechanger

Baltoff: the Old One on Westla who was manufacturing the drugs that Thenos used to overthrow the government of Altar.

Barquel: The main god worshipped on Freinana

Blair: Owner of the Landoor ranch. Good guy.

Brala: Shaara's friend on Westla

Chaslow: Shapechanger working for Thenos, blew up nursery on Westla & hunted for Shaara

Clofa: one of Altar's two moons. It was where the old Shapechanger liked to retire. Thenos blew it up.

Crimson Black: The horse-like landoor Shaara befriends

Flar: Freinana housemaster that Shaara stays with. Husband of Frieda

Flaorth: A tracker implant which Shapechanger insert under the skin of females for identification purposes.

Frieda: Freinana housemistress that Shaara stays with. Wife of Flar

Goria: Pseudo wife of Pathe. Former lover of Shaarvan. Bad person

Isandor: The commoner who owns Shaara on Freinana. Bad guy

Landoor: An animal that looks like a horse

Mandar: A landoor the Guardians bought Shaara on Westla

Megloztar: Theinian slaver who kidnaps Shaara

Parthrol: An Old One who lived on the former moon. He was thought to have known an antidote for what poisoned Tevor and the other Council members.

Pathe: Son of Tevor & Teea (brother of Shaarvan & Thenos) Doctor, good guy

Saberey: Symbol of the Shapechanger & their origin

Shaara: College student. Wife of Shaarvan and later Stegthal (Thal) Renamed numerous times: Susan, Sletttha, Sleena, Skeva, Thalia, Thenosa

Shaarac: (**Thaarac, Thenon**) Shaara and Shaarvan's son
Shaarvan: Steals his wife, Shaara, from a college campus, Altarian Shapechanger
Skeva: Name given to Shaara on Freinana
Sleena: Name given to Shaara on Freinana
Slettha: Slaver's name for Shaara on Freinana
Spelon: One of Shaara's guardians. Shapechanger Warrior
Starnkor: Teea's Second Husband
Stegthal: (**Thal**) He becomes Shaara's Second Husband. Good & bad
Stubra: The small goat-donkey animal found on Deathstar. They were mostly used to carry loads but were friendly creatures that Shaara and Shaarac treated as pets.
Susan: Shaara's original Earth name
Targone: Shapechanger who arrives on Freinana to verify that Shaara is Shapechanger
Teea: Shaarvan's mother, lives on Altar, wife of Tevor (and later Starnkor)
Tem: Head of Westla, Uncle to Shaarvan, Tevor's brother
Temina: Wife of Tem, mentally unstable
Tenor: One of Shaara's guardians. Shapechanger Warrior
Tessa: High Priestess
Tevor: Shaarvan's father, lives on Altar, husband of Teea
Thal: Stegthal's name on Deathstar
Thalia: Shaara's name on Deathstar
Thandar: Shaara & Thal's son
Thedar: One of Shaara's guardians. Shapechanger Warrior
Theinian: Another species, usually slavers and most often gay
Thenos: Son of Tevor & Teea (brother of Shaarvan & Pathe) Bad guy
Tren: Owner of the casino and of Shaara. Good guy to Shaara
Tura: Westlan Priestess who flies to Altar with Shaara
Westla: Huge artificial satellite. Only Shapechanger may go there or girls and servants

Additional Terminology:

Tide: Approximately one Earth day. Tides are usually grouped, as in a five Tide, twentyTide, etc.

Pass: Approximately a year. A halfPass and quarterPass are common expressions.

Shapechanger: Never found in the plural. The Shapechanger are an artificially derived species that are capable of shape change, most often as a Saberey (tiger-like cat), This also includes many sensory improvements and abilities.

The Names of Shapechanger: Names beginning with T or S denote Power. Those Shapechanger are deemed Lords. Formal testing on Westla ranks them.

Warrior Shapechanger: Those who meet qualifications of specific battle readiness. Ranking is by formal tests on Westla.

Priestess: Females who have achieved a ranking on Westla denoting their ability to stand up against Shapechanger Power. Always capitalized.

Chapter One
Scholarship Interview

Susan

I desperately needed this scholarship. The one I'd been counting on didn't receive the funding they expected. Their slip-up left me desperate. Registration fees and the cost of my semester's books took most of my savings, and I scarcely had enough left to pay dorm fees. My job and the money the government sent me helped, but without a scholarship, I'd be in big financial trouble.

Which is why I so desperately needed this *new* scholarship. I'd filled out at least five different forms for it. No other application asked so many personal questions, and the last questionnaire had been really bizarre. Why would a scholarship ask applicants to write about what they'd do if they were transplanted to a desert environment or were suddenly forced to live in a bubble under the sea?

I was a fair writer. My imagination had come up with several ideas about surviving in odd locations. I had my fingers crossed that the scholarship committee liked my writing, and they had called me back for a second screening.

So, as I walked into the school auditorium, I felt great about my chances . . . until I saw about two hundred women sitting around waiting for their turn at the interview portion. I paused at the threshold, looked down the aisle, and searched faces. Were all the women as desperate as I? How many scholarships was the *Women's Promotional Foundation* offering?

I spotted an empty chair, plopped into it, and prepared to wait. Resting my elbows on the armrests of the seat, I glanced about but found it hard to concentrate on doing any kind of headcount. The sound of the gum chewer in front of me was irritating. The girl kept blowing a hefty pink bubble, leaning her head back, then shooting it upwards like a smoker working on a smoke ring. Each time the wad was full enough to pop, the girl coolly stabbed it with one of her crimson nails.

I thought about saying something, but it would have been silly. The girl had every right to chew gum. It was my fault for being bothered by it.

A moment later, the girl next to me, Shannon, she said her name was, started talking. "This is the final screening, you know. I'm sooo nervous. Imagine having to go talk to the officials *in person.*"

Shannon's eyes did a quick examination of me as she nervously tweaked her hair. Apparently, I passed her inspection because she whispered the next bit of information as if she suspected someone might be listening.

"I hear this scholarship is being sponsored by a rich company needing the publicity. I was told that whoever they are, they have oodles of money and are searching for just the *right* women to make them look good. It should be a piece of cake for *us*, know what I mean?"

Actually, I had no idea what Shannon meant, but my hopes went up a little. I liked the sound of "oodles of money."

All around us, girls sat talking, fidgeting, reading books or studying. I wished I'd brought my history notes. I didn't have time to waste. Why hadn't I thought to bring something? I could have finished the reading for psych class.

Shannon kept on talking. "Loosen up, girl. You remind me of my kid sister. She figures an undone button is a crime. Do you think she's going to get a scholarship when she goes to college? No way. You gotta give a little *oom papa*. You know?"

Shannon was showing lots of *oom papa*. Her dress dipped low in the bodice, and it was obvious she wasn't wearing a bra. The skirt of her outfit had a slit that displayed slim thighs. I wanted to dislike her . . . she was everything I wasn't . . . but her smile looked friendly, and her cheerfulness felt contagious.

She stopped talking a moment as the official behind the microphone began to call out names. The designated girls lined up at the front, were checked off one-by-one from the man's list, and then a few of them headed back behind the stage curtain. Strangely, it looked like some of the girls were rejected. You could tell by the way their faces looked as they walked toward the exit behind us. Why had they been told to show up today if they weren't in the running? Had there been some kind of mix-up?

"See what I mean?" Shannon said, jabbing her elbow into my side. "Notice any ugly women going behind the curtain? The scholarship committee is only taking pretty girls. It's just like I said."

I began comparing the retreating applicants to the ones still in the line-up. A girl covered with crimson tattoos strode angrily up the aisle. Her eyes glared right and left. She looked ready to spit . . . or to sock the first person who looked at her. I shifted my glance back to the front.

Shannon elbowed me to get my attention. "My sister's *a brain*," Shannon said. "Are you?"

I shook my head and turned to look at her. "I get good grades, sure, but I'm not that smart." I sighed and thought about how I wished I were. For a moment, I heard a memory of my father's voice, "You got the smarts, kiddo, to be whomever or whatever you want." He used to say that all the time, his form of encouragement whenever the going got tough, but stuff like that didn't count. Parents always believed their child to be the smartest, prettiest, and most capable of all.

Yet, Shannon couldn't be right about needing to be a beauty queen. Scholarship committees didn't reject people based on how applicants looked. There were laws about such things. Weren't there?

Six more girls walked onto the stage and passed behind the curtain. Four returned, walking back toward us and out the entrance. They looked angry. One of them was crying. Shannon had correctly predicted in every case which girls would be rejected and which ones would continue on through the curtain.

I began to worry more. If the scholarship people wanted only perfect candidates, would I qualify? Maybe I'd worn the wrong dress. Did my shoes look cheap? They were only plastic, but I'd thought they'd be OK for an interview. My hair wasn't very stylish, either. I hadn't had time or money to get the split ends cut.

Shannon didn't seem worried. She was smiling like someone had invited her to a party. I wished I were as confident as she.

It didn't take much to keep Shannon talking. She babbled on and on about her little sister, the brain. Why did Shannon think I resembled her sister? Was it because of the way I looked? Did I look like a "brain"?

I nodded occasionally when Shannon paused, cleared my throat, and spoke when I thought I was supposed to answer her, but mainly, I continued watching as the auditorium slowly emptied.

"You're serious, just like my sister," Shannon continued. "I bet you're a good student. She gets straight A's. You got better looks, though, than my sister. She's stuck in her role. You could . . ."

"Shannon Gray," the announcer called out.

Shannon stood. "That's me. Good luck, Susan," she said. "I hope you and I **both** get this scholarship. Don't forget now, the committee wants women who will make them look good. You got to show a little leg when you go up there, Susan."

I whispered, "Good luck," and watched as Shannon left. It was hard to believe she could be nervous; she looked perfectly poised as she walked toward the stage. She turned once and waved back at me. I copied the gesture, then noted how her leather shoes looked expensive.

When Shannon reached the man who'd been doing the announcing of names, I could tell she was flirting with him. She was tossing her hair about teasingly and smiling up at him with the little twist of the neck some girls have down perfectly. The guy smiled back. The two of them continued to chat for a couple of minutes, ignoring all the other girls waiting in line. I wondered if the man was asking Shannon for a date. Maybe he was promising to put in a good word with the scholarship committee. Shannon was sure to win. It was probably pointless for me to sit and wait for my turn.

I glanced down at my clothing and brushed at a speck of lint. I'd worn my favorite dress — navy and white, with a splash of red in the pocket. It wasn't anything expensive, not like the outfit Shannon was wearing. Hers had probably cost a couple hundred dollars, not counting the designer shoes and the little purse hanging from her shoulder with the name "Lane Bersher" on it.

My dress was only polyester knit, the kind of thing you could toss into the washer and it would still come out looking good. Tina, one of my roommates, always sneered at such dresses. She said anything you could wash, faded and looked old quickly. She didn't even put blue jeans in the washing machine but paid to have them dry-cleaned.

I sighed and watched as the gum chewer in front of me stood up, then squeezed through the row of empty chairs and girls who sat, still waiting their turns. The chewer's hair looked shaggy, and I thought her dress was too tight, but she was pretty. Would the committee accept her? As if she felt my eyes on her, the girl turned and glared. Once more, her gum blew outward, forming a perfect light bulb before collapsing inward. She turned to stride haughtily down towards the announcer.

I wondered how Shannon was doing. She'd been one of the ones to go through the curtain. Was she being interviewed now?

I shifted my legs and accidentally scuffed one of my shoes. They were new. I'd bought them for the interview at a discount store. I licked my finger and rubbed at the spot. Sure, the shoes were cheap plastic, but you couldn't't tell. They were a perfect match for the red decoration in the corner pocket of my dress.

The gum chewer was talking to the checkpoint man. He held up a small garbage can and made her spit out her gum. She passed his screening and walked on through the curtains. Maybe it didn't matter if you weren't perfect. I felt relieved.

But the checkpoint man wasn't our interviewer. Maybe it was later when a polyester dress and plastic shoes would matter. I sighed and shifted in my chair. The chair's padding was not very thick. I stood up and stretched, then sat back down.

It was too late to change my dress into something different. Besides, I had nothing in my dorm room closet that would be any better. I started worrying about what Shannon had said. My outfit *was* pretty unrevealing. I looked down. The dress was pleated, which meant when I sat down, the skirt had room to flare over my legs. I hated dresses with the tendency to inch up, showing your thighs whenever you moved. I never wore tight skirts or short, short ones.

But, maybe Shannon was right; I was too conservative . . . still, I wanted to be an elementary school teacher, not a Playboy bunny. Just for fun, I played with the skirt of my dress, flapping it about to show a little leg.

A glance at my watch told me I'd been in the auditorium for close to an hour. How much longer would this take? When would they call me?

All around me, I saw vacated seats. I glanced at the remaining applicants. There were a lot of half-buttoned tops and slinky skirts with slits up the side. I guess most of the girls agreed with Shannon. Had I worn something too old-fashioned?

Another group of names was called. A girl with a ring on her nose and spiked hair walked up to the announcer. Would she be rejected? The official started shaking his head at her. I think he indicated she shouldn't't stay, but the girl began to argue at full screech. Her middle finger rose up and taunted him. Everyone was watching.

A second man came through the curtains and strode down the steps. Perhaps he'd heard the noise and been bothered by it. Would the interviews have to halt while the girl's tirade lasted? The new man talked to the girl. She gave him the finger, too, but strangely, she then accompanied him up the stairs and through the curtains. I guess it paid to make a scene.

Why were none of the interviewed girls returning through the auditorium? Was there an exit at the back? I supposed that made sense. Anyone who came walking back down the aisle would probably be badgered into telling us the interview questions.

The number of girls in the auditorium grew smaller and smaller. Being one of the final contenders made me nervous. What had happened to alphabetical order? My last name was Baker.

"Felicia Peters, Sara Theep, Susan Baker . . ."

Finally. As I walked up to the front, I saw there were only about twenty of us left. Was being last bad or good?

Felicia was sent through the curtain. Sara was rejected. Then, it was my turn. The announcer turned cold, gray eyes on me. I shivered. He held out his hand to shake mine as he had done with the others. I reached up and took it. His grip was strong but not painful.

For some reason, his eyes softened, and he smiled at me. "Please proceed on through the curtain, Ms. Baker. They are ready for you now."

The man's touch and the way his eyes had gone from cold to hot unsettled my stomach. I wanted to run. I wanted to follow Sara back up the aisle and out the entrance. I stood for a moment in indecision.

"Go up the stairs, Ms. Baker," the announcer repeated.

I looked up. His green eyes startled me. Hadn't they been gray a moment before? My legs began to move. One step creaked as it felt my weight, but I continued climbing the short, steep staircase. Then I walked across the stage towards the full-length crimson drapes. I parted them and passed on through.

Beyond the curtains was a second flight of steps, descending into what was probably a practice room. No signs were posted telling me where to go, but the only other option was a locked door. Gingerly, I stepped down the stairs, listening for voices. Only dimly could I hear the sound of the announcer's voice behind me. At the bottom, I came to a passage marked "dressing rooms." One of the officials for the scholarship committee was waiting there. He touched my shoulder, halting me. He had gentle-looking, soft brown eyes. I was glad they weren't green.

"Your name?" he asked.

I gave it to him, and he checked me off. Then he took my arm and led me further down into the maze until we reached a large room filled with cellos, drums, and orchestra stands. On the opposite side, I saw four men, two of them standing, hovering over a third who was busy feeding data into a computer the size of a dorm room refrigerator. The fourth man was standing in a darkened corner. All I could tell about him was how large he was. I stared, fascinated. His chest looked as broad as the doorway I'd just entered.

"This is Susan Baker. She has scored a 41," my hallway guide said.

"Is that good?" I asked.

"You will sit here," the guide said, indicating a folding chair next to the computer. The other two men drew closer. The computer geek stood up to join them. Why were all the interviewers men?

Very gingerly, I sat down in the chair, worrying about its collapse. The thing felt unstable. Why did I have to be interviewed in a rickety chair? I wanted to complain about it, but I didn't.

As long as I sat still, the chair appeared willing to hold my weight. I planted my feet just in case I needed to bolt up should the chair suddenly give way, but in the process, I forgot to worry about whether my skirt should or shouldn't be showing my legs. I looked down. My knees were uncovered, which would have been fine, except they were shaking with nervousness. I tugged at my skirt and set the chair quivering.

The guide left. I think he had more girls to escort to their interviews. I wished he'd stayed. His eyes had looked kind.

The three men standing around me were studying their clipboards. They spoke in a language I couldn't't understand. The computer guy returned to his chair. His chair didn't wobble. I wished I could trade.

The two guys by my side were older men, their faces lined, their skin leathered by the sun. They looked alike. In fact, in their matching three-piece suits, I found it difficult to tell them apart.

One of the men cleared his throat to gain my notice. "We have a program we want you to try, Ms. Baker. The other applicants have been willing. I assume you are?"

It was the man on the right who'd spoken. His heavy accent was exactly the same as the guide's and the announcer's. Where were the men from?

I nodded about the computer program. How could I say anything but "yes" when all the other applicants had agreed? But before I'd even given my answer, the geek was already hooking me up.

The computer program used wires they taped to my wrist and the sides of my neck. I wasn't too happy to see the second man wrapping tape around my wrist. It would hurt when he pulled it off.

"What does the program test?" I asked.

"You must listen, Ms. Baker. It is important you follow directions."

This was too bizarre. Perhaps I didn't need a scholarship. Taking out a loan wasn't really that bad. Lots of people did it, and I'd be able to repay the money with my first teaching job . . .

"You are not listening, Ms. Baker."

"I'm sorry. What did you say?"

"You are to tell a lie."

"A lie?"

The man nodded at me. He was the only one saying anything. The other guy seemed to be the quiet type. The twin had disappeared.

I drew in a deep breath and let it out slowly. "I am *not* an outstanding student who deserves this scholarship," I said, looking my interviewer in the eye.

The man smiled. He had laugh lines about his eyes. I liked that. Also, he smelled like peppermints.

The big guy in the corner turned around to look at me. It was funny how I could tell when he did so. He wasn't in my line of vision, but I could feel him starting to focus on me. I turned to peek.

"No, you must sit still, Ms. Baker. Tell me another lie."

I smiled at my interviewer and considered for a moment. "If you give me this scholarship, I will *not* study hard."

This time, the speaker laughed. "You are persistent, Ms. Baker." He turned away and began talking with the computer person in a strange language. I listened, hoping to catch a word I'd understand. They were not speaking French or Spanish.

I glanced over at the giant. He was still watching me. I wished I could see him better, but the shadows cloaked him. All I could make out was the hugeness of his shoulders and chest, his great height, and his striking gray eyes, similar to those of the announcer's. But Shadow Man had eyes even more luminous. Cat eyes — except gray. But that was crazy. Maybe it was merely the dimness of the corner where he stood that made me think that.

"Tell me something truthful," my interviewer demanded abruptly.

I inhaled deeply and thought. "The world needs good teachers, which is what I will be if I get this scholarship. No," I said, pausing slightly to emphasize my correction. "Actually, I will be *better* than good; I will be a *great* teacher."

Maybe I was laying it on too thick, but there had been at least two hundred girls in the auditorium, and I wanted these men to remember me when they examined their computer data.

The back of my neck goose bumped. Shadow Man was giving me 100% of his attention, like his eyes were traveling up and down my spine. I tugged at my skirt and then wished I hadn't. Shannon had warned me to show my legs. Now, the interviewers would be lucky to see my ankles.

The computer was evidently set. The man with the laugh lines and the shiny black hair tightened the tape around my left wrist and began asking me questions of a different type.

"Tell me your favorite class in school."

"French and Spanish," I said. "I believe it's important to learn languages to understand the people of the world."

"Your hobbies," he asked.

I swallowed nervously and then said, "Equitation, but since I don't own a horse, I exercise and train other people's horses. Jumping is my favorite sport. Also, I love to hike on nature trails and identify the trees and flowers, and I'm learning about the different birds I see, too."

"Do you like children?" the man asked.

"Of course," I blurted out. *Why else would I want to be a teacher?* (Of course, I didn't put it like that.)

"Do you like to travel?" he continued.

I sighed. "Yes, but travel is expensive, and I can only sightsee if someone else is paying."

"Who would offer to pay?" The question came from Shadow Man. His voice was like velvet: rich, smooth, and deep. Velvet or, perhaps, chocolate syrup. I licked my lips. I bet the guy could do commercials for men's cologne. His voice was the loveliest, most delicious, sexiest sound I'd ever heard.

I steeled my beating heart and turned to meet the mystery man's eyes. I almost forgot to answer him. He'd decided to walk closer, and his walk was like the rippling of a tiger's muscles. The power of his chest, his arms, and his legs was almost frightening and . . . hypnotic.

Eyes like dark emeralds (how could I have thought they were gray?), teeth like a toothpaste commercial . . . the guy was gorgeous. Star quality dripped from his pores. How could I not have noticed? The way Shadow Man looked, you'd have thought my heart would go into stasis just from proximity. It took me a moment to recover my breath. I breathed in deeply and tried to find my calm.

"I sometimes travel with tour groups around L.A.," I answered the man.

Why was I so out of breath? My voice sounded winded. I felt a great weight on my chest, as if the air were too thin for my lungs or as if the man's eyes had absorbed all my oxygen.

"My way into the museums . . . is paid for . . . in exchange . . . for being . . . a gopher."

The man's eyes smiled into mine. "A gopher is a small animal. I do not understand."

He, too, had an accent. His was less noticeable than the other men's, but he had to be from the same place. It was an enchanting accent. I couldn't't place it, but I loved it instantly.

"To be a gopher' means . . . that . . . I . . . *go for* things."

"You will explain more."

The way Shadow Man said it, I think that was supposed to be a question, but it sounded like an order. I tried to pull my eyes away from his, but how could I look in another direction? His eyes held the answers to everything. I had to obey.

"Mainly . . . I go on tours . . . with the elderly. They . . . have wheelchairs . . . or canes they've left in the lobby . . . *Breathe*, I told myself. *Stop this jerkiness. Breathe.* "I go get . . . their things for them. I get coffee . . . and souvenirs . . . while they rest . . . Whatever . . . they need me to go get . . . that's my job, which is why . . . they call me . . . a gopher."

This explanation seemed to satisfy Mr. Gorgeous. He stood there, staring into my eyes, thinking.

I breathed in deeply two or three times. My lungs hurt. My breaths were still too shallow. I craved air.

How old was the man? Was he married? Did he date applicants? Why was it so hard to breathe when his eyes were commanding me?

The other man, my original interviewer, had moved back. Shadow Man, my gorgeous Shadow Man, must be the one in charge. I hoped the interest he was showing meant I'd get the scholarship . . . or at least, perhaps, he'd ask me out. It was hard to remember how important the scholarship was while staring into such unbelievably, indescribably delicious gray, green eyes.

"Give me your hand," the man ordered.

All the air left me again. I stood up gingerly, half expecting the computer guy would say something about staying still, but he didn't speak. Both he and the interviewer were acting subservient to Mr. Big Shot. I held out my right hand (luckily, the one taped to the computer connectors was my left). Shadow Man didn't wish to shake it. He turned it over and studied my palm. His long index finger traveled the lines.

"Where I am from," his soft, velvety voice told me, "much can be learned from the soft flesh in the hand. You have heard this?"

I nodded. His finger didn't feel like any palm reading I'd ever heard of. His finger was sending shivers of delight up and down my spine, and something in the man's eyes told me he was aware of it.

"Another custom of my land," the man said, "is this." He lifted my hand up to his lips and gently touched the center of my palm with his mouth.

Whoa. A whole symphony started playing inside me. Suddenly a breeze blew all around me with oxygen . . . pure and delightfully, intoxicating oxygen. And the air whirled with colors and sounds so pleasurable I wanted to cry, to laugh, to sing, to shout, to dance all about. I closed my eyes and held my breath.

Then I jerked my hand back. This was all wrong. The interview frightened me. What was going on?

I dropped my eyes and took a step backward. I glanced over at the man who'd begun my interview. He wasn't paying any attention to me. He was filling out forms. He must have felt my eyes on him, but he didn't look up. Couldn't he feel the tension in the room, the strangeness?

I couldn't look at Shadow Man. He shouldn't have that kind of power over me. He shouldn't make me melt with his touch. I needed to get away from him. I no longer wanted a date, not if I couldn't breathe when he was near me.

But the scholarship . . . I needed the scholarship.

"I assume you find the time to date," his velvet voice continued. "What do you like to do on your dates?"

I swallowed hard. The man hadn't done anything wrong. European men kissed the hands of women. I'd seen it in the movies. It wasn't *his* fault his proximity made me feel strange.

I raised my chin. Concentrate on the scholarship, I told myself. Concentrate on the scholarship. Just to be safe, I looked at the wall beyond him instead of meeting his eyes.

"I don't have time to date," I said. "I work a bunch of jobs, so I can afford to attend the university. When I'm not working, I'm studying or attending classes."

My chest was starting to hurt again, and my voice sounded shaky. "I need this scholarship . . . to pay for my tuition and . . . housing . . . I'll . . . save . . . dating for . . . after graduation."

The man's smile was dangerous. It drew my eyes. I could feel how easy it would be to get sucked into those dreamy eyes and that dazzling smile. The chemistry between us was so good a lighted match would set the air on fire.

The biology wasn't too bad, either, I decided, as I once more became aware of the man's powerful build. He had the arms of a wrestler, a chest like a swimmer, and . . .

"I'm sorry. What did you ask me?" I questioned, trying to pull myself together.

He laughed gently. Bells chimed. Angels sang.

" I said I have no more questions *now*. You are an excellent contender for the scholarship, Ms. Susan Baker. However, there are a few details we should meet to discuss. You will come to my apartment this evening. Shall we say 9:00?"

The innuendo was as clear in his eyes as it was in his voice. He was dripping with insinuation. I couldn't believe it. Right there in front of everyone.

My anger broke right through the enchantment. I reared around so abruptly that I knocked into the chair, and it fell. I felt sick with embarrassment. "I have to go now," I said, throwing the words over my shoulder as I took a step backward.

I know. Dumb line. I should have said I was reporting the man to the College Board. I should have uttered something so snappy it would have soured his ego forever, but I was crushed. I'd thought the man liked me. I'd thought the chemistry between us was more than just . . . I tore off the computer hook-ups and fled toward the door.

"What about the scholarship?" Mr. Gorgeous asked a second before my hand reached for the doorknob.

I twisted the handle. It didn't move. "I don't need your kind of scholarship," I said. "Now, unlock this door."

"Take her," said the velvety voice.

"What?" I looked back, but my glare never reached him. The interviewer and another man were shoving a malodorous towel in my face. A green towel that smelled of dirty socks. I fought the odor almost as much as their attack.

"Keep her separate. She is mine," I heard Mr. Gorgeous say.

I couldn't breathe. The towel was smothering. The room turned into a compact disk, going round and round.

I felt awful. A strange man was holding me tightly against his body, and an ugly green towel was pressed over my nose. What a lousy interview, I reflected as I fought the hold. That was my last thought.

Shaarvan

When the girl entered, I hardly paid any attention. Her test scores were high and strong in all areas, but she was not my type. I preferred tall, well-proportioned women. This one was too small, almost tiny, and her body was clothed in so much material it was hard to see what she was hiding, but I was positive it wouldn't be ample.

But she was extraordinarily strong-willed and verbally skilled, which caught my attention. I found those characteristics enticing. Then the youthful eagerness in her attitude, the way she teased with her quick sense of humor, the faint touch of innocence when she pulled her skirt lower. They drew me closer.

The girl's hair, full and long in a fine chestnut brown, suited me. The curls, falling down her back, were as saucy as her tongue. And, in spite of her size, I had to admit, the girl's face and body were pleasing. She had nice eyes of a deep blue color, much larger than one would expect, with lashes dark and inexplicably flirtatious. She thrust her tiny nose up into the air with such arrogance I clenched my hands not to claim her instantly.

I tested the little Terran with my words and touch. She was amazingly responsive. I felt the rise of passion in her from even the lightest probe. Unconsciously, the girl wet her lips, too inexperienced to realize its implications. Her lips drew me tantalizingly. When her eyes flared with temper, she was exquisite.

As she attempted to run from my final test, I made my decision. I ordered her capture. Her eyes widened with fear, but she fought with the spirit of a wild cat. It pleased me. I knew then I had chosen well.

Chapter Two
On Board

Susan

I woke to find the Shadow Man hanging down over me. He smelled nice, like a forest of pine trees. Lovely.

I thought, at first, I was only dreaming. I smiled into his eyes and sighed. Then I blinked a couple of times to clear away my sleep apathy, but that didn't seem to help. The man was still there.

Why was I lying down? Had I fainted? I tried to sit up. My legs and arms were strapped to the bed. Fastenings secured my chest and thighs. What was going on?

Shadow Man stood towering over me, watching. "How do you feel?" he asked.

"Um . . . fine. If you let me up, I'll . . ." My voice came out creaky, and my throat hurt. I didn't feel well at all. In fact, at that moment, my stomach informed me that I was about to throw up.

"Lie still," the man ordered sharply.

He reached over and grabbed a reddish-orange tube. He squeezed it twice. Just as I started to ask him what its purpose was, he plunged it into my arm. Like a bee sting, the pain of it didn't start at once but rippled across my arm in widening circles.

I wanted to scream, but the room was whirling worse than before. I shut my eyes and fought the nausea.

In a moment, although my arm still throbbed, my queasiness was gone. Cautiously, I opened my eyes. The room no longer spun. I felt better . . . except for the fact I was still strapped on a doctor's examining table and had just had some stranger jabbing at me with the most outlandish syringe I'd ever seen.

"I'm better now. May I please get up?" I croaked.

His hand clamped my chest. "You must stay still," he said. "Your body needs time to awaken properly."

I stared at his jumpsuit. What was he wearing? The fabric rippled as he moved, causing little rainbows of light against its shiny gray, rather like a disco ball in the skating rink when it turned round and round.

"I don't understand," I said. "Was I asleep?" My eyes studied the room. Where was I? The walls were blank, blank white, a white so strong it hurt my eyes to see it, a white which blinded me.

"Be quiet, little one. Listen."

Gray eyes stared at me, eyes with an intensity that halted my words. I wanted to keep talking. I wanted to argue, but I couldn't, not with those eyes staring into mine. I tried to draw in air.

"You have been sleeping for five of your weeks, Shaara. The transition is . . ."

"Why do you call me 'Shaara'? My name is . . . Five weeks. Are you nuts?" I struggled against the ties again, but there was no give in them. "Let me up, or I'll scream," I warned.

He didn't move. His eyes observed me dispassionately.

"I'm warning you," I threatened again, but his eyes held no fear. He stared unblinkingly.

I screamed at full volume.

I thought I was loud, but the slap he administered to my face sounded thunderous in the tiny room. And it stung. I shut my mouth and stared at him. He said nothing, looming over me, a sycamore tree scaling up to the ceiling. His gray eyes peered, cold as two icebergs. I swallowed hard and stared back. My body began to shake.

When he saw that, he reached out a hand and touched me. It rested on my stinging cheek.

"There was no scholarship, Shaara," he said softly. "The screening was solely for the purpose of determining which girls were suitable. You intrigued me. I am keeping you for myself."

I ignored the last part. Sometimes, there's only so much you can deal with. "Who are you?"

"I am Shaarvan, the captain of this ship. We are bound for Altar."

I closed my eyes and drew in a full breath. I couldn't believe the conversation. It was preposterous. But, I was also feeling less than able-bodied. I felt disoriented like I was fuzzy or changed in some way. When you wake up feeling like that, you just have to wait for your brain to catch up and for your body to switch back to normal. At least, I figured that at the time and kept on talking, just like I believed everything the "crazy" was telling me.

"Where is Altar?" I asked.

"It is far away. You would not understand the distance."

His hand was still touching my cheek, stroking it. I shivered, but that didn't halt his caress.

Why would he say I wouldn't understand? Did he think I was an idiot? When was Mr. Madman going to unbuckle me?

"Is Altar a city or another country?" I asked, trying to keep him talking so he didn't do anything worse.

"It is a planet," he said.

Truly a nut case. I had to get away. But how? And where was I? Why was nobody responding to my scream?

" Why do *I* get to go to Altar . . . because I like to travel?" I said, trying to joke the guy out of his weirdness.

His grin would have knocked me over if I hadn't already been flat. How could somebody so devastatingly gorgeous be deranged?

"Altar needs women, as do the other planets where we will land," he said with a straight face.

"Wonderful. Can't they do without me? I'd like to get my teaching credential first. I'll apply later."

He laughed. The *fruitcake* was really enjoying himself, and I was ready to cry. This was so absurd; no decent science fiction story would have an alien who looked like Shaarvan. Aliens were supposed to be horrid looking. And who would believe aliens would abduct Earth women from a *California* university? I could just see the movie title: **Scholarship Bound**, or should it be **Scholar-Ship-Bound**?

I didn't have time for this nonsense. I had a history test to study for. I started to tell Mr. Crazy about it, but he interrupted my thought.

"You are calm," he said, nodding his head. "Good."

If he was rating me on a scale of one to five, I'd say I was somewhere between hysterical and terrified. I concentrated on my breathing and tried to get my brain to assimilate everything. I desperately wanted the jerk to untie me, but I wasn't too clear about what would happen afterwards. Could I knock him down? Could I escape through the door before he caught me again? How crazy was the guy?

He unfastened one of my arms and picked up my wrist. I wondered if he was going to do his palm reading again, but it wasn't his fingers that traced my skin. His lips traveled across my hand, spreading kisses. I tried to jerk my hand away, but he wouldn't let go, and then, it was too late. Every pore of my body asked for more. I couldn't help myself. I groaned. His tongue licked the lines of my hand. It sounds really gross, but it felt like a Puccini opera, and I melted into romantic sighs.

"Shaara," he said.

Kisses and Puccini drugged me, but obediently, I opened my eyes and stared into his.

"Shaara," he said again. "You are mine. I have claimed you by Altar and Westla. And, now, according to the laws of your planet, as captain of this ship, I hereby pronounce us husband and wife. I shall kiss my bride."

I was in a daze, but the part about husband and wife really snapped me out of it. "No, I . . ." His lips lowered to mine. I locked my mouth closed and concentrated on not feeling the warmth and the seductive sweetness of his lips. My body was strapped to the couch, but I had one free hand and arm. I used it to fight him.

"My foolish wife," he said, chuckling. "Do you truly believe your delicate, little fist can defer my intent?"

He forced my arm down to my side and secured it with his body. Then his tongue burst through my sealed lips.

His tongue was a whirlwind. I couldn't think. I couldn't fight him. I was sucked up into the tempest.

They say electricity is only charged electrons. I understand now. My body tingled with it, every pore and every particle. And when Shaarvan's lips withdrew from mine, it was as if the current had been brutally disconnected. The loss was a pain so intense I whined in the agony of his withdrawal.

The eyes that met mine understood how I felt. He smiled down at me with an almost kindly indulgence. "I suspected it would be like this, my wife. Your palm told me you were full of fire."

I closed my eyes and took in a long, deep breath. I fought for sanity as I tried to still the lust inside me. What was wrong with me? I tried to think, to reason it away. How could I have let him kiss me? How could a stranger have made such an impact?

"I am not your wife. I'm . . ." I began to argue, then stopped as a new idea hit me. "This isn't a frat pledging, is it?" I asked, grasping at the idea.

He studied me for a moment, like a professor trying to figure out how to explain physics to a second grader. "What is frat pledging?" he asked, his eyes flashing with amusement.

I sighed and breathed in deeply, fighting for calm. The surface of the ceiling had small white pockmarks like an albino with acne. My scrutiny of it brought me no tranquility.

"Some kind of candid moments on the web?" I said, but his gray eyes didn't register any recognition. The ceiling lights reflected off his hair, giving it a golden hue. A single strand kept falling into his eyes, a streak of sunshine in the austere room.

"Shaarvan," I said, tasting the sound of his name on my tongue. "What is it you want from me?"

His eyes softened. His hand stretched up to rub my cheek again. "A wife, Shaara, and the sons you will give me."

"Please . . ."

His hand was stroking me like I was a cat he thought would purr. He moved his fingers under my chin and continued rubbing. His eyes were fastened on mine so hard you'd have thought they were magnets. I couldn't look away. Why was I getting goosebumps?

I fought his power: his eyes, the touch of his fingers. *History. I must think about my history test. What was it we were studying? Concentrate.*

Shaarvan's hand stopped. I wanted to beg him to continue. *The Industrial Revolution. What were its components?*

"You do not accept my words yet," he said. I looked up. His eyes had darkened like rain clouds before a storm. He took a step backward from me and turned.

"I shall leave you to feel the motors of the ship, to study the room, to wonder why no one came when you screamed. Listen well, my wife, and *learn.*"

No, stay and pet me, my mind whispered, but I didn't say it. I was watching Shaarvan walk away.

"Wait, untie me first." I cried out.

The door whooshed closed behind him. He hadn't even paused. The silent echo of my words haunted me with their sad, plaintive bleating.

It was hard not to be frightened. The news broadcasts were full of weirdoes and sickies doing horrible things to people. "Dear God," I prayed. "Please, don't let Shaarvan be one of those. Please, help me to get free and away from him. Please, God. Amen."

I spent a few minutes attempting to unbuckle the left strap and the one across my chest, but I couldn't find a release button, nor could I tear them. In a panic, I wrestled with the lower bonds, my whole body rocking against them, straining and fighting the tethers. They wouldn't loosen, either.

I screamed, then. I don't know why I'd waited so long. Perhaps Shaarvan's slap had frightened me so I hadn't had the courage to try again. But with him gone and the silence seeping into my bones with its cold numbness, I filled up my lungs and blasted the walls with shrieks and bellows and with tears and cries for help.

I stopped, finally, when the echoing walls brought me nothing but a headache and a throat scratchy as a pinecone. Then I lay there and panted. I had no more tears left. My body ached, bruised by my struggles against the straps; I was thirsty, scared, and miserable.

The room wasn't cold, yet I began to shiver violently. "This isn't fair," I yelled. "I shouldn't be here. What did I do to deserve this?"

I sobbed, drawing in quick, short breaths of air. "It isn't fair. Do you hear me, Shaarvan? This isn't fair."

There was only silence. The walls of the room stared back at me, cold and uncaring. The pockmarks in the ceiling gloated.

Why was this happening to me? Why?

I tried to remember what had occurred after the interview. I could picture the green towels and the men preventing my escape. I recalled Shaarvan watching from a distance. What had he said? He'd ordered the men to use the towels on me. Why had they done so? Employees didn't kidnap someone just because their boss told them to. None of it made sense, not unless what Shaarvan had said was true. But his story was laughable. It wasn't possible. He was crazy. Maybe the others were insane, too.

"I hate you, Shaarvan," I yelled at the door, and my anger swelled again. I thought of the things I'd say to him when he came back. I practiced saying them out loud. I organized my arguments. I prepared my battle.

But Shaarvan didn't return.

I wiggled on the high examining table and stretched my limbs, no longer fighting the bonds, accepting I couldn't break free of them. My bottom had become numb, and my legs were stiff. I tried to do an upside-down caterpillar crawl. The movement helped. The stinging needles in my bottom told me all parts of me were waking up.

When the tickly pains stopped, my eyes searched the room, probing for clues. Where was I? Maybe it was a practice room, which would explain the soundproofing, the reason why no one had come when I'd screamed, but why would there be a doctor's couch in a music room?

A metal chest of drawers, where the red-orange tube still lay, took up the wall across from me. It had no knobs or decorations on its series of drawers, but you could see where the drawers slid out. It could belong in a doctor's examining room, but where, then, were the charts of the human body, the warnings about what you should and shouldn't do in life, and the certificates of graduation from medical school? Where were the nurses and the other patients? Why had no one come to let me out?

I didn't want to look at the tube Shaarvan had used to give me a shot. It was like no hypodermic needle I'd ever seen, and he'd left it there in plain sight. Shouldn't he have thrown it out? Yet, there was no garbage can in the room, not one visible to me from my horizontal position.

Why couldn't I see any needle at the end, gray and pointed, like an elongated stinger? Had Shaarvan tossed it out when I shut my eyes? The red-orange color of the plastic was an unusual color for a doctor's tool, and the chubby nature of the syringe looked different, too, but it was possible it was just a new kind of injection device, wasn't it?

Where was Shaarvan? When would he return? Why had he left me? He'd told me to listen to the ship. I closed my eyes and concentrated. There *was* a faint hum, but it could be an air conditioner or ventilation pump. How would I know if it was the sound of a spaceship zapping across the galaxy?

Yet I'd listened, done what he'd ordered me to do. Investigation: inconclusive. My screaming was finished, my hysterics concluded. Shadow Man was still in absence. What should I do subsequently?

I suppose I should have planned my escape. It would have been the logical thing to do, but my mind drifted. I began thinking about what a beautiful day Saturday had been. Why did I never go to the beach to study? I could have gone to the park and read in the shade, listening to the birds and watching squirrels chase each other around and around a tree. I wished I had a book with me. I could read then and wait for Shaarvan to let me go. Would he? Would he ever? Or would they find my body stuffed in a garbage can or buried in the woods somewhere?

What if I *had* been asleep for a while? Would anyone miss me at work? This weekend, I was supposed to work in the administration office, but I was usually the only one there on Sundays. That helped me get all the filing done since no one was around to interrupt me. But it also meant there'd be no one to notice if I didn't show up. I needed to exercise a horse after that, but the stable wouldn't notice my failure to arrive. It wasn't like *Sugar Baby* could tell them.

My roommates were both gone for the weekend. They wouldn't wonder about my absence until Monday, and the elder group had no activities until the following week. The depressing part was that *nobody* would worry or be overly concerned even if I never . . .

A tear slid down my cheek and fell onto my arm. I didn't wipe it away. What was the point? I was too miserable to care. I missed my parents. I wished I could call them and talk like my roommates did with their folks.

It surprised me to find I was sobbing again. I'd thought my tears were gone. It was remembering about my parents that started me off again. I always tried *not* to think about them. It was always difficult to recall how things used to be. Their silver Volvo with its crushed-in front seemed to overshadow every good memory.

Shaarvan

Stars, she was a spunky little thing. Scared as any newly captured girl, yet still feisty enough to challenge me in spite of the patterns I had used on her. Delightful.

I smiled, recalling how she'd continued her saucy banter even in the midst of her fear. The little Terran had broadcast her thoughts more clearly than a highly trained sender. She was strong, almost as gifted as my mother. And the girl's concentration against the *Power* was astonishing. Would it be a complication? It might prove a hindrance to the others on the ship. I would have to blanket her projections.

Ah, but she would be worth it. She was a delight sexually. And when I bedded her, her projections would be most favorable. I would take great pleasure in training her to my needs. But, first, I must break her resistance. Her strength of mind would require great skill.

I suspected I was going to need enormous forbearance. She would be a challenge. I would have to find more patience with her than I had ever had with a girl before. I must not forget how many Shapechanger ended up killing a girl who harbored her ability and courage. It was the biggest danger with defiant females. Yet the sons this girl would bear me . . . the sons would make the added effort worth it.

I was eager to return to her, but I would wait until the fourth watch. She would be unbalanced then from her isolation. Not even the strongest female could tolerate the sensory deprivation of being locked in a white room for long. When I returned, she would be far more accepting.

Susan

The door whooshed open. I turned my head to see. It was not a rescue as I'd hoped, only Shaarvan back to taunt me with his wild stories. Still, my heart beat faster, and I felt the most indescribable joy at the sight of him.

He stopped and studied me. I met his eyes, and again, I felt the strange magnetic pull that secured me to him. He walked closer and bent over me. I could feel his hands detaching the straps binding me, but yet I couldn't free my eyes from his.

He straightened up. For a moment more, those green-gray eyes of his held their power over me. I trembled.

"Sit up now, Shaara," he ordered softly.

I didn't argue over the name this time. I was too eager to get up and out of the room, but his commanding voice still rankled. Even worse was his laughter when I freed my eyes from his. Just to please the jerk, I raised up. I could feel the remnants of the drugs in my brain; the room was still swimming. A wave of nausea hit me. I almost flopped back down.

"Easy, my little wife. Sit quietly for a moment. It will pass."

I didn't dare move. I breathed in low and steady breaths: in and out, in and out. As the nausea receded, the feel of the guy's strong hands gripping mine became the center of my attention. He was offering support; why was the touch of his hands sending waves of desire? I shook myself like a dog ridding its coat of water.

"I'm fine now," I said.

Once more, the jerk laughed, but he loosened his hold. My eyes were drawn to the hands holding me. I studied the exquisite perfection of those long, slender fingers. Michelangelo could not have crafted them as flawlessly. I noticed, of course, that the fingers were also ringless. If Shaarvan had a wife, he didn't display it.

"You may stand up, Shaara."

His voice recalled me. Why should I care whether the jerk was married or not? I flung my legs over the side of the couch. The movement sent a jolt of pain to my head. My headache returned to full volume. I ignored it and proceeded on. It was not a graceful leap, but the feeling of foot on ground gave me a measure of success. I gripped the side of the couch and waited for the spinning of the room to slow down. In spite of my nausea, my eyes traveled the distance to the door and then glanced away, not wishing Shaarvan to know my purpose.

Then I gritted my teeth and closed my eyes for a second. I needed another moment to regain my balance, but I sensed Shaarvan's movement when he turned about to pick up the hypodermic needle. It was what I'd been waiting for.

I charged the door. The lunge forward brought the nausea forefront, but I didn't have time to let it stop me. I swallowed hard and focused on the door. I had studied it sufficiently. I knew there was no knob. With both hands, I flung myself against it, expecting it to whoosh open as it had for Shaarvan.

The colonel of fast food fame could have fried himself a whole batch of chickens off the juice the door sent through me. From my shiny pink toenails clear up to my brown, curly split ends, the door let me have it. I'm not talking static cling like what happens when you get the socks out of the dryer. I mean, major pain, agony, distress, alarm. It knocked me down and out.

Shaarvan must have picked me up and carted me back to the couch. When I woke again, I was right back where I'd started, except my ears were ringing, and my brain felt like a construction worker had drilled a hole in it. No, I felt worse than that. I felt like I'd just survived an attack by killer bees, and my body was still buzzing from the consequences.

I must have been slightly hysterical, too, because Shaarvan placed his hand on my forehead for a moment and said, "Easy, girl," and I latched onto his hand like I thought I was drowning and he was offering to pull me out of the water.

Shaarvan disengaged his hand from my wrap-around grip and backed away. I wished he hadn't. A whole herd of cows came stampeding over my brain. I needed his hand to . . .

I saw the red-orange tube ascend upwards, and then it reversed itself and plunged down into my skin. With all the delicacy of a baboon-playing doctor, Shaarvan rammed the pricker into my skin.

"Ow." I cried out, but the shriek sounded more like it came from a wounded pelican than me. The echo hurt my head something awful. I clamped my jaws shut, closed my eyes, and gave in to the nausea. Mt. Vesuvius was about to erupt.

Once more, Shaarvan's hand rested atop my forehead. I didn't throw it off; I couldn't move. I kept my eyes shut and listened to the faint hum of the whatever it was. All the while, the touch of the jerk's hand soothed my head. His fingers circled around and around. I moaned.

"It will be all right now, Shaara. I know you had to test the door, but that is over. Relax."

Either the shot or his hand eased my pain. I was no longer sick, and my headache began to recede. A tangy scent floated in the air. I suspected it was from the medicine he'd given me. I inhaled and closed my eyes, but already the smell had dissipated.

Again Shaarvan lifted me up to a sitting position and then helped me to stand. I was feeling so wobbly, for a moment, I almost thanked him for his support.

With his hands on my shoulders, he half-guided, half-shoved me towards the door. My legs rocked unsteadily; I was leaning against him, allowing him to sweep me forward, but a foot from the door, I stiffened and tried to stop. "No," I said, shaking my head.

"You must learn not to argue, my wife," Shaarvan said, and his grip on my shoulders tightened painfully as he pushed me onward.

"Don't make me do it again. Please." I cried out in panic.

I was fighting his grip, attempting to pry his fingers off my shoulders while struggling to break away, but my resistance had no effect on Shaarvan.

He thrust me ahead, placed his hand on the door, and whooshed it open. "Behave," he ordered sharply as he pushed me through the doorway.

The door had opened into a hall at least twenty feet long in each direction and was filled with white walls, white floors, and shiny, white doorways at measured intervals. Of course, Shaarvan didn't allow me to stand there gawking. As we entered the hallway, he let go of my shoulders, grabbed my hand, and pulled me forward at a pace much faster than my poor, shaky legs wanted to go.

Several times, as we proceeded down the long corridor, I shot glances up at his face, thinking about asking him to slow down, but the granite hardness of his eyes as he met mine kept me from begging. Still, even though the pace was greater than I would have liked, my eyes were busy studying the hall and the doors we passed, attempting to count them in case I needed to retrace my steps. (Why I would ever want to return to a sterile white room, I didn't know, but wasn't the examination of a scene necessary whenever a crime was committed?)

I had counted twelve doors when we came to a major intersection, or at least the place where we had the opportunity to go in four different directions. There were no pictures on the walls, no pattern or color anywhere. Even the flooring was white. Did no one know paint came in shades and tints?

Motion sensors gave us lighting. Some kind of recessed illumination lit up the walls as we passed. The fixtures were so skillfully hidden I could see no demarcation of any kind — no panels, no plastic or glass covers, no switches, not even buzzing florescence. At times, I smelled fresh air and a faint odor of something like newly mowed grass. I wanted to stop and analyze the sensory input, but Shaarvan kept tugging me forward.

We headed down the passage on the farthest left, continued walking five more doors, turned left again, then right two doors down, and in and out of different halls until I realized I'd completely lost track.

My legs were no longer shaky by then. My steps had grown steady, except for the occasional jogs thrown in to keep up with Shaarvan's much longer legs. My shins, however, had begun to ache from our speed, and my breath had grown labored.

"Where . . . are we . . . going?" I asked, panting from my efforts.

Shaarvan's answer was silence. He looked down at me. I knew he'd heard. He just didn't seem inclined to offer any information. What a jerk.

He yanked me forward slightly as if I'd stopped, and we passed several more doors and went down a couple more turns and twists, which all looked the same to me. I noticed that, after my question, Shaarvan had slowed his speed somewhat, adjusting his step to my shorter legs. For a while, I no longer needed to take the extra jogging step.

His grip on my hand had tightened slightly when I'd asked my question, but when I hadn't persisted or pulled back, he'd once again loosened his hold. Perhaps loosened wasn't the right word. A vise that holds a board so tightly it dents the board can be released slightly so the board is not damaged. It was that minor a change.

Shaarvan's hand was immobilizing and strong enough to give damage to my hand, but he didn't do so. My hand felt small, buried in the hugeness of his, but his grip was not crushing. It gave me no pain.

As the corridors turned, and the maze we walked in seemed ever increasingly unending, I wondered where on earth we could possibly be. I was familiar with the administration building of the university. I worked there in my time off from classes. But there were no places in that building with halls this long or this barren of decorations and color. Shaarvan had to have taken me off the campus while I slept my drugged sleep, but where?

It was amazing the guy could find his way in such a rat maze. How could he orient himself? Or could it be possible he was as lost as I was? I sneaked a glance at his face. His hand squeezed mine instantly in the slightest contraction of a warning. I hadn't paused or slowed, nor had I spoken. The warning, if it had been one, perhaps had been no more than a reflex or an unconscious twinge. I risked a second look at the man's face and felt the same reaction. Yet, he said nothing, and our pace didn't change.

What would he do if I suddenly bolted? Would he . . . ? Once more, I felt the tightening of his hand, the quick, gentle warning. This time, his eyes rested on me. I studied the flooring and walked slightly faster.

Was it a coincidence? Yet those eyes, that strange luminous gray, or at times, eerily green, and always cold as ice water, were so perceptive . . . so aware. I shivered and kept my eyes lowered, my thoughts on safer things.

We continued walking through halls and corridors of unending sameness, yet Shaarvan didn't act unsure of his way. He walked like a man who knew where he was going. I had to trust he was acquainted with our destination. I hoped, like every rat maze I'd heard of, there was food at the other end. My stomach was beginning to talk to me.

We stopped at last. It was in front of a door that looked just like all the others we'd passed. Shaarvan placed his hand on it, whooshed it open, and pushed me inside. We had walked a vast distance to arrive at a room only barely bigger than where I'd first been held prisoner. Like everything I'd seen that day, the room was stark white and absolutely devoid of decoration.

The door whooshed closed behind us. At that moment, I realized I'd only exchanged one prison cell for another. I was still ensnared by a madman.

Shaarvan

Shaara, my wife . . . interesting feeling that gives me calling her wife. I need constantly to remind myself of it. Wife. I laugh at myself. The title of it is almost bigger than the girl is.

How disappointed I had been to see the girl's true size as she slept. Her figure and face were fine, and her body pleased me, but I hesitated as she lay there, wondering if I had chosen correctly. It had been the memory of her response that had steadied my hand as I cut into her arm to start the medicine. Even so, I think I half-hoped her body would not accept the transformation process.

But my doubts are gone now. I am positive I have chosen wisely. When the girl is awake, when the fire in her makes her seem more of a normal woman's height and mass, then I remember fully why I chose her. She calls to me strongly.

She is very young, younger than the others I have captured. Will it be an advantage, or will it make her mind too fragile for adaptation? Will she be able to endure the changes?

I worry needlessly. The girl yielded quickly to the confinement I gave her, and she learned the lesson of the door quickly, both points in her favor. She should have submitted fully to our departure from the room, it is true. Does she not have the sense to realize she cannot win against me? It should not be necessary to use force on her. She should see the obvious.

But, I shall give her time. Perhaps she is still in shock. I shall be lenient for a while, but if her stubbornness persists, she will feel my displeasure.

Yet, I must temper it. I must remember to be cautious in my punishment. She is too small to use much of my strength. The feel of the tiny bones in her hand warns me of this. I am glad she will be my last training; I grow weary of female disobedience.

Susan

Inside the room, the crazy man ignored me. He walked over to the far wall and put his fingers on it. Panels started springing out from the touch of his hand, and there was suddenly an enormous computer taking up the whole long wall. Three wide screens, with lights in flashing colors, positioned themselves higher than I could reach.

Shaarvan sat down on a stool, then spoke in a foreign language. A rectangular box, the size of a file cabinet, answered him in the same babble. I stood at a distance and watched. The man seemed to have forgotten me, he was so involved with talking and studying the flashing lights.

That was fine. I wanted the guy to ignore me. It was safer, but I was hungry. "Will we be staying in here long?" my mouth said, without my intending it.

I was almost surprised when the guy responded. "This is your new home, Shaara. You may explore. There is nothing in here you will disturb. I must prepare the computer program for you."

New home? I already had a new home. It was called a dormitory, and there were only girls in it.

Hesitantly, I moseyed over to the doorway to study it. I was mainly concentrating on not giving into my feelings of violence, for I was wishing strongly I was a black belt in Karate or Judo or had something really hard I could throw at Shaarvan, like a brick or one of my textbooks.

I knew Shaarvan was aware of the direction I was headed. I could feel his eyes on my back. When there was no reaction from him, not even a sharp order about staying away from the door, I figured the special shock system, which seemed only to affect me and not him, was alive and potent. Of course, it was possible Shaarvan wanted me to think so, and the door truly had no such system.

I turned around and looked at him. His eyes, gray this time, met mine, but he said nothing. I took a step closer to the door. Did I see a smile in the corner of the man's lips? Was he amused by my indecision?

That did it. I raised my hand and brought it close to the door. The tiny little hairs on my hand responded to the electric field. They wiggled and danced, like in the experiments we'd done in school where a comb could make your hair stand on end. My little experiment told me exactly what I wanted to know. This baby was as hot as the first door I'd come in contact with. Whatever Shaarvan used to get through doors, I sure didn't have it.

Shaarvan was grinning openly now. "Clever girl," he said. "It will be much easier on you if I only have to discipline you once for a lesson to be learned."

I didn't like the way Shaarvan talked about disciplining. It didn't encourage me to think that my captivity would be a pleasant, peaceful retreat from my studies.

I forgot about wishing for a brick. I decided a slingshot would be perfect. It would be very enjoyable to knock away some of the cocky attitude of the freak.

I shot a glare at Shaarvan and turned to the left to survey the rest of my prison cell. Shaarvan turned back to his computer, and I observed a second door in the room. As quietly as possible, I tiptoed towards it. Maybe, just maybe, I could find a way out of the mess I was in.

I didn't have to test the door with my hand. The door slid open in my proximity. I had a moment of wild jubilation, but the interior turned out to be a potty room, not an escape route.

I was sorry it wasn't a way out, but it wasn't called the necessary room without reason. A hole is a hole. There weren't too many ways to be imaginative. I tried it out, and when I was finished, I looked around for toilet paper, but I couldn't find any. As I started to lift up, the john sprayed my privates and then dried me instantly. It was a really weird feeling.

I tried to figure out how to flush, but the toilet performed the service automatically the moment I moved away from it.

A shower, I think, was next to the toilet. It had no water faucets, but still, it was similar enough, with the same four-walled cubicle appearance. What else could one put in a bathroom anyway? I saw no buttons to push. I wondered how you turned on the water.

There was no sink to wash my hands. I thought about sticking them into the toilet to see if I could get a wash there, but the idea repelled me.

It would have been nice to brush my teeth, too. They felt like they really needed it. If Shaarvan was right about my sleeping a whole month, I'd probably have a ton of cavities. I'd be sure to send him the dentist's bill.

I missed not having a mirror. I'm not vain, but everyone likes to check how they look. I mean how does one know there isn't something stuck in your teeth or toothpaste on your cheek or something? I couldn't even see if my hair was sticking straight up or puffed up on one side or something.

I sighed. There was nothing I could do about it, obviously. Maybe Shaarvan was a vampire. Weren't they the ones who couldn't look in the mirror? Or was that witches? I didn't have a brush or comb anyway. I wondered if they had convenience stores? What did aliens do when they forgot to pack their toothbrush?

I stepped towards the exit. A sudden cloud of mist surrounded me. It was tingly and warm. In a second, the cloud disappeared, and the door whooshed open. My skin had been scrubbed clean, and my teeth no longer felt stale and grimy. I felt clean all over. I hoped the cloud had also done something about my hair.

Isn't it funny how the appearance of bathrooms is so much the same? How much could you vary one? Yet, I felt like I'd entered the next century. This Shaarvan guy must work for the World's Fair, where they showed off future inventions. Perhaps I'd just visited the bathroom of the 2899 exhibit.

Shaarvan turned to watch me as I came out. His right eyebrow lifted with a mocking look like he dared me not to believe his story now. I admit I didn't think it was a frat prank anymore, but the honestto-God truth was I didn't know what to believe. I was quickly running out of theories.

"Shaarvan, are you a time traveler?"

He laughed. "You are an obstinate girl," he said. "What will it take to convince you? Will I have to open the ship's door and push you out into the void?"

"Please. That would be very persuasive." I nodded my enthusiasm.

Shaarvan shook his head and continued talking to his computer, all the time chuckling away.

His occupation with the computer left me free to continue my explorations, not that there was much to see. There was a panel of buttons off to one side, well-blended into the white wall. I put my hand up close to check for shock treatments, but there were no dancing hairs on my hand. I started to push a button in the middle of the group, but I decided I should go in order so I could remember what each button did.

The top button on the right lifted a table up out of the floor. One moment, there was a soft, white carpet, and then the next, there was a flat-topped mushroom growing at fast-forward. When it stopped, it flattened out and formed a round surface for a workspace or for dining, I guessed. I touched the table curiously, but it felt like plastic, nothing more — smooth-edged and scratch-free, but ordinary white plastic. Somehow, I was rather disappointed, although I don't know what I expected. I suppose after seeing the bathroom, I thought the table should have diamonds or gold flakes across its surface, anyway something a whole lot more exciting than cheap plastic.

I pushed the left top button, and a chair grew, or rather, a cube-like stool. On top of it lay a covering of what felt like squished marshmallows. I touched the marshmallow and thought of *Alice and*

Wonderland. Maybe I'd find the sign that said eat me. The top felt cushy, as I'd said, but the texture was springy, although thankfully not sticky. Who'd want to sit on a sticky marshmallow?

The chair was remarkably comfortable. When I sat down, the stool adjusted to my height, which was kind of a nice touch.

I got back up and pushed the button again, hoping to get rid of the chair, but instead, another chair grew. Again, I pushed the same button, and a third chair rose up. What would happen if I pushed the first button again? Another table? I tried it, but the table only melted down into the carpet. A moment later, it was like the carpet had never been disturbed. I reached down to touch the carpet. I couldn't even feel the place where the table had risen up.

Now, the three chairs moved to face each other. I hadn't pushed any buttons at that point, so it was really weird, like the chairs needed to see each other better. Again, I pushed the same button on the right. I wanted to see if the chairs would move if a fourth chair joined them. Instead, all the chairs melted down into the carpet like the table had done.

Once more, Shaarvan's eyes were watching me. They were curious, amused, and horny? I hoped not. I had no defense against crazed sex demons. I didn't think sprouting chairs and tables would keep Shaarvan away if he decided to make serious moves.

I guess his interest wouldn't have bothered a lot of girls. Shaarvan had a great body, and his face was like a movie star's. My roommates in the dorm would have welcomed him, brain-dead or not, but I couldn't. It was not like it was a religious thing or anything like that. I hadn't made a pledge or taken vows. It was just that I believed a first time should be really special, so special I'd spend the rest of my life with the guy.

I know, romantic bunk. It wasn't like I hadn't seen divorces right and left. I was Californian. It was part of the culture. It was only that I hoped somewhere I'd find a guy who felt like permanence was a good thing, and maybe he'd be glad I'd waited.

For a moment, I thought about my parents. They'd had a great relationship. As far as I knew, when their car had crashed that rainy Sunday, they'd still loved each other as much as the day they'd gotten married.

I remember how I used to tease them about kissing in the kitchen. I'd told them it was disgusting for parents to do stuff like that, but I still remembered them sneaking off to wash the dishes together and how flushed Mom would be afterwards. I wanted someone who'd still kiss me in the kitchen twenty years after our wedding.

I don't know . . . maybe the truth was I just hadn't found anyone who lit me up. None of the guys I'd gone out with were worth the worry of AIDS, pregnancy, and dropping all my dreams.

Now, it looked like I probably wouldn't be a virgin too much longer, so all the waiting was for nothing. If I stayed locked up in this room with Shaarvan, I doubted if he'd care about my dreams and goals. Yet, he hadn't moved to attack me. Maybe, oh please, God, maybe Shaarvan was gay?

Then, I remembered the way he'd kissed me when he'd claimed we were married. He hadn't acted gay then. He'd been really into it.

I watched Shaarvan concentrating on the computer. I'd met guys who were computer buffs. They acted like a computer was something animate, like it was their whole life. I wondered if Shaarvan was like that. What was so fascinating about a machine full of lights and data bits? You couldn't pet it or play with it. You couldn't talk with it and know by watching its eyes that it was responding to you. It had no feelings. You turned it off, and it was dead. More or less, it was like getting attached to a mirror, only a reflection of what you programmed into it.

I went back to punching mystery buttons. The next one brought up a bed. I quickly punched that back into the melt zone. The next button offered beverages, I think. I wasn't sure what kind of liquid it was. It could be coffee; it was black and smoking, but I suppose it could be poison, mouthwash or computer oil. I punched the button to take it away.

The next button deposited what looked like an unwrapped granola bar. It smelled like seaweed and molasses. I wasn't tempted to see if it was edible. I was hungry, but not that hungry. The only thing it would be good for was as a weapon against Shaarvan. I pushed the button quickly to take it back. The temptation was too great. As a projectile, the bar might give me a second's satisfaction, but Shaarvan's muscles were as solid as a tank. I couldn't picture the tank halting due to a granola bar missile.

The next button delivered a screen with a printout. I couldn't read anything. It was all scribbles and hieroglyphics. I touched the screen once more, and two pills fell out.

Shaarvan stood up and turned to glare at me. "Drop them back in, Shaara." His voice brooked no argument.

I did as he ordered. I didn't want the pills anyway.

Shaarvan clapped his hands twice, and the screen and all the buttons disappeared. It was like the meltdown of the table and chairs. Suddenly, there was only wall. Things were getting scary. I had to have gone into the future. I know, don't laugh, but what other explanation was there for all I'd seen. Going into the future was a tad bit easier to swallow than buying Shaarvan's explanation he was an alien from Planet Altar.

"Come here," Shaarvan said. His voice was gruff, but his eyes held no threat of lust. I thought it safer to obey than to argue about his bossiness. I walked slowly towards him, watching his eyes. Was this where he pulled out a knife and stabbed me?

I got no closer than a step beyond his reach before I stopped. I chewed at my lower lip. It was a bad habit I'd acquired at some point in time. It was the main way I dealt with my nerves.

Shaarvan held his hand out to me. A lock of his hair had fallen out of place. It made him seem younger. He didn't look crazy. He made no sudden moves toward me. He just stood there waiting, his hand palm-up and ready for my obedience.

I took a big breath of air. Then, I gave him my hand, but I was shaking. I figured I must have pleased him because he smiled at me and nodded. I was still scared he'd pull me closer, but he only led me to the door, saying, "You must be hungry, Shaara. We will go eat now."

"Where?" I asked.

He didn't answer. How much of this could I take? Already, my nerves were telling me I couldn't handle caffeine today.

Shaarvan had used his left hand to touch the door. Was that what he'd done before? Could the door shock a right hand and open to a left? Somehow, I doubted I'd discovered the answer, but it was worth trying later.

Had I read somewhere that lefties were more inclined to have deviant personalities? Or was it they just made better bowlers? I couldn't remember. I'd thought that chapter in the psychology text wasn't important to a teacher major. If I ran into psychos in second grade, I knew there'd be a panel of psychiatrists to help me.

I never thought about dealing with the rest of the world. Maybe you needed to know all about wackos just to get through day-to-day existence. Now I wished I'd memorized the book. Every chapter of it.

Why didn't textbooks offer the answers you needed? College and high school kept telling us they prepared us for life. Well, Life 201 didn't seem to help me here. I could speak French about European history, give Shaarvan four verb clauses or a thesis if he'd prefer, and explain the difference between a parabola and a parallelogram, but I'd never read anything about what to do when an alien kidnapped you.

Newspaper etiquette experts, could I write to you from outer space? Did they have a Pony Express via satellite? Maybe one needed to attach letters to a meteorite and hope they didn't burn up in transit. What kind of stamp should I use?

"Shaarvan, do you have post offices in Altar? I really need to mail a letter."

I didn't expect him to answer, and he didn't. He just chuckled.

Shaarvan

I had to admit Shaara was entertaining. We were not melded yet, but stray thoughts fluttered about her mind like leaves drifting on wind currents. I tried to concentrate on the program I was completing for her, but she distracted me most enchantingly.

I was not unaware of the delights of her body, but it was not that which disturbed my concentration. It was the quickness of her mind, her darting leaps of ideas, and the playful frolic of her imagination.

She was like a garden of children, giggling and happy, even amid her fear and distress. She beguiled and intrigued me, and I could not regain control over my thoughts for fear I would miss some delightful flood of reflections streaking across her mind. I was beginning to realize it was going to take considerable determination to ignore the babble of her thoughts.

It pleased me how easily Shaara transferred her understanding about the door lock to a new room. The test for electric current she contrived was an excellent demonstration of her intelligence. Her method of classifying the buttons was commendable as well. In general, the girl had proved herself to be both methodical and logical and displayed a high level of reasoning skills. To be exact, she had reflected precisely what her tests had foretold.

I wished her hand were not so tiny in mine. She was such a little thing. Would she be able to give birth to my future sons without problems? The thought concerned me.

Chapter Three
I'm Troublesome?

Susan

Again, we strolled down the long, slender corridors. Shaarvan wasn't much of a talker, and I didn't know what to say. I was the guest, so it was really up to him. However, I was pretty sure Shaarvan hadn't read a lot of etiquette books. His manners had so far been extremely antisocial. Maybe they didn't have rules on proper behavior where he came from which left the ball in my court.

But how do you discuss politics with someone who thinks he's from outer space? In the next election, are you planning to vote for the Bug Men from Venus or the Green Martian Militia? Certainly, water is an issue for Mars, but I don't think draining the Atlantic Ocean is a viable answer, even if the land could be cultivated, and it would end our overpopulation problem.

I decided to avoid politics, religion, and what was the other one? I forget. I had unavoidably left all my etiquette books at home. I settled for a neutral subject.

"Do you have any great restaurants onboard your ship, Shaarvan?"

The look he gave me could have burned rubber. It sure put a speedy end to the conversation I was attempting to instigate.

Our hike ended up in a large, white (of course, was there any other color here?) sterile-looking room. There were tables and chairs and men sitting around eating.

People. I could get away from this creep.

"Help." I screamed out. "He's kidnapped me. Help, please."

I pulled and wiggled like a fish on a line, but I couldn't break away from Shaarvan's hold. I lashed out with my foot and tried to kick where I knew it would do the most good, but Shaarvan only pulled me closer and wrapped both arms around me. I couldn't reach him to kick, and I couldn't get loose from his gorilla grip. I continued battling for a few minutes, lashing out with both feet, screaming and yelling, "Help." but I didn't hear anyone rushing to my aid.

I was winded when I halted, and I broke off to breathe a moment. That wasn't easy since Shaarvan's arms were squeezing my middle like jeans on a fat day. Panting heavily, it took me a moment to realize no one had even *paused* in their dining. All the men sitting around the room had completely disregarded my screams.

I continued to huff and puff and looked about. The men were all wearing the very same gray workman's overalls as Shaarvan's. They must all be part of this elaborate hoax or members of the same mental hospital.

A couple of the men looked up briefly as if wondering if my display was over, but their mouths continued chewing, a herd of steers ruminating over their grassy pasture. I hated them. I wanted to yell at them, call them names, and tell them what I thought of them, but I could feel Shaarvan's ribs heaving in laughter, and the sound of his chuckles hurt worse than any insult I could think up.

"You are finished now?" he asked casually.

I wanted to shriek and boot him again with my feet, but instead, I pulled in a deep breath and expelled it slowly.

"For the moment," I snapped.

I felt Shaarvan's arms stiffen minutely with the same instinctive reflex he'd demonstrated before. My heart sped up, sensing danger.

"I have been lenient with you, Shaara, because you are my wife, but be warned, there is a limit to my patience." He whispered the words into my ear unemotionally, but my body identified the threat. The danger meter had just indicated a rise in temperature.

Shaarvan's arms were still wrapped around me, and after my energetic struggles, I was anything but cold, yet shivers raced up and down my arms, legs, and backbone, and my teeth began to chatter. Terror hit me with a punch in the stomach.

Apparently, my fear relaxed Shaarvan's tension. He turned me around to face him. "Easy, girl," he said as his hand stroked my cheek. "Your inner senses have alerted you to something you are not ready to understand."

What did he mean? I wanted to step backward, to flee from him, but my lungs were empty, my body frozen.

He continued to stroke my cheek. "Easy, girl. Easy now," he repeated over and over until my shivers died away, and I could breathe again.

He drew me closer, his arms still about me but less painful. "You have felt the fear, my Shaara. It is a lesson that may protect you. I do not wish to hurt you, and I will not do so unless you force me into the necessity of it. Remember your fear, my wife.

"And as to your tantrum — these men are used to the antics of captive girls, although few as *troublesome* as you."

I felt Shaarvan smiling down at me. I looked up into his eyes. He was no longer angry. With this knowledge, my fear lessened. It felt good to breathe in and out freely.

Again, his hand stroked my cheek. "The men on board the ship will never interfere, Shaara," he continued. "They will not talk with you or listen to you. They will not respond to you in any way. Do you understand?"

I nodded. I was mainly just appreciating being able to breathe normally again.

Shaarvan continued to smile as he led me over to a table away from the others. I was glad we didn't have to sit close to them. I hated the men. They'd humiliated me with their disinterest.

I collapsed onto a chair stool and waited for someone to bring us food. Shaarvan sat down, too, but there didn't seem to be any waiters. How were we going to get our dinner?

While I waited for Shaarvan to figure out the problem, I glanced about. I had listened to Shaarvan's words, but I hadn't believed them. The reaction of the men still made no sense to me. I mean, I wasn't drop dead gorgeous or anything, but usually, when I went places, men gave me the kind of attention which said they appreciated the way I looked. You know what I mean. My hair was long and full, curling even when I did nothing to it. So it was brown, not blonde, but the highlights were reddish-gold, and I was comfortable with it.

My body was good, too — not perfect. My top could have been fuller, and my nose was too short, but I had good eyes in a rather odd color of aquamarine, and everyone said my lashes were too long to be real (although they really were).

I still had on the dress from my interview. It had a little polyester in it, which I know is a sign of its being cheap, but it also meant it didn't wrinkle easily. Which is to say that with my slinky nylons, my red heels, and my navy and red dress, I probably still looked OK.

Even if my hair was a mess, which was probably true, but usually my hair only got tousled like a sex queen on a magazine cover, as one of my roommates said.

So why would all the men just ignore me? It was like one more shock piled up on top of all the others. I wasn't used to being slighted. Maybe this whole place was gay.

Shaarvan's eyes mocked me like he could read my thoughts. "The men do not look at you, Shaara," he said, "because I do not permit it."

My mouth dropped open. Was it a coincidence? Could Shaarvan truly read minds? Just in case, I concentrated on burning his brain like a French fry forgotten in the frying grease.

Shaarvan didn't seem the least bothered. His brain didn't cook, and he didn't look like he got a headache from my thoughts. In fact, he laughed at me again.

When he finally stopped chuckling, he pressed down on something in the middle of the table. The button or communicator, or whatever it was, started humming like a woman doing heavy oneness with her meditation. The humming only stopped when a server unit, a robot, came over to the table. The robot, a real one, not the kind with someone inside just pretending, looked almost human, but its eyes were like doll eyes, glassy and empty, and they were flashing synchronized blinking yellow lights.

Shaarvan spoke to it. Once more, I wondered what language he was using. Could it be Arabic or Russian, perhaps?

When the robot left, I asked.

Shaarvan's eyes smiled his amusement. "Altarian," he said, "but the robot handles many other languages."

I sighed. "English?"

Shaarvan's lips curved. I thought I'd die from the waves of charisma this guy sent out. Did I tell you he had dimples? Between his dimples and his deep, sexy laugh, I could barely remember what I'd asked.

"No," he laughed, like English was too insignificant for a robot to know.

I was so captivated by the laugh it took me a full minute to realize Shaarvan was putting down my native tongue. I started right in on defending it, but before I had time, the robot waiter returned with our meals.

The food came in white glass TV dinner trays with clear plastic wrapping over the top. Yummy . . . TV dinners. Shaarvan placed them in the center of the table, and they sank. The table melted back over them.

I couldn't believe it. I hadn't eaten in a month, and Shaarvan fed the table. Unbelievable. Wonderful lunch. The table eats, and we watch. I *must* be dreaming. There could be no other answer for all this madness.

A minute later, like the mushroom table and the chairs, our meals rose up from the center of the table. Shaarvan scooted my dinner towards me and pulled away the covering. The air filled with the smell of wild mushrooms, olive oil, and sausage. I watched, salivating, stomach growling, ready to dive in. At first, I could see nothing but steam rising, and it carried with it incredibly delectable smells. Was that a hint of garlic? I waved my hand back and forth and peered down. When the food finally became visible, I wished I hadn't looked. It was a plate full of worms, writhing like they do when a log is first lifted, and they are startled by the light. I couldn't help my screams. I reared back and away from the table faster than a ping-pong ball hitting the wall.

I wasn't paying the least bit of attention to Shaarvan. He was like a snake striking at its dinner rabbit. His hand darted instantly and seized my wrist in a most unpleasant manner. Perhaps that's what a boa constrictor around your wrist feels like. All I know is the hand gripping me started tightening like a vise, and the pain of it halted me in the middle of my leap.

"Sit down," Shaarvan ordered. There was no amusement in his eyes. I could see I had irritated him.

I lifted my chin and gave a glare strong enough to wilt a tulip. A sudden spasm of pain was my reward. It called attention to the fact that Shaarvan's grasp on my wrist was steadily tightening. I could read the anger in his eyes. I knew at once he would keep squeezing until every bone in my wrist would be crushed if I didn't obey.

A flash of memory recalled a football jock I'd seen compress a beer can into a one-inch hardened lump of metal. I needed my wrist. I dropped my eyes. At once, the pressure lessened.

"The worms . . ." I said. "I can't . . ."

The fury in Shaarvan's eyes was burning me. I couldn't look at him. I didn't dare, but I could still feel the heat of his rage.

"Sit down," Shaarvan ordered again. Once more, his hand tightened on my wrist. I couldn't argue when my wrist was breaking. I sat down gingerly, avoiding looking at the plate full of writhing worms.

Immediately, my wrist was freed. I held it with my other hand. The skin was puckered where Shaarvan had squeezed so hard, but the pain was almost gone. I attempted to rub the ache away.

I felt Shaarvan's eyes still focused on me, studying me. I feared to look up.

He sighed as if trying to find patience. "They are not worms, Shaara. It was only the heat," he said at last.

The anger was gone from his voice. I looked up. Once more, amusement was back.

"Look, Shaara."

I peeked, scarcely believing the worms would have vanished, but Shaarvan was right. There was only a plate full of food, something resembling curly spaghetti.

I felt like an idiot. My eyes teared in relief. They met Shaarvan's. His were softer, not smiling, but the hint of it was there.

He picked up something which looked like plastic tweezers and placed them in my hand. They were long, skinny things, like the long-nosed pliers I'd seen in a copy machine repairman's hand. Shaarvan placed the implement in my hand and squeezed my fingers shut on the tweezers. It worked. I got a tweezer full of noodles. Yummy.

I laughed and began squeezing the strange utensil. It was incredibly fun. The noodles were easy to tweeze, but you needed to dump them all into your mouth without biting the plastic. You had to get the grip just right, or the whole wrapped-around mess plopped back into your plate, and then the tweezers became a bear to hold because they got all slippery.

It became even more complicated when I started laughing. I giggled when I missed, and then inevitably, it all plopped down again.

I was having an absolute blast when I looked up and discovered that Shaarvan had not even begun to eat. He was sitting with his elbows on the table, his hands intertwined, his chin on them, chuckling as he watched me trying to eat.

"Aren't you going to eat?" I asked.

"Later," he said. "Right now, I'm enjoying watching my wife."

Without thinking, I smiled at him. When he smiled back, I almost dropped the spaghetti, tweezers and all. What a politician the guy would make — if he didn't tell everyone he was running for senator of outer space or something.

"This is a great invention." I told him. "It's going to be the latest thing in all the Italian restaurants."

Shaarvan didn't correct me, and I didn't think about how if he was telling the truth, I'd never get to introduce them anywhere.

The food wasn't that great — about like the food on an airplane or in a cafeteria, but I was amazingly hungry. I ate more than I needed, and still, there was a big pile left on my plate.

"Is this Altarian food?" I kidded Shaarvan.

He'd finally started eating, and I wasn't sure if he'd answer me, but I felt a lot better with my tummy full, and I absolutely could not be quiet.

"Actually, this dish is from Grenobilitob," he said.

"Oh." A great conversation stopper. Shaarvan continued to shovel the stuff in. He was a neat eater, though. None of it ended on his dark gray overalls. Give him a plus for tidiness. On the last date I'd had, the dumb jock had dripped all over himself and me.

"How do you know what foods my body can tolerate?" I asked. "I mean, people could be poisoned by foods from an alien planet." I figured that two could play the alien game.

"Your body has been altered. It will process the same foods as mine."

"Altered for Altar, huh?" I joked. Shaarvan ignored me.

"Actually," I continued. "I have already trained my body to accept hamburgers, French fries, and colas. Don't you have any of those?"

"You will find that our foods meet all your nutritional needs. We do not eat animals or empty calories."

"You take all the fun out of life then," I complained.

I guess Shaarvan liked the spaghetti a lot better than I did. He finished all of his. Then he pushed our plates into the center of the table. The plates were immediately gobbled up. I was delighted to learn that Shaarvan didn't expect his *wife* to wash dishes.

Shaarvan's finger reached up to stroke my cheek. He drew a pattern downwards and traced my lips. It was strange how his fingertips set me on fire.

"You will discover we *do* know how to have fun, Shaara. I will teach you."

"You mean like parties with dances and lots of hoopla?"

"Not on the ship. On Altar, there is that." His eyes held mine. I knew he was searching for words. "You will see, my wife."

Shaarvan reached into an inner pocket and pulled out a small brass, bullet-shaped capsule. He twisted it, and something white fell out. Shaarvan held the tablet out to me. "You will take this medication daily for another of your months."

I took the pill from him. It looked like aspirin. I fake-plopped it into my mouth. I thought I was very clever about pretending to swallow it, but Shaarvan wasn't fooled or pleased. A flash of anger made his eyes like granite. With a painful jerk of the same wrist he'd almost crushed before, Shaarvan pried open my hand. I cried out, but I don't think he noticed.

This time, he held the pill to my mouth. "Open," he ordered. I wanted to lock my lips and bar his entrance, but he was twisting my wrist with his boa grip. I heard my wrist crack. I opened my lips, and the pill went in. I pretended to swallow the stupid thing, but Shaarvan held a cup to my lips and ordered me to drink. The pill, like a sugar cube, dissolved instantly in my mouth.

It was bitter, and the taste was not at all like aspirin. It tasted like a combination of hot mustard and horseradish. I gagged and drank more water. Then I coughed and coughed as the pill dissolved, burning my throat, my esophagus, my windpipe, and all the other parts deep inside me. I emptied my glass of water and eyed his. His hand gestured for me to take it. Only after I'd emptied the contents of his did I start to feel better.

Shaarvan laughed. The sound echoed even longer than my coughing. Perhaps I'd made a face. Maybe it was just that I'd given in to him. I lowered my eyes and hated him for several minutes, but I fumed silently. Perhaps he was the conqueror this time, but every Nero met his downfall.

Eventually, Shaarvan stopped laughing. I saw his eyes narrow as he realized I was supporting my injured arm. "Give me your wrist," he demanded.

I didn't want to. I didn't want him to touch me, but I also didn't argue when he took my hand and brought it closer. Almost gently, he examined my wrist, waving my hand back and forth, his manner as impersonal as a doctor's. He flexed the bone. I gasped at the pain. His eyes studied me a moment. "It is not broken," he said. "You are lucky."

I opened my mouth to speak, but I didn't know what to say. I closed my mouth and looked down.

He held my wrist a moment more, then placed my hand down on the table as if he'd lost interest. Yet I felt his eyes fastened on me. I couldn't stand it. I looked up. As if he held some power over me, I couldn't look away. I was frozen, a deer in an auto's headlights.

"Be careful, Shaara," he said finally. His voice had a stern, father's lecture quality like the injured wrist had been my fault. "I am unused to disobedience."

A shiver went through me. Shaarvan was frightening me, as he'd done earlier. It wasn't the words but something in his voice. It was the tone of authority, the policeman's assumption you wouldn't argue when he held a gun to your head.

No, I had it wrong. It wasn't like that at all. The force of Shaarvan's voice was much stronger; Shaarvan was so confident in the strength of his power over me that he needed no gun.

Shaarvan

Little Shaara has fire, no question of it, but when she rebelled the first time in the cafeteria, I could only laugh at her attempts to fight me. Did she not see how ridiculous her efforts were? I could crush twenty good-sized men in the space of a few minutes, and she, the size of a youngling, dared take me on. She has much courage but little wisdom.

There was a moment when she felt the Power. Her body recognized my nature, yet not even that prevented her from her challenge at the table when she was frightened over the appearance of the food. I could have injured her gravely, but still, she defied me. Will she learn? Can she be taught? Was she what my mother was like when my father first conquered her? It is possible. But my mother's judgment is good. Will Shaara be trainable?

Susan

Shaarvan led me through corridor after corridor. We walked through a maze just like before, passing doors and turning left and right at different places where the hall offered options. I was soon so confused I knew I could never retrace my way, yet I still struggled to hold the directions in my mind. I kept thinking it might be important to know the route.

Several times, Shaarvan shortened his steps as he realized his long strides were beyond me. He looked down at me then as if he'd forgotten my presence, but he said nothing, and we continued on without pause.

"Where are you taking me this time?" I asked.

"You must learn to be quiet, Shaara. Altarian women do not ask questions without permission. They do not speak at all without their husbands granting them leave to do so."

"Then it is a good thing I'm not an Altarian woman," I said before I had considered whether it was wise.

Shaarvan halted on the spot. He whirled around to face me. "Do you challenge me, Shaara?"

I was kind of unclear what he meant, but I was afraid to say "yes." I shook my head.

"Then learn to obey."

This was not the moment to take a stand. I lowered my eyes and followed Shaarvan silently.

We continued, winding around, in and out. At times, Shaarvan held his left hand to doors that whooshed open, then closed behind. I realized then it didn't matter if I tried to hold a mental map of our course. It would do me little good. I couldn't go through those doors. Shaarvan's eyes met mine, and I saw the knowledge in his eyes. He'd known I was counting every door, attempting to memorize the directions as we'd walked.

I wanted to protest the cruelty, but his finger planted the *shush* sign on my lips to remind me to be quiet.

At last, we arrived at his intended destination. It was a room filled with men. They looked up as we entered. I started to ask for help, but it was the same reception as in the cafeteria. It was as if they didn't see me. To them, only Shaarvan had entered through the door, and I was like a book he carried, noted, but unimportant.

I ignored them, too, and let my eyes scan the room. The large screen at the front attracted my full concentration. It supposedly showed us the outside, which was black as the sky on a cloudy night. A sudden streak of light flared. It was an incredible brightness as it moved across the emptiness of the screen. Then it was gone, and the darkness felt like the bottom of a well.

Shaarvan was watching me. He must have known I couldn't keep on doubting his words when I saw this. He lifted my chin with his fingers until he had captured my eyes. "I will never lie to you, Shaara. I promise. What I have told you about Altar and the ship and about being my wife is all true." He held my eyes another moment, and then he let me go.

I had not wanted to believe him. I had wanted this to be a dream I would wake up from tomorrow. I would go back to school, laugh about the silliness, and maybe tell someone what a ridiculous nightmare I'd had. I didn't want to be staring into a stranger's eyes who promised me he'd never lie about stealing me away from all I'd ever known.

"This is the control room of the ship, Shaara," Shaarvan told me. "You will be absolutely silent here always. No questions, no complaints. Understand?"

I nodded. I was too shocked to think straight. I couldn't decide whether to cry, to scream, or to lie down and die, and this man was ordering me to be silent.

"You will sit here, Shaara," he ordered. I sat down like an obedient puppet, but inside, I was Dorothy from Earth, and I wanted to click my heels together and go back home.

The seat Shaarvan had pointed to was the closest thing I'd seen to a real chair since I'd encountered Shaarvan. It had fur like a shaggy dog but was beanbag shaped. I sat down in it, and it lowered until my feet rested comfortably on the ground. Then, it kind of shifted gently, and the back crept forward to meld with my body. I almost jumped up, it surprised me so, but my movement brought the eyes of Shaarvan. I stayed put, accepting the lesser of two evils.

When Shaarvan turned away, I breathed more easily, and my eyes began to explore the room we were in. It wasn't like a *science fiction movie's control room,* but it was close enough. I would have known it was the piloting room without Shaarvan's labeling it so. The panoramic screen showed a great immensity, like being on the ocean, far from land, and looking out across the enormity of it, wondering how there could be so much water. This vastness of space made the oceans of Earth look like the tiniest droplets of liquid, and the blackness was further than I could see, further than Terrans could ever go.

For a long while, I watched the wonder of it. The splashes of light, I figured, must be giant suns streaking by so quickly that they, too, seemed like mere droplets in the limitlessness of space.

For an undefinable period of time, I developed a hope this was still all a hoax. I felt if I watched closely enough, I would catch some impossible error, and I would suddenly prove the fakeness of the scene, but other than science fiction movies and reels from science clips of various voyages to the moon or Mars, I really had no mental image of what I should expect to see. I knew Shaarvan's ship was more advanced, compared with anything on Earth, that even an error I thought I'd discovered could merely be something beyond my Terran understanding.

Every moment we traveled, we were leaving my planet farther and farther behind. How many years would it take to journey out of our solar system? A lifetime? Yet this ship was so far from my home. I couldn't even see the Sun anymore. We were probably already beyond Earth's charted realms of space.

Hope is hard to give up. I kept stumbling over *what-ifs* that belonged in fantasy/sci-fi novels. What if Shaarvan got tired of me and returned me to Earth? What if I met someone who would take me home? What if I took over the ship? What if Shaarvan fell in love with me and took me back to Earth because he'd rather live without me than see me unhappy?

The real truth was I couldn't be like Dorothy and her magic shoes. Maybe I'd have to be Scarlett O'Hara and say, "I can't think about this today. If I do, I'll go crazy."

I forced my eyes away from what I didn't want to acknowledge. I concentrated instead on viewing the rest of the room. The panels of instruments and the men peering down at them offered little interest to me, but on the right, individual screens showed scenes around the ship. One screen viewed a room full of caskets. The camera touring the room showed controls and individual faceplates. There were girls inside the caskets.

I forgot I'd been ordered to sit in the furry rabbit chair. The sight of those caskets drew me towards the video screen. I peered in, watching the faces. I looked for one I might recognize. I forgot about Shaarvan.

His eyes glowed angrily as he yanked me around to face him. "You were told to sit."

I was caught up in my fascination with the casket dwellers. His words didn't penetrate, nor did I give credence to the expression on his face. "They're the girls from my college, aren't they?" I cried out. "You've kidnapped all of them."

"Silence." he demanded. Shaarvan's words were the slap that broke through my distraction. His eyes inspected the room. Only when he'd completed his assessment did I feel the full force of his anger. He grabbed my hand, whirled me around, and pulled me from the room. As we marched down the corridor, I tried to pull back to slow him down, but he wouldn't allow it. He kept me at a half jog and strode on, his long legs galloping up the distance. When he rounded the corners, I felt like a dancer at the end of a Cancan line.

The return to his room was none too soon. I was out of breath and panting. Shaarvan punched a button, and a large double bed grew out of the floor. I backed against the computer.

His fingers flashed a message into the air, but it had no meaning to me. I knew he was demanding something, and I was supposed to obey. Impatient with my ignorance, Shaarvan grabbed my wrist to pull me over. I didn't fight him, but I cried out in pain. It was the same wrist he'd hurt before. He dragged me down on the bed beside him and then let go of me. I started to move away, but he flashed another sign with his hand and said, "Stay." I was debating whether to obey when his hand grabbed my other wrist. When I jerked to move away, he began his tightening and twisting on my good wrist. I froze.

He was glaring at me, his head shaking back and forth. "You are difficult," he said. He stressed the *you* part like no one else had ever caused him any trouble.

My mouth flew open. I was difficult? I had more or less done everything he'd told me. He'd given me no choice. How could I be difficult when he was so ready to crush my wrist into smithereens?

"Wait a minute." I said, "I haven't . . . ."

"Enough." His hand rose up as if he planned to slap me. I cringed and shut my eyes. He didn't hit me. He sighed and dropped his hand.

"The others did not require the explanations you do, nor did they constantly rebel. I do not know whether you are too young to understand the dangers or just stupid."

"What others?" I blurted out before I could stop to think whether it would anger him.

Shaarvan shook his head at my rashness. "We have raided many planets, Shaara. I have had many girls. You are the first to cause so much inconvenience."

This conversation could not be happening. I was imagining it. I was dreaming it. I was making it up . . .

"Then take me back," I shot out at him. "All returns accepted."

"You are my wife."

"So were the others. Where are they now?"

"You are the first I have called my wife."

"Why me." I threw the words at him too forcefully. Shaarvan's eyes grew dangerous. "I'm sorry," I cried out. I knew it was cowardly, but I also knew he'd hurt me if I wasn't careful.

It was close. I saw it in the tension of his posture. The stiffness of his anger ebbed slightly.

"You have much to learn," he said, his voice heavy with warning.

I gulped and looked down.

His eyes studied me. He did that a great deal. What was he searching for? How was I so different from the other girls he'd had? Why had he made me his wife? Where were the other girls? Were they dead . . . or sleeping like the girls I'd seen? Why was I awake here with him while the others were sleeping? My mind reeled question after question, but I didn't dare ask a single one. I kept my eyes on the velvet white of the carpet.

"Better," Shaarvan said.

I should have kept my eyes lowered, but his tone angered me. I looked up and glared with all the force of my Irish heritage.

Once more, Shaarvan shook his head from side to side slowly. "You *are* like Teea," he said, and there was wonder in his voice.

And in that instant, for some reason, he was no longer angry with me, nor was he mocking me with his laughter. Stunned by the change, I forgot my annoyance and gaped in bewilderment.

"I have known other Terrans," he continued while the knuckles of his free hand caressed my cheek. "Many are spirited, but you are *different*. I think perhaps you are . . . All right, Shaara. I shall be patient with you. Perhaps you *are* worth the extra effort."

The monologue confused me. I didn't know what he meant. Who was Teea? Yet, I realized something had changed. It was like back at the screening when I'd thought he liked me. For a moment there, Shaarvan had seen me. He had seen me as a *person*.

"Come," Shaarvan said, standing up. The conversation was obviously over.

He led me to the computer and placed a kind of earphone on my head. It fastened around my head securely. "Attempt to remove this, Shaara," he warned, "and the pain of the shock will be like when you touched the door."

Then he walked away and lay down on the bed, leaving me to face the torture the computer inflicted.

It was a learning machine, unlike anything I'd ever seen on Earth. It hummed coarsely, smelled of old tires, and, even worse, gave me no choice whether or not I wished to learn its lessons. Failure and incorrectness brought on pain.

There were degrees, I discovered. Lack of effort was rewarded with a higher jolt than a simple wrong answer. I struggled harder than in any language lab, but the language was far more difficult than French or Spanish because there was nothing familiar. There were no cognates or words that sounded similar, and I had nothing written to help me remember, nor could I take notes because I had no pencil or paper.

When Shaarvan finally freed me from the machine, I was limp. There was no rebellion in me as he led me to the bed. He pushed me down on it and moved my legs up onto the bed. I trembled at his touch.

The lights went out, and Shaarvan lay down beside me. I rolled onto my side, away from him. Shaarvan's hand traveled languidly on my thigh. I felt disgust, revulsion, and the shock of absolute horror. I froze, not knowing what to do about it. Protest, fight him, lie still, and pretend it wasn't happening?

His hand moved to rest on my buttocks. He squeezed my bottom, then pulled me nearer. In the closeness, our bodies molded together like two puzzle pieces that fit. I felt his hardness against my skin. That brought me to the brink of panic. Although I rarely cry, my dam broke then. The day's hardships had undone me. My tears began slowly but quickly turned into a torrent of misery. Like a ship anchored in a storm, I bucked and plunged, attempting to break away, but there was no freedom. I was at the mercy of the captain, and I already knew that the captain had no compassion.

Shaarvan

The whole day, I had made mistake after mistake with the girl. Why had I not seen she was on overload? Why had I not been gentler in my training?

I had taken Shaara to the control room. From her expression, I think she finally believed all I had told her. I was behind schedule, and

I left her sitting in the visitor's chair. I thought it would be good for her to think about her new life and to find acceptance of it. It did not occur to me that she would have time to search the room. That quick mind of hers not only discovered the other girls but, in doing so, disturbed the concentration of the crew.

I took my wife back to our room. She had wearied me beyond my patience, yet I attempted once more to explain to her how her attitude was dangerous. Wisely, she fears me. I see it in her eyes. But when I trampled her pride, she reared up like a she-tiger. My satisfaction with her curious dignity robbed me of my ability to discipline her properly.

I put her on a learning sequence, then. She did poorly, fighting against it instead of giving in to the machine. It is my fault I so poorly predicted her nature. I shall redesign the program tomorrow.

My worst failure was in attempting to take her on her first night. She was worn out with stress and the fatigue of adaptation. I thought she would find the joining enjoyable, and it would relax her. I was wrong about that, too.

The only positive for the day is my discovery that I have achieved my aim. I wanted a wife as strong and capable as my father's wife has proven to be. My mother, Teea, has been a delight to him. She was a good breeder and mother, and she companions him well. I was sure I could find another like her in her home world, and I am positive that I have done so. Shaara has all the attributes I esteem in Teea. Perhaps Shaara's troublesome nature may merely be the reflection of those qualities.

Tomorrow, I shall begin again in my training of her. I understand now she will require an inexhaustible quantity of patience. Stars help me.

Susan

Shaarvan did not take me then or in the night. I think it was my tears that saved me. When I woke, he was dressing. I was afraid to look at him. What would I see in his face? Would he be angry with me? Would he retaliate? What would happen to me next?

"Shaara," he said when he saw I was awake. He uttered a string of words that I presumed was Altarian. I had no idea what he was telling me. I figured from his gestures he wanted me to use the bathroom. I did so.

When I came out, Shaarvan handed me a dress. It was pretty material in a pale yellow color. The material was soft to the touch but slightly stiff in texture, like corduroy. I went back into the bathroom with the dress clutched in my hand. Shaarvan followed behind me.

Did he intend to watch me change? Would I have no privacy?

"You will dress in Altarian clothing from now on," he instructed me. "The fastenings go in the front, but they are to be kept tightly drawn. Nothing may be worn under the dress."

"You don't mean . . . ?"

"You will wear nothing underneath the dress. When you come out, you will give me your Terran clothes. You will not wear them again."

Shaarvan motioned something with his hands, and then he left. I didn't understand his gestures but I knew what his eyes had said. A flash of warning in the eyes is multilingual.

I did not dare leave on my bra or panties. I placed them in the pile with my other Terran things. The dress Shaarvan had given me was long-sleeved and full-length to my ankles. It fit me perfectly in size, and although I didn't usually wear long dresses, it was pretty enough to be tolerable. The color was nice, a margarine shade that suited my reddish-brown, gold-streaked hair. The skirt was loose enough to be walked in comfortably.

The underside of the dress was soft against my skin. It felt like the material had been coated with fuzz. Even under the arms, it would not chaff. I wished I had a mirror to see how I looked.

When I was dressed, I was shy about departing from the bathroom. I was the kind of person who wore panties to bed. Now, Shaarvan expected me to go about the ship without them *or* a bra?

I was taking too long. I didn't wish to begin the day by angering Shaarvan. My wrist still ached from when I'd annoyed him the day before. I took a moment to do some deep and heavy breathing, and then, still feeling naked, I stepped out.

Shaarvan immediately jumped up and came towards me. His eyes questioned as he took my Terran clothes.

"You wear only the dress?" he demanded.

I nodded hesitantly and felt my face grow hot. I stood with my head down, staring at the floor.

Shaarvan didn't say anything else. He turned and carried my clothes to a place I hadn't noticed. He pushed a button on the wall. A circular mouth opened. Shaarvan was shoving my clothes into it before I realized what he intended.

"No, please . . ." I cried out as my brand-new red heels disappeared into the hole. "I just bought them," I said sadly.

"You have no further use of them, Shaara."

"But you didn't give me any shoes. Am I supposed to go barefoot?"

Shaarvan didn't respond. He was busy stuffing my favorite dress into the gap.

"Couldn't I at least keep them as a souvenir?" I asked.

Down everything went. My nylons, panties, and bra soon joined. With their departure, I felt even more exposed and unprotected, as if I were a knight whose armament had just been seized. I crossed my arms and glanced about, wishing for someplace to hide.

Having demolished everything I'd owned, Shaarvan pushed the button again, and the hole disappeared. Then, he looked at me. "Turn around slowly," he ordered.

The warning I saw in his eyes gave me no choice. The room wasn't cold, but I shivered.

"Drop your arms. I wish to see you," he ordered.

It wasn't one of my favorite moments. I was used to men looking at me, but this was different. I felt exposed, unprotected, and weaponless.

For a moment, Shaarvan eyed my body as if I were a statue. Then he nodded his approval. "Good. You have obeyed well. The dress suits you, and you look better without excessive garments against your skin."

He walked over to the chair by the computer and picked up a pair of yellow slippers. They were made of cloth the same color and texture as my dress and looked rather like ballerina slippers except with thick rubber-like soles.

I took them from him, sat down on the chair, slipped them on, and then began to tie the shoestrings.

"No. That is wrong," Shaarvan said, shaking his head. He bent down, moved my hands aside, and instructed me on the correct Altarian way to fasten shoes.

When he decided the lesson had been learned suitably, Shaarvan pulled me up to a standing position. Once more, his eyes surveyed my body. Again, my face grew red. I wanted to cross my arms, but Shaarvan's hands held me still.

He released them, but it was only a second before he'd gripped them both again in one strong grasp. His other hand rose to touch my face, caressing my cheek, then slid down around my neck and lower.

I was shivering from fear, but I didn't move, nor could I have, since his legs secured my lower body, and his hand still held me close.

"Shaara, why do you tremble? I will not harm you unnecessarily, my wife."

I felt like a mouse in a hungry snake's cage. There was no place to run.

"Do not fear our joining. I shall pleasure you," he murmured.

Did the snake tell the mouse not to be frightened? Was it not the mouse's nature to be afraid?

"You paint pictures in your mind, Shaara, but they are wrong. I shall not pounce on you to devour. I shall gentle you. I shall show you lovely things. Relax, my wife, my Shaara."

He pulled me closer. His lips breathed warmth on my shivering neck. His touch sent goosebumps down my spine. How could he believe I could relax?

"I shall not take your body now, my wife. I shall only awaken you. Trust me."

His eyes met mine, gentle and warm, yet I was so frightened I could barely stand. But I couldn't move either, for his eyes held me captured. I felt frozen under the spell of those sparkling silver eyes, eyes that pulled me in. I was drowning in their liquid mercury. Oh, luscious feeling. If Shaarvan's eyes were the magnets, I was the little iron bearing that clung to the pull of his magnetic force. His eyes enticed, mesmerized, and my resistance deserted me.

His hand on my breast squeezed the nipple. It didn't hurt me. I shuddered. The water in my blood began to whirl. A spasm rocked me. Was it pain or delight? I didn't know.

Shaarvan's eyes were captors, but I didn't resist. His hand stroked and petted. He allowed me no outside thought. My whole world was his hand and the pleasure it gave, the hand rhythmically circling, sending tremors of heavy, sensual feeling inward and throughout my body. Like a pebble thrown into the pond, waves of delight expanded wider and broader across my body. I whimpered. It was all too much. I could scarcely breathe.

Tony, my roommate's brother had said I was frigid. He'd tried to awaken me, but his lips had been slurpy-slimy, and I'd felt nothing but revulsion. His hands, as they'd crawled from my waist upwards, had only been tickly and bothersome.

Boy, had Tony been wrong about me. Shaarvan's hands didn't make me laugh. His hands made me tingle and sing. I was so alive; every cell in my body was doing cartwheels. I was so hot I could have melted the North Pole.

Shaarvan broke off from his cascade of kisses to smile down at me. "You are relaxed now, Shaara, but your brain is still fluttering all around. No more thinking, my wife. Focus on what you are feeling."

Shaarvan took my hand in his and brought it up to his mouth. His lips touched the back of my hand. His tongue darted across my skin in a pattern. I couldn't look away.

He turned my hand over and began at the wrist. His tongue spread ripples downward, clear across my palm. It was painful, but a different kind of pain, a pain I wanted, needed, craved more than life. I didn't understand what it was I was feeling, but the torture was exquisite. I was frightened by it, but still, I wanted him to continue.

"Shaarvan," I said. "Please . . ."

I didn't know what I wanted to say. Please go on? Please stop? He knew. His eyes smiled full force into mine, and he nodded. Then his lips rose. They took too long to reach mine. I met them midway. I was so eager for the touch of his lips that I couldn't wait. I remembered how his lips had been like this before when he'd proclaimed me his wife. The taste of him had driven me wild.

His lips seized mine, and I fell into another world again. Once more, the lips drove me to abandonment. I had no room for outside thoughts then. There was only Shaarvan.

His hand deserted my breast. I whimpered. He chuckled softly, but his lips were devouring mine. I gave into the luscious feeling, lost in sensation. My body sagged into him. His lips were all that held me upright.

I felt his hands on my buttocks, cupping and squeezing. I wanted to protest, to pull back against this intimacy, this invasion, but he pulled me tighter, and I could say nothing. I reveled in the feel of his body pressed against mine. I felt the rock hardness of him, but Shaarvan brought me no fear now. I was beyond fear. I wanted him closer, closer until his essence was part of me.

Delicious waves of longing traveled through me. I felt his skin, the hard, strong muscles in his back. They flexed and rippled, urging me on. I was alive, more alive than I'd ever been. I couldn't get enough of him, his lips, his tongue, now plunging into my mouth. I wanted him.

None of this was like me. I was the ice maiden, my name in the dorm because I wouldn't *put out*. But I was slush now. I was liquid. Shaarvan would soon have to swim to me.

But something was wrong. I was ready to fly free from the rational world, free from responsibility and common sense. I was ready to join with the poets and lovers, but Shaarvan was starting to retreat. His tongue had stopped teasing me. His fingers had stopped painting patterns of burning desire all over my skin. He was cooling the flames raging between us.

"No," I cried out. Shaarvan's lips returned, but his kisses were less. They no longer consumed me. His embrace grew gentle and sweet. The blaze between us was lessening. He was pulling back, tamping off the fire. His kisses moved to my neck, languid and easy, but I wasn't ready for that. I didn't want him to take his mouth away from mine. I knew there was more, and I wanted him desperately to show me, to share all he knew.

But, gradually, he withdrew. His hands smoothed my hair gently, calmly, forcing me to quiet until only his eyes held me to him.

"Shaara," he said at last, in a voice of incredible gentleness and patience. His lips darted a quick kiss to my face. "You are full of fire, a luscious delight." His hand moved up to brush his knuckles down my cheek. "I have chosen well."

The velvet way he said it, full of lust and hunger, once more sent shivers through me. I knew I'd pleased him. His eyes weren't mocking me. He wanted me as much as I wanted him. I read it in his eyes, and

I felt it in his body. I didn't understand. Why had he stopped? I stared into his eyes, full of questions.

Shaarvan's hand continued to brush teasingly down the side of my face. It was a calming, tranquilizing sensation. My face craved his touch, but his touch was no longer sexual. Shaarvan picked up a lock of hair that had fallen down into my face. He smoothed it back in its place.

My eyes watched his every movement. How had he gained such complete possession of me? The touch of his fingers halted my breath. Again, he brushed his hand down my cheek. It was such a gentle touch with so much promise.

"Shaara, you have been slumbering until today. Just now, you have begun to rouse, but you are still half-asleep. Tonight, your eyes will open, and you will see. I will teach you everything you yearn to know. Tonight, I will make you my wife in more than name. Think about it all day, Shaara. Think about the touch of my fingers on your skin, my hands caressing your breasts, my lips tasting yours, my tongue plunging down inside you. Think about it, Shaara, and be ready."

Chapter Four
First Times

Shaarvan

The girl's fear of joining seems to be greater than I have felt with the others. In my studies, I have not read of this. Perhaps it is merely an individual characteristic. She is not immune to my Power. She was swayed easily when I played her body. She will not resist me this night, but I must go slowly with her. She is not a mere girl to be passed on when I tire of her. I must remind myself I have begun the training of a *wife*. As such, my own impatience is detrimental to her future stability.

Side note: Shaara is small in stature, it is true, but her body is well-developed. Beneath a proper dress, she is quite pleasing to the eye. The day will be long, but I shall anticipate the night. A treasure is worth the wait.

Susan

Shaarvan promised me ecstasy but then strove off into the sunset, or at least, wherever captains go when they have work to do. And not only did he desert me when I needed him most, but he also left me there to be tormented. He hooked me up once again to the sadistic machine that pounded my brain cells with volts of agony and expected me to understand a language beyond my ability.

"Please, Shaarvan," I'd begged. "I can't do this. I try, and the computer zaps me anyway. Please don't make me stay here."

"The program will teach you the Altarian language. It has succeeded with thousands of girls. As quick as you are, and with your exposure to different Terran languages, you will pick up Altarian readily."

"I am good with Earth languages, but your Altarian is different," I'd argued/begged.

"Altarian is easy. You will find it so once you begin to learn."

"I will do better if you disconnect the punishment part. I want to learn, and I will. I promise I will, but please, don't torture me."

He'd laughed at me then. "Torture. You are a child, my wife. You do not understand how gentle I have been with you. I shall waste no more time with your arguments. You will adapt to the machine, and you will learn."

He'd left me there with the computer, his eyes unbending and uncaring. He was right. It *was* pointless to argue; he would never be influenced by something someone else wanted. How could I have been deceived by his kisses and the touch of his hand on my face?

Through my suffering, I did my best, but I was frustrated, and I felt the lesson did me no good. It drilled me for hours, and I was forced to speak into it, be corrected and shocked, and it went on and on. Its dribble grew longer. I think it was giving me whole sentences of meaningless repetitions. I kept on going because I had to. The pain, or my fear of it, drove me without mercy.

When Shaarvan returned and detached me from the horrible, horrible machine, I flung myself into his arms and began sobbing. For a moment only, I felt his strength, but he gave me too short a time to feel any comfort.

"Enough," he ordered abruptly. "You will become accustomed to it."

I stared at him in shock. This was the man who had brought me to the point where I'd offered him all of me? How could I have let lust sway me from myself? I'd never given into it before. How could I have been brought so low by a man I despised? A man who was rough and unfeeling, a man who ordered me about, a man who would only use me as he'd used the others, then cast me away.

Shaarvan seemed unaware of my turmoil. Why should he care what I felt? He wasn't in the mood for it now. His compassion and kindness were like window wipers, to be used only when needed.

I raised my chin and backed away. I fled into the bathroom to cry. He didn't follow me. He didn't care.

When I came out, my tears had all been removed. My eyes were not even scratchy, and I felt better. Thank you, modern technology, I whispered to the bathroom mist.

My tears had restored my resolution. I would not donate my virginity to such a stone-hearted, slithering snake. I would fight him with all my power. If he hit me or beat me for it, so be it. It would be easier to hate him.

Shaarvan, like the typical male, was not aware of anything amiss. He probably accepted my silence as the obedience of his latest concubine. I expected him to start to whistle *Oh, What a Beautiful Day* at any minute.

When he took me to the cafeteria that day, I refused to look at the food directly after the heating unit performed its function. He laughed. "What, no worms today?"

I glared at him, but he ignored it and only laughed more. His laughter echoed cruelly, but none of the others paid the least attention.

Shaarvan didn't take me to the control room. He took me, instead, to the ship's gym. I was glad. I had anger to burn.

I tried to use the machines, but my dress interfered. It would not let me spread my legs to mount any of the exercisers, and, at one point, all the excess material in the hem became caught in the cogs.

"Stand still," Shaarvan demanded after he'd torn the material free. He knelt beside me and tied my dress at mid-thigh. The knot he made wasn't easy to do with the thickness of the material. It took great strength to pull the knot tight, and I understood he needed leverage to do so, but I don't believe he needed to reach underneath my dress to do it. And when it was done, and he stood there with his hand on my inner thigh, just resting it, not moving, his eyes burned into mine.

"Your thigh is soft, Shaara. Is that how you feel all over?" he asked with a teasing smile which hinted of things to come.

I felt my face turning hot. I remembered how Shaarvan had tossed away my undergarments and how, underneath the dress, where his hand lay, I was naked. He watched me with that look of his, the one which said he knew exactly what I was thinking, and he laughed again. His laughter should have made me angry, but it was low and knowing, and it shot heat throughout my body, and again, I wanted his lips on mine.

After that, I needed the workout more than ever. There was a treadmill, not dissimilar to the ones I'd used before. It had so many combinations of buttons I was afraid to push any. Although Shaarvan had walked it up the walls and over the ceiling, my dress and lack of underwear kept me firmly on the ground.

Still, I preferred it until Shaarvan allowed me to try the *horse.* He said he'd programmed it just for me; I found the statement hard to believe. The exerciser was a kind of riding machine, but it felt more like an interactive computer. I could trot and canter and jump over a course, and the screen would let me think I was no longer trapped and out of control of my life.

I would have stayed there forever, but Shaarvan turned off the machine. "Come," he demanded. "You have enjoyed your sport, but tonight, it is I who will be the rider." He laughed, and his laugh was a knife stabbing at my moment of contentment.

We returned to the room to freshen up. A trip through the mist of the bathroom exit was all it took Shaarvan to get clean, but he made me change to another dress since mine had been torn by the exercise machine.

We left again almost immediately. There was a concert going on in one of the large assembly rooms. Close to eighty men were sitting in seats ready to watch musicians play their instruments. It wasn't extremely different from an Earth concert. The seats circled around the performers and rose up in rows. The musicians played a variety of instruments, sometimes at the same time, sometimes individually. The music had an odd sound, and I was the only female in the room.

Shaarvan had seated us away from the others. We were in a special box with a small plastic-looking wall all around us. The wall allowed us to see through it and obviously to hear through it. I couldn't see any reason for its presence, but Shaarvan was in one of his *don't talk* modes, so I didn't ask questions.

The musicians were mostly plucking some kind of string instruments, except for the scattered few who had watermelon-like drums. One man played an instrument larger than the others. It reminded me of an accordion because it swelled up and got smaller as the man played it. I don't know how he made it expand and contract because he was busy stroking it with a bristly bow.

The music was almost atonal at first, but as I sat there listening, I began to trace the pattern, flitting in and out like a butterfly among roses. Lighthearted disguises of the melody seemed to play the dominant role. Every time I'd lose the strains, they'd haunt me from new, different directions, slipping in for a delicate surprise.

I wouldn't say the music was beautiful, yet it was intriguing, and my mind couldn't leave it. Each time the piece ended, I wanted to clap at its success, but there was only silence like it was a ceremony we needed to meditate on.

Sometimes, I tried to scan the faces of the men around me. They were solemn and contemplative. The audience appeared not to savor the music at all, yet no one left, or spoke, or looked bored. Shaarvan, beside me, often closed his eyes and placed his head back against the neck rest of the beanbag chair in which he sat. Only a couple of times did his eyes meet mine, but then they were glazed, and I don't think I registered on him.

We were at the concert for a very long time, probably four or five hours, and I was ready to leave long before, but I didn't dare suggest it. Isn't there an expression about letting sleeping dogs lie? I figured Shaarvan wasn't forcing me, at the moment, to work on the computer program, and he wasn't angry with me, and nothing bad was happening, so the concert was more or less one of the better things to do.

Unfortunately, after working out in the gym for hours and face it, I hadn't exactly been on a stress-free diet lately, I was kind of exhausted. At some point in the concert, I drifted off into a really nice dream. I guess Shaarvan didn't notice right off, but when the concert ended, he wasn't pleased with me.

"You were given the opportunity to travel. I thought you told me you liked to visit new places."

"I do, but this was a concert. We didn't go anywhere."

"The concert was a journey to the world of Gadoor. Music is always a voyage."

"I didn't mean to fall asleep, and I didn't hear anything about a door."

"Gadoor, Shaara. Music must be listened to through your other sight: your feelings, your emotions, the undercurrents of your soul."

"All I heard was a butterfly," I said sadly.

"A butterfly is a Terran insect which flies about? Perhaps you did tap into the mood of it then."

"Listen, my wife: There was a theme throughout the piece aired by each instrument in various modes and melodies. It was about wandering homeless with no roots or permanence. The Gadoorians require stability in their residence, and solar flares have been disrupting their environment, causing the forced evacuation of millions. This concert was their plea to the universe for constancy."

"How do you get all that out of just listening to musicians playing instruments?"

Shaarvan shook his head at me and sighed, "I listen, Shaara, instead of falling asleep."

His hand was stroking my cheek with his knuckles. He was amused, not angry. I was relieved.

We ate in the cafeteria, then or rather, Shaarvan did. The food was tasteless to me and smelled of old bananas. Even worse were Shaarvan's eyes on me. They were a steady irritant to my hunger. His food was only half-eaten when he took my utensil and placed it down on the table. "You distract me," he said.

I looked up, afraid. I had not meant to be so restless. My thoughts had been far away.

"Be easy, Shaara," he said, stroking my face with his hand. "My appetite is not for food this night."

The relief I felt at not angering him was replaced by a new anxiety. I wasn't eager to return to our room.

Shaarvan didn't touch me on the walk back, yet I felt an almost electrical charge. It was like holding my hand near the doors that held shock potential.

Far too quickly, we arrived at Shaarvan's room. As his hand touched the doorway, it whooshed open. I hesitated to go in.

Shaarvan misunderstood my hesitation or else had thoughts of his own. He swept me up in his arms, saying, "I believe this is one of your Terran bridal customs."

He carried me over the threshold and stood there looking down at me in his arms. "I shall be your devoted bridegroom tonight, my wife." His eyes held promises which both thrilled me and frightened me.

As he carried me further into the room, his eyes were already undressing me. I felt ill. My terror drew in the icy breath of frost. My teeth began to chatter and my nose to run.

At the touch of his hand, the bed materialized, and Shaarvan set me down on it. I, the ice maiden, was so close to hysteria that I couldn't stay. As Shaarvan began to remove his shoes, I darted into the bathroom. I knew I'd bought myself only a few minutes, but I couldn't go through with this. It was madness. The man was a stranger. I knew almost nothing about him, and what I did know, I didn't like. How could he expect me to . . . ?

I sat down on the floor of the bathroom and drew my legs up. Holding them tightly, I sat and tried not to cry. What a mess I was in — and there was no way out. My mind leaped from idea to idea, searching, running through plans, attempting to find any answer which would free me from my circumstances.

Shaarvan gave me only two minutes before the door slid open. He stood there, half-undressed, staring down at me in bewilderment. "What are you doing?" he thundered.

The sight of him there, demanding, ordering, expecting me to pounce into his bed . . . I couldn't help it. I started to bawl like a baby with a booboo. I knew he would be angry, but I had no control over it. The tears gathered force, and, in a moment, I was sobbing so hard I couldn't get my breath.

"Not again, sweet wife. Not two nights in a row," he said. There was stern determination in his voice. I heard no understanding, no leniency.

Ignoring my sobs, his strong arms scooped me up and carried me back to his bed. With one hand holding me down as I fought him, he began to strip off my dress. My fingers clutched at the material, attempting to hide my nakedness, but it didn't slow Shaarvan greatly. He ripped the dress from my fingers and tossed it onto the floor. I was frantic then, completely without thought. I wrestled him like a crazy woman who thinks she's possessed by demons.

Shaarvan ignored my tears and my struggles. He held me anchored to the bed by one hand, with a leg thrown across my thigh. With his other hand, he began to trace patterns on my skin. I barely felt them. My mind contained only the thought of escape.

"Shaara, calm down," he said then, but although my mind heard his words, I couldn't respond. I could barely feel his hands on me. My panic was too overwhelming.

I knew Shaarvan was going to rape me. I knew I was making him angrier as the minutes passed, and he couldn't reach me. I stopped my struggles and lay there frozen, an iceberg he couldn't warm. His lips traveled me. Earlier, their touch had warmed my heart, but now I was detached from it. I felt his fingers dancing on my skin. Why was he drawing patterns on me? I knew his touch couldn't heat through the thickness of my ice.

One part of me protested it would be safer to let him waken me. That part of me yearned to open up my ice and let him feel the warm core of me, but I couldn't invite him in. If he raped me, I'd give him nothing of me.

I expected Shaarvan's violence. I waited for the pain, but, strangely, he didn't seem angry with me. I felt his withdrawal. The kisses and the odd designs he drew on my flesh stopped. He drew me up onto his lap and tried to calm me down, petting my hair and speaking soft words in his own tongue.

Then, I began to cry again. The torrents were gone. These sobs were the tears of heartbreak. I think, at last, Shaarvan comprehended. He began to speak to me in English. "Shaara, hush now. Do not cry. I will *not* take you with violence, my wife. You have misunderstood my intent."

I didn't trust him. I flailed out, attempting to be free.

"Shaara, calm down. I do not wish to hurt you, my little one."

He had my attention. His arms were fastened around me. I already knew I couldn't break his hold. And, it was true. He hadn't been rough with me. My sobs lessened a little.

"I frightened you. It was not my intent, Shaara. I thought I could break through your resistance, but you have to calm down first. I cannot reach you like this."

He still intended to take me. Once more, I panicked. I jabbed with my elbow. I think I hit his rib. He inhaled sharply.

"I'm sorry," I said, but I think it came out garbled with my tears.

His arms tightened around me. He rocked me back and forth. "Shaara, Shaara, listen to me. You have forgotten what I taught you this morning."

One of his hands moved up to stroke my face. At his touch, I went wild again. He sighed loudly, opened his arms, and let me go. I scurried to the farthest corner of the room and curled up into a shaking bundle.

He stood up, pushed a button, and then came walking towards me.

"No. No. Please, don't," I cried out.

"You do not understand, Shaara. You will find pleasure in my touch, not pain."

"Please, don't touch me," I cried out, not daring to look up at him.

His only response was to lay a blanket across my shivering body. I gathered it around me. The whooshing door as he left almost sounded as if he'd slammed it.

Shaarvan

How in the planets did I fail her this evening? I thought she was ready. She had shown her acquiescence in the morning, yet as the night grew later, I could feel her drawing away from me. Why had I not observed the signs?

The girl is Terran and is not even through the transition. How was she able to ignore my patterns? She should not have had that kind of resistance. I will test her tomorrow, but her strength of mind is an enigma. She should not have been able to defy the patterns of my touch.

We Shapechanger do not rape. It is against our code. Never a problem before. Females always succumb to the Shapechanger patterns, All of them but this one. How does one deal with a woman who is so afraid AND resistant?

My second brother would be delighted with my difficulties. He would say it serves me right. He does not approve of our way of stealing and selling women. He stays single to avoid such a crime, as he calls it. But most Altarians and those from other worlds do not agree. They see it as the only way to perpetuate our species. On most non-Shapechanger planets, females are the majority. They represent at least 52% of the population, with some even higher. We just help even out the ratio. What is wrong with that?

Susan

I was asleep when Shaarvan returned, but I woke when he picked me up and carried me to the bed. "Be at ease, my little wife," he said. "You are safe."

I was still half-asleep. I kept my eyes closed and accepted whatever he would do to me. I was too tired to fight him anymore.

Shaarvan lay me down on the bed, stretched out beside me, and then drew me back into his arms. His lips moved close to my ear.

"My sweet Shaara. I know you are awake. It is late. I shall not take you now, but know well you have sorely tested my patience, and such resistance is not wise."

His lips kissed my hair, and then his hand brushed a lock of my hair back so he could touch his mouth to my cheek.

"I thought you were ready, little one. Tomorrow, I shall be sure of you. You will learn there is nothing to fear from these kinds of lessons, only pleasure."

His words didn't frighten me, nor did the sweet lips which planted kisses down my face. Tomorrow was far away. This was now, and Shaarvan's body felt warm and familiar. I sighed happily, and his arms hugged me gently. Contented, I slipped back into sleep.

In the morning, Shaarvan was gruff. He tossed me the dress I was to wear and ordered me to hurry. I was disgusted to see it was the same color and style as yesterday's. This was getting tedious. I wished he'd let me do some programming. The material could be purple, and the drawstrings in the bodice could be black. I'd scoop the neck a little; the sleeves wouldn't be quite as full, and the length would be . . .

"Shaara." The warning was back in Shaarvan's voice.

I turned my back on him and went into the bathroom. I was changed into the butter lady quicker than fat melts in the microwave.

Shaarvan kind of grunted at me when I came out so quickly. He looked like he'd wanted me to be slow. I think he was hoping to yell.

We went to the cafeteria, and Shaarvan forced my hand up to a food machine. "It is time for you to learn to choose your meal, Shaara," he said.

The machine tingled my hand as it registered my print, but it didn't hurt. He ordered me to pick something. How could I know what to choose? I wanted to see what he would choose, but he had a strange look on his face. I tapped my hand on the first box at the top.

The machine dropped a frozen plate of food down to the bottom, like a food machine dispensing candy bars. This was a much better machine, though, because it apparently needed no money.

Shaarvan took his food and mine, and we went to the drink machine next. Again, he insisted on repeating my hand imprinting, but he told me he would choose my drink. He picked the fourth button down.

I thought his hands looked full, carrying everything, and I offered to help.

"It is a man's job to take care of his wife. I do not need your assistance," Shaarvan told me gruffly.

No dishes, no cooking, someone to take care of me . . . maybe Altar wasn't such a bad place, after all.

Shaarvan led us to the table and did the cooking, or, rather, the table did. He removed the plastic for me and set the food in front of me. I wondered if he was planning to cut it up and feed me as well.

My meal tasted like sandpaper, or at least, what I think sandpaper would taste like — all gravelly and bland. I ate it when I saw Shaarvan's laughing eyes. I attempted to pretend I thought it was delicious, but I could tell from Shaarvan's amusement he knew how I felt. I will not choose number one at the top again. The beverage was hot. It tasted like a cross between cocoa and coffee. I liked it.

Shaarvan ordered me to swallow the daily pill. I caused him no trouble this time. I suppose if he wanted to poison me, it would be easy enough. He could even give me another of those injections like he had when I'd awakened the first time. If this was to be my life, I wasn't sure I cared anyway. Let him poison me. Death would probably be a lot easier than putting up with Shaarvan's constant orders.

This time, the pill did not burn so badly. Only my throat stung from its passage. I emptied my water and again drank some of his. He didn't laugh this time, only nodded he was pleased.

We went to the control room next. At the door, Shaarvan stared warningly into my eyes. "Behave, Shaara," he ordered. "Punishments in Altar are swift and painful."

I sat in the fuzzy chair and said nothing. The control room wasn't the most exciting place, but it sure beat the computer torture.

Shaarvan turned off the video cameras, which showed the sleeping girls. I didn't understand why he cared. I certainly couldn't do anything about it. Why was it such a big deal to him?

His eyes were on me when he dismantled the cameras. I knew not to speak. I dropped my eyes and watched the carpet. When Shaarvan was no longer hovering and had gone back to his work, I continued my observations of the room.

One of the men kept glancing at me. He didn't do it in an obvious manner, but I could tell he was aware of me. He was younger than Shaarvan, maybe younger than I was. I smiled at him. He changed colors and dropped a data file. Then, he shot a quick glance in the direction of Shaarvan.

The man was rather cute. I wondered if I'd embarrassed him. Surely, he was used to women flirting with him. Was he afraid of Shaarvan? If Shaarvan was the captain, I suppose he did have power over the man, but would that make others *fear* Shaarvan?

I wondered what would happen if I winked at the kid. Maybe I could wave at him. It might be amusing. It might even send him through the ceiling. Perhaps I could show a little leg like Shannon at the scholarship interview had told me to do. Where was Shannon? Was she one of the girls sleeping in the coffins? If Shaarvan had let me view the faces, would I have seen her?

The man was feeding his data disks into the computer. He didn't look at me again. He had probably forgotten me. I watched him from the corner of my eye, but his concentration on his task made him boring.

I began to focus on other members of the crew. Would a crewman feel my eyes on him? Would he glance at me? Could I get him to see me as a person? I stared openly at several, directing my full attention at them, but they didn't react. I knew when someone stared at me, it bothered the heck out of me. Why couldn't they feel me staring at them?

I was testing one of the older ones when Shaarvan caught me.

"What are you doing?" he demanded in an accusing tone.

I fixed Shaarvan with one of my most innocent looks. "I was just wondering what was on the screen the man was watching so carefully."

Shaarvan studied me for a moment. His eyes nailed me. "You better hope, Shaara, you screw better than you lie."

It was a slap in the face. I dropped my eyes and felt my face grow red. How had Shaarvan known I was lying? I was a good actress. He couldn't possibly have known what I was up to. What would he do? I was frightened again. I had tried so hard not to get in trouble. How could I have been so stupid?

It was then the meaning of Shaarvan's words hit me. I ran them again in my memory. I couldn't believe Shaarvan had said that to me. Had anyone else heard him? My eyes scanned the room. No one was looking at me, but that didn't mean they hadn't heard. Did any of them speak English? The interviewers had all spoken my language. Maybe the whole ship spoke it. How could Shaarvan have said such a thing to me? In front of them.

Had it been a threat? The words kept echoing over and over. Shaarvan had meant the words to sting, but had he meant it as a threat? I better screw better . . . What if he found me unacceptable in his bed? What if I didn't know how? Would he get rid of me? Would he choose another and put me into one of those caskets where the other women were?

I had no hopes of pleasing him. I didn't have the first idea of how to pleasure a man. I should have gone to see an X-rated movie while I'd had the chance. Now, how would I learn? I'd taken a college class during the summer of my senior year, and the professor had given us a choice of assignments: discuss pornography or violence on TV. Why had I chosen violence on TV? That sure helped me a lot here. So far, I hadn't even seen a TV, and if Shaarvan were a typical Altarian, I could already predict the rest of them would be far more violent than Earth males.

What was I going to do? All the things my roommates had told me started running through my brain. "Don't let him take you in the backseat the first time." Really useful. "Make sure he takes you somewhere really romantic and different." I don't know about romantic, but going to Altar was sure different. "Make sure he's prepared." Birth control? What did aliens do about birth control? Did Altarians have condoms? Did they have AIDS? Did they even make love in the same way as humans? Suppose we didn't fit? What if his sex organs were in his feet or something.

Shaarvan came back towards me. He stood, looking down at me, but I couldn't meet his eyes. I wished he'd leave or at least stop staring at me. His intensity made all the tiny hairs on my arms stand at attention.

I think he was debating what to do. He must have made his decision. "Come," he said abruptly, and his hand reached down and grabbed mine. I stood up like a robot, but I felt more like wilted celery.

There was just too much stress in outer space. Being kidnapped by an alien had to rank up there with losing a job on those insurance charts. All the adrenalin pumping away in my body in double time couldn't be good for me. Would Shaarvan care? Should I tell him my blood pressure was too high for sex?

If the hand holding mine noticed I was shaking, Shaarvan didn't mention it. He led me forward and out of the control room without another word.

We went to a garden. One moment, we were in the sterile, white, and insipid corridors, then through one tiny door, and I suddenly felt like I was back on Earth. There was dirt on the ground. Soft, padded earth. I wanted to touch it, to pick it up, to roll in it like a dog. There were small flowering trees, ferns, and bushes with tiny fruits and flowers. I saw a pretty stone bench to sit on under a tall, green-leafed tree.

I forgot my fear of Shaarvan in my awe of the sight and the luscious smells — a blooming yellow vine with a scent just like honeysuckle, flowers in pinks, oranges, violets, and blues, all of them bursting with full-throated blooms of color which wreathed the air with a happy, flowery bouquet. My heart skipped a beat at the sight of all the greenery with heart-shaped leaves and bushes forming perfect ovals of plump or feathery olive, blue-green, and velvety forest hues.

And there were trees — real trees with bark and branches and deliciously dangling leaves bursting with the shine of emeralds as the sun, directly overhead, shone down all warm and cozy. The ceiling of the room was rich with blues and puffy white clouds. It was summer, a perfect summer day in a park.

"It's Earth." I cried out as I spun about, trying to look at everything, attempting to absorb it, to experience and savor what I'd missed so much. My stress was being soothed, all right. I'd gone to heaven. I was smiling for the first time — no, beaming. That's the word for your expression when something this stupendous hits you in one surprising moment. Beaming.

Maybe Shaarvan would let me spend the whole day relaxing here. Maybe he'd noticed I was all tense and needed a break. Maybe he was trying to be nice for a change, to show me he was — well, maybe not human — but close to human?

"It is not your planet," Shaarvan said briskly. "It is Altar. I told you they were much the same. Come, sit," he said, pointing to the empty place on the bench.

I joined him, but my eyes were still darting about. "Oh, look at the roses," I said as I marveled at their perfect symmetry. Each bloom was at least six inches across, and the colors were a blending of orange, yellow, rose-pink, and apricot — like a sunrise when the sky was just a little bit smoky from a nearby fire. Deep-hued. Vivid. Color so bright your eyes couldn't move away. Like you were mesmerized by the splendor.

Shaarvan seized my hand before I could stand up and run over to look, smell, and touch them.

"Shaara, they are crilla. Say it."

"Crilla," I said, not looking away, still mesmerized. "But they look like roses to me," I added, not meaning it as an argument. I was still spellbound by the magical garden.

Shaarvan didn't take offense. He, too, was quiet. He waited a moment, then said, "Such a little hand. You are smaller than I would have liked. It is too easy to crush tiny bones like yours."

I didn't like this monologue at all. I tried to pull my hand away, but he wouldn't release it.

He chuckled. "Your body is small, but your spirit is big, and your courage is considerable. I treasure those qualities, but they make you difficult."

Here comes the stress again. I didn't know if I should say anything or not. I stayed quiet. Besides, I think Shaarvan had already told me this before. Would I hear how difficult I was on a daily basis?

"Terrans require more effort to tame, it would seem. My father warned me. I have tried to be patient with you, Shaara, but you have exhausted my patience."

Resolutions to be quiet just went down the drain. Words came tumbling out of my mouth. "I don't suppose you could take me back to Earth then?" I was hopeful as I looked up into Shaarvan's eyes.

"Be silent." He said it automatically, with no tone or inflection. I think I really was wearing the guy out.

I did kind of wonder what Shaarvan was talking about when he'd said I'd been difficult. Did he mean last night or in the control room? Which thing had I done which had tried his patience the most?

"Shaara, pay attention," Shaarvan demanded. "*First* — you will not look at other men."

"I wasn't looking at them. I . . ."

"Silence."

What a temper. It wasn't like I'd done anything wrong. If Shaarvan didn't want me to stare at the men, maybe he should give me something to do.

"Shaara, listen."

How did he always know when I was tuning out? I returned my eyes to him. I hoped he felt the anger in them.

'*Secondly*, you will not speak unless you are spoken to.'

"What?" This was too much. I stood up to tell him a few things.

He pulled me done *mucho pronto* and started telling me about signs he'd flash with his fingers. What, I was a dog now?

He took me through "sit," "stay," "no argument," "be silent," and three other different warnings. They weren't difficult. It was a great deal easier than learning his stupid language.

"You will obey these signs, Shaara, or there will be consequences."

The way Shaarvan said *consequences* sounded like the bell of doom. I could pretty well figure out what he meant by it, but my mind kept wandering, and I hoped I hadn't missed one of his commands. Had the hand signs been rule number three?

"*Fourth*. He didn't tell me to listen again. I guess he figured it was hopeless. He grabbed my chin and brought my eyes up with it."

"If I ever catch you lying to me again, I shall whip your bottom until it hurts to sit."

I didn't think much of number four. And how had he known I was lying? I couldn't figure that out. I wanted to ask, but I was afraid to.

"*Fifth*." He was still holding onto my chin. I couldn't budge. His mouth moved down to punctuate number five with a peck of a kiss on my lips.

"I have locked us in here, Shaara. No one may enter. The day is lovely. There is a smell of flowers and greenery in the air. Our business is finished. We may pleasure."

Faulty grammar construction, Mr. . . . What did he mean by "We may pleasure?" He treats me like a dog, making me learn doggy commands. He threatens me with violence to my body. He says we're going to "pleasure" . . . whose — his or mine?

Shaarvan stood up, all six feet, four inches of him. I didn't like his expression. His hands pulled me up slowly, next to him, too next to him. Suddenly, I knew what he meant by number five.

Shaarvan picked me up in his arms and carried me to the grass. He lay me down on it and stretched out beside me. The grass was soft. It smelled like Earth grass, newly cut and fresh as the summer. I hoped no dogs had been there first. I wiggled into its coolness, relishing its pleasantness, its squishy texture. I sighed in contentment and closed my eyes.

A moment later, Shaarvan's hands began to stroke my face. My eyes popped open. Apprehension tingled the depths of my brain and traveled alarmingly across every pore of my body.

Shaarvan's dark gray eyes were soft and like a chasm as they swept me in. He took my eyes into his and held them hostage while he ran his index finger across my lips. Nervously, I fidgeted, sending fresh waves of grass scent into the air. But I couldn't let that distract me from saying what needed to be said. Shaarvan's finger caressed my cheeks, touching me as if my skin were rose petals, and he was acquainting himself with their texture.

The words he'd said in the control room — words about his expectations kept running through my mind. I had to warn him I wasn't any good at making love. I didn't want him to be disappointed or, even worse, angry at my ineptitude.

"Shaarvan . . ." I tried to talk, but he used a finger sign on my lips, the one which meant, "Be silent."

"Please," I begged. "I have to tell you . . ."

His finger left my lips and gave me the "no argument" sign. There was warning in his eyes, enough to light a fire.

I was stuck. I couldn't prepare him for my lack of experience. I was pretty sure I couldn't back out of the situation. I didn't think tears would work for a third time. From the look in Shaarvan's eyes, there could only be one result from this position — bye-bye virginity.

At least we weren't lying in the backseat of a car, and it was a romantic spot. I guess it was time for me to learn what I'd been missing.

The only thing that bothered me was that he was probably about to rape me, and I couldn't even scream.

Shaarvan

Stars, she was a handful. She was feisty in the cafeteria, eating *Gregan Slipsh*, with her mouth all pursed and her face as legible as a data disk, yet she did not air one complaint. Instead, she cocked her chin as high as a pennant and ate a fair portion.

Her pride and sense of humor bolster her. Without them, she would be easier to train, yet I cannot help admiring the pluckiness of her spirit.

I was understandably annoyed with her actions in the control room. It seems that when I provide her with a respite from pressure, she unfailingly finds trouble. Yet, it is difficult to punish her for such mischief. Her conduct was more in the realm of a playful child than in direct disobedience. But, as the wife of a captain, such behavior cannot be allowed. I cannot be lenient with such disrespect of the Laws.

The men dealt with her admirably. Young Teban shows promise for future positions, but he will need to be watched with Shaara. She draws him. The others were not bothered in the same way, which was wise on their part.

It is possible Shaara is far enough along in her adaptation that her impishness is partly caused by my failure in not servicing her needs. I cannot allow this situation to continue. Whatever she requires, I shall give her. I shall be patient as a grandfather, but I must persist this time despite those eyes of hers mirroring her every thought of misery, fear, and the flow of her unceasing distress.

But I will not relent again. I will reach her this time. I will initiate her Shapechanger senses and make her my wife.

Susan

We lay there, staring into each other's eyes. I wondered if Shaarvan thought about the fact we really didn't know each other. Did such a small detail bother a man as it did a woman? I wished he would give me more time to know him before . . .

His fingers were traveling slowly over my lips again. His eyes urged me. I couldn't believe the charisma of this guy. My heart was thundering with worry and yet, I didn't want to move, didn't really even want to escape. I craved the feel of his touch, the magic rippling my senses and making me weak.

His hands stroked my face softly and with a new gentleness. The caress left a trail of tingling. His fingers, like a blind man's, traced me as if I were a work of art. And, all the while, his eyes continued to watch me, insisting, demanding, forcing me to feel something that left me almost queasy in my need.

And those eyes of his — deep, dark gray eyes which locked me to him with unspoken promises. Eyes which spoke of gentleness and patience, yet nothing he had shown me so far in his personality or his great size and strength had taught me he could be gentle. I feared him. I cowered before him. Yet the tenderness of his enticement and the slowness of it, for he wasn't forcing himself on me — not exactly. He was wooing me. That's what it used to be called. Slowly, methodically, perhaps, but soothingly.

Then, his lips met mine. They didn't linger. They stole to my neck, to the same places he had stroked with his hands. He awakened my skin. Already, it craved his touch. I was a morning glory arching towards the sun, opening to him, feeling his warmth.

I'd never felt the rough touch of a man's fingers before Shaarvan's. I'd never known the power of their touch. The hands, caressing and playing, tantalizing me with their fondling and teasing. His touch stole the part of me which had kept me detached. I was liquid, flowing towards him as he tilted me.

His fingers traced strange patterns on my neck. I couldn't move. I almost couldn't breathe. Again and again, his fingers trailed desire. It was irritating, maddening. Oh, God, don't stop. My skin was in torment in every place he touched.

Again, his fingers moved back to trace my neck lightly, a whisper of agony. His lips seared me with kisses. Please, don't stop, I wanted to say. I didn't have to. His fingers returned to my lips, tracing, playing, and opening my lips to him.

I was ready for his mouth on me, but it didn't come. His lips teased me further, approaching, slipping away to escape down my neck with kisses so hot, so delightful my body was ensnared by it. Then, back again came his lips to torment my mouth. A kiss on the left, on the right, missing the lips. I hungered for his lips. I couldn't play this game. My lips searched for his. Finally, he allowed me a minute of tasting him. It wasn't enough. When he moved to bathe my neck in kisses, I groaned, "Shaarvan."

At once, his lips rejoined mine, and then, no longer did he tease. There was fire now and intensity, which should have alarmed me, but it didn't. His lips were rougher, abandoned, driving me on. My only existence was in his lips.

I felt his hands moving downward. They cupped my breasts. Yes, yes, my body urged him. Touch me. Touch me. My breasts tingled and burned. My nipples hardened to his touch. A moment later, he retreated. I thought I'd die. "No," I cried out, but he was only slipping the dress over my head.

As he lifted me, his lips descended on my breasts. I imagined there could be nothing more thrilling than that. How wrong I was. His lips made music. I arched, and he lay me back.

Once more, his eyes met mine. "One moment, my sweet wife. I want to feel your skin on mine."

The very word *skin* sent shivers up and down the length of me. I bit my lips. Then I wet them. His essence was in my mouth, my nostrils, in my brain. I was filled with the pinecone smell of him. Like redwood forests and greenery, Shaarvan's fingertips gently stroked and teased.

As Shaarvan lifted his arms, I watched, my mouth slightly open, my lips dry again. His belly muscles rippled as he stretched to remove his shirt. His arms flexed. The bulging wideness of his arms drew my eyes. Powerful arms — tight and strong. No wonder I couldn't fight him, couldn't pull away, couldn't defend myself against such power. He was Popeye, Tarzan . . . Apollo.

The wide expanse of his chest drew a gasp from me. His body was beautiful. He was everything a woman dreamed of — at least physically. Once more, I nibbled at my bottom lip and thought about how the golden brown of the hair on his chest made me yearn to stroke him, to feel those hairs against my skin, squeezing against me, slightly scratchy against the muscled hardness of his body. I knew I would drown in the warmth of his body. Drown or go mad.

Shaarvan's eyes, as he watched me studying him, were knowing. The way he unbuttoned his slacks teased. I tried to look away, but his eyes still held me, still touching my skin even from the distance. He liked my watching him. I could tell. I was glad. I wanted to observe him like this — at a distance, in safety. I wanted to stare at him forever.

He turned around, his back to me. I watched the broadness of him, the play of the muscles on his shoulders and arms. They rippled as he moved — an athlete with a hard, firm carriage.

He was taking off his pants. I saw he wore nothing beneath them. The shock made me blush, but again, I couldn't look away. His butt, something I'd never even thought about — was as pleasing to me as the rest of him. I wanted to touch its slope, to feel his skin with my hands, to cup the rigid compactness of it.

Shaarvan turned to remove the final pant leg. The heavy muscles of his thighs were as tight as his belly. That was the last sane thought I had because as he turned and walked towards me, it was not his thighs which held my eyes, but his manhood . . . All right, his penis, like a knight's jousting sword, was fully erect. That unnerved me. Never had I seen the enormity of a male. The pictures I'd giggled over in the girl's gym with my friends had shown an erection at half-mast and never up close, never approaching me to stab me with its massiveness.

"No," I cried out as I curled up like a baby.

Shaarvan said nothing. He lay down beside me and began to stroke my back. I was tense and rigid. I wanted to flee, but I was trapped. I knew he wouldn't let me back out — not this time.

"Shaarvan," I said softly, fearfully. "You don't understand. I don't know how to do this. I don't even know if I can."

"Sh. It is all right," he said, turning me over onto my back.

I didn't fight him, but I lay stiff. My hands crossed automatically over my breasts. I shivered as if the room had suddenly turned cold. My nakedness made me feel defenseless.

Gently, Shaarvan moved my arms down to my sides. His tongue licked my swollen breasts, but it only made me colder. I retreated slightly away from him — only an inch, no more. His arm lay across me. One leg covered my left.

He let go of my hands and then stretched out his arms on each side of my head. He made no further move. He looked down at me. He wasn't angry. His eyes were still gentle.

"I know, my little one. I know it is your first time and that you are frightened, not rebellious. I shall be as easy as I can with you."

Again, he began his stroking and teasing. I wasn't receptive anymore. I was too frightened. I was scared he'd become impatient and take me unwillingly. I fretted he'd be rough and hurt me or that I'd fail to please him.

I whimpered once, not because I meant to. It embarrassed me. I started to apologize again, but my teeth were chattering. I couldn't speak. I felt frozen, chilled — panicky.

But Shaarvan didn't stop. He spread warm kisses on my neck. His finger played my face like a musical instrument. He stroked me over and over.

And finally — gradually, I felt the heat calling up within me again, and I began to relax.

My mind was foggy, but at some point, I realized Shaarvan kept repeating the same patterns on my skin like he was tracing something over and over. I couldn't hold on to the thought of what it was, although I tried to focus. Again and again, he persisted, his fingers sketching, his stroke insistent and firm. His touch had grown hotter. It burned me, yet not painfully so, more like a quiet smoldering fire growing bigger.

I knew I couldn't take much more. I started to wiggle, not to get free, but to stop the endless teasing of it. My body ached. I wanted something, but I didn't know what it was. I wasn't thinking clearly. I even moaned several times — low-pitched and almost purr-like. I thought at first it was a sound from the ship, a tree limb batting against the wall, or some strange animal hidden away inside the park-like room.

But then I caught myself. It was me making the noise. Me.

"Shaarvan," I cried, but he didn't heed my plea if that's what it was. He didn't ease off. The patterns continued.

I twisted and turned as if, by my movement, I hoped to entice him to move to another part of me. Stroke me, kiss me, rub me like a purring cat, I might as well have said. Where was my pride? What was he doing to me?

But no, I was not some well-satisfied kitty. I was a fly caught in a web. Soon, my limbs were no longer free. I couldn't move then — not to shift slightly in the grass — not even to twitch. Shaarvan controlled me that skillfully. I lay trapped in some kind of spell.

His lips met mine then, and I was more than ready for them. Their touch on my mouth was like throwing a buoy to a drowning man. At that moment, I welcomed his power. I no longer had any will to resist.

Shaarvan's hands descended lower, traveling my body. Everywhere, his fingers gentled, caressed. I felt sensations I'd never known. My body trembled, but not with fear, but still I flinched when his hand found the part of me I both feared and longed for him to touch. His hand rested there a moment as his lips fastened onto mine. Ah, sweet ecstasy. I understood kissing. I was comfortable with his lips. But then his tongue plunged into me, and it drove all conscious thought away. Like a twig on a raging river, I was swept along, floating, bobbing, consumed by what was happening to me.

His hand crept downward again. I hardly noticed. It felt right. It was still doing its patterns, still stroking and weaving spells. And yet . . .

"No." I broke away. I turned my head. "Don't." I cried out, for he had pushed his way inside me, touching me where no one had ever touched me before.

Fear awakened. I fought his hand. Again, I tried to cover my nakedness.

"No, my wife," Shaarvan said as he raised up to look down at me. I lay still, staring up into his eyes, while the finger, that dreadful finger, lay inside me.

"I . . ."

"No, wife. You will not fight me," he said, and I shivered at his voice. Something in it resonated inside me. I felt the danger that straddled the words. Shaarvan was not angry, but there was power in his voice, power which controlled, commanded, and warned me not to dispute his claim on me.

One of his hands gathered up both my wrists and twisted them about to my right side. He was gripping them tightly, and he wasn't gentle, but yet, he didn't cause me pain.

Of course, I had the good sense not to fight him, and in truth, I was still reeling from the shock I'd felt at the knowledge of his *power*.

His other hand wasted no time. Inside my private realm, it began to stroke and probe more intimately.

"Shaarvan, please don't," I sobbed as the finger invaded deeper.

"I shall please you, Shaara. Do not fear my touch."

For some reason, I wanted to please him, to let him have his way, but I couldn't. I was frightened. His touch was too invasive, too much like the weapon at his loins.

I locked my legs, trying to force him out. Had I consciously thought, I wouldn't have dared to do so, but it wasn't deliberate. I had no awareness of anything — anything but my fear.

Suddenly, my wrists were freed, and Shaarvan moved off me. I thought he was giving me my freedom, but instead, he pried my legs apart and held me still. Then, his head lowered towards me. I fought the hands on my thighs, the head sinking down inside me.

"No," I cried.

Shaarvan's warm mouth was where his finger had played a moment before. His hands, with a grip so tight my legs couldn't close, still didn't hurt me even though I was flinging myself about. But my rebellion was short-lived. In seconds, great waves of lust lost me in their swirl. I couldn't fight then. My mouth was open, but I didn't protest. I no longer knew what I wanted. Shaarvan's tongue was lapping, his lips tormenting. He drove me deeper, deeper into something so alien to me that I had no words for it.

Again, I moaned, and I didn't know who had voiced such a sound. I gasped. I sobbed. I cried out, "Shaarvan?"

And, then, when the utter abandonment of it came, I danced across the liquid stars of paradise.

I no longer had any will of my own then. I was Shaarvan's to use, and when he drew his body across mine, I did not protest his possession. I wanted him as part of me. I knew he would take me now, and I almost welcomed the pain of it.

Yet, Shaarvan didn't stab me with his weapon. His sword dipped inside me, but it brought only more pleasure. He rocked it back and forth, never pushing hard where I knew he'd go. With his penis stroking me, forming its own patterns, once more, he made me lose myself. Then, as fresh waves of delight cascaded inside me, he plunged down through my hymen.

Of course, I cried out. The pain was beyond imagining. It burned like a thousand bee stings or a knife thrust through my skin. Shaarvan stopped, arching himself up. His lips sought mine to harbor there. While deep, deep inside of me, he held himself completely still.

"It is over now," he whispered in my ear. "It will not hurt again," he promised.

He had brought such delight and such pain. My eyes searched his with questions. I didn't understand. Who was this stranger who played my body and conquered my mind? His eyes read my thoughts.

"I am your husband, now, Shaara, and you are mine."

His words were a brand echoing in my brain. His eyes seared me with their impact. A shiver traveled down my spine, and deep inside of me, his organ throbbed. He took me to other places I had not visited. He drove me beyond all-knowing. He rode me with a fierceness which should have frightened me, but I craved it.

When it was over, I understood. Shaarvan had given me the pleasure of supreme gratification, but he'd also claimed me with his sword, and although he had brought me many times to the brink of madness, it was by his dominion and by his will.

The fires within us were extinguished. Shaarvan's staff was limp then, yet still, he held me and stroked my arms. His eyes were soft and satisfied. He seemed well-replete. The fire he'd built inside of me had made me his. A part of me had reveled in it, but there was a part of me which felt consumed.

He grinned as if reading my thoughts. "Yes," he said. "Recognize it, feel my scent upon you, the ache of my brand between your legs. You are mine completely now, my wife. Every cell of your body."

His eyes were glowing strangely. I lowered mine in fear. I didn't argue with his wording. I cowered.

For a while, Shaarvan let me lie there, still shaking a bit, but his hand stroked me quietly. His touch, which should have frightened me more, somehow reassured and eventually calmed me.

I had no cover for my body. My clothes were on the bench. Shaarvan's eyes roamed freely. I was dreadfully embarrassed. It was all too new to me — not just the physical joining, which had unbalanced me so much, but everything that had occurred between us. It was as if he had stolen my detachment, my separateness. I couldn't meet his eyes.

After a few minutes, he sat up and looked down at me. His hand cupped one of my breasts. Then he leaned over and kissed my lips. "It was good between us, Shaara, but it will be easier for you next time."

I was afraid he meant right then. He laughed at my startled look, and his knuckles stroked my face. "No, my wife. Not now. I shall give you time to heal. You will be sore for at least a day."

He helped me to put my dress back on. I couldn't tie the gathering in front. My fingers were still shaky. His huge hands tightened and tied the ribbons. How strange that felt. How startling to see he could be so gentle.

I felt his eyes examining me. My face flared with heat. He didn't speak, just turned away to clothe himself.

I couldn't watch it. His body now seemed heavy, harsh, and rough. He had taken my virginity. My maiden fear had been removed, but now I feared his largeness and his strength, and most of all, I feared his power to steal my self-control.

Shaarvan's arm wrapped around my shoulders. It was a common gesture, but I resented its possessiveness. He held me close. His eyes were knowing as if a link had formed, a link of ownership.

We returned to our room, walking slowly. He was right; I felt sore. I ached. My body felt bruised and beaten.

When we entered our room, his hands once more removed my dress, although he'd told me he would not take me again that day. I had nothing left in me to protest. I watched him as he stripped off his clothes. I kept my eyes down and sighed.

I thought he'd put the bed down, but he didn't. He merely took our clothes and recycled them. He took clean ones from the machine. Then he turned to face me, and I saw his gallant sword was not fiercely ready to battle. I was relieved.

He stretched out his hand and took mine. Then he led me to the bathroom, and we showered. The water was warm and comforting, but Shaarvan insisted on soaping my body. I did not want him to, but I was too tired to argue. Besides, it would not have done any good. He would have done as he wished anyway.

His hands were large and strong. They had gripped me earlier, twisted me about, secured me when I would have fled, but in the shower, they were tender, loving, even gentle. His touch, in fact, was efficient and thorough, not sexual at all. He made no attempt to build up my desire, although each place on my skin he touched tingled, and when he pulled me up against his body to soap my front, the warmth of him against my backside made me feel weak. My stomach spasmed. Unbelievably, I yearned for him again.

He showed me how to bathe him. I tried, but I didn't know how to deal with his manhood. I avoided it. His hands brought me back. My touch made his penis swell large again, but it didn't threaten. When we were finished, although his rod demanded compensation for my touch, Shaarvan only kissed me on the cheek and halted the water's fall.

We walked out through the bathroom exit and were instantly dry. I was glad I wouldn't have to dry him with a towel. His nearness made me shiver.

Shaarvan dressed me then — like a doll. He attached a cloth to catch the blood still dribbling down my leg. It embarrassed me when he did it, but he didn't seem concerned.

Had he done all this before? How many virgins had he conquered before me? Was I just like all the others? Did he lie to me about being the only one he called wife?

As he slipped the dress over my head and began to slide the material down, his hands stopped to linger at my breasts. His lips bent to suckle. He only paused a moment and then let my dress fall the rest of the way down to my feet. Where his lips had been, it felt cold.

He dressed himself. I stood watching. When his eyes lifted, they gently mocked. My face grew warm. I lowered my eyes.

I hoped I'd earned a day's peace from the language torture, but it was not to be. Shaarvan sat me down at the computer and made the connections.

"Shaarvan . . ." I started to beg, but his hand flashed no argument. Stupid signs. I couldn't pretend a lack of understanding.

He left me there. His departure was a sudden wrench. I had no reason to miss his presence. Shouldn't I be grateful he was gone? I wanted to analyze the day and my feelings, but the computer began its horrid language drills.

Hours later, when Shaarvan returned, I was drained in mind and body. I felt empty. I was Susan. I struggled to remind myself, but the name seemed unrelated to me, part of another lifetime.

Shaarvan

It is done, although it surprised me how little pleasure I took in it. Shaara's body is a luscious feast, which makes my mood all the more inexplicable. I have tasted her. I have pleasured myself in her warm, wiggling body. I should feel sated and content. Yet, our joining was not the completion I had envisioned. I want her body *and* her soul, and she has not freely given either to me.

"Patience," the great ones would say. "Is the bud which opens slowly any the less pleasing when the fullness of its bloom is achieved?"

But I have been patient. I have tasted the nectar, and it only tantalized me. It gave me no reward. Wife, how long will it take to open you? How much more can you need from me?

It was her fear which dulled my appetite. Where I expected challenge, I felt only her tearful eyes and the desperation of her spirit. I drove her to the heights several times. I would not be Shapechanger if I had not done so. Yet, for her, it was still not enough. What is it she needs for her body to accept my touch?

And when I took her, it stunned me how much it hurt her. It lanced through me. I could barely continue. Her pain should not have been that great. I have never known a girl's hymen to be that resistant. It was not so with the other Terran girls in the hold. And afterward, Shaara continued to bleed when the others had not. I will check her when I return to the room, but I must not allow her to know that this is not normal. I do not wish her terror to return.

Yet, I ask myself, why should her feelings be so prominent in my thoughts? Why did I feel her panic so strongly?

That never happened with the others. It can only be due to her adaptation process. But how can she project so clearly only Tides past the introduction of Shapechanger DNA? Our union made it twice as strong. Every thought Shaara felt after our joining was an assault.

I must shield myself strongly, for she has power already. How is that possible? So little, yet so strong — the feel of it is delicious. She will need testing.

The incorporation of a wife into one's life is much more complicated than I had imagined. How much easier it was to simply capture and trade the girls who passed through my days. No wonder so many of my compatriots have not taken advantage of the opportunity for such a link. Had they perceived, as I have not, how assimilation alters the male as well as the girl? Or am I reading more than there is? Is Shaara unique?

Chapter Five
Communication is a Good Thing

Susan

The cafeteria, when Shaarvan took me there later, was empty. I chose dish number two from the top, working down the list. Shaarvan's eyes were amused, but he said nothing. When my meal was heated, I looked down in disgust. The meal I'd chosen had the color of creamed spinach with lumps of red tomato. It was a strain to even get it near my mouth. One swallow and I knew I couldn't eat it.

Shaarvan laughed at my expression. "I will trade if you like, Shaara. Shloosh requires an acquaintance of time. You *will* learn to enjoy it one day — just as you will learn to enjoy the demands I make on your body."

Darn him. Would he never stop making me blush? I looked down at the shloosh, pretending to be fascinated with its appearance. Shaarvan laughed and pulled it towards him, then pushed his dinner into its place.

His laughter hurt me. I wiped a tear.

"Shaara, look at me."

I didn't want to meet his eyes, yet I knew I couldn't disobey. I was surprised when I glanced up and saw his gray eyes were not scornful. They were smiling at me in an almost kindly manner.

"Shaara, I enjoy you. You see things through different eyes than mine, but my amusement at your difference is *not* ridicule."

Once more, I blushed. I appreciated his words, even though I wished he hadn't said them. When Shaarvan explained something or when he said something nice, it made it so much harder for me to endure captivity. I wanted to hate him. It was easier when I could. Loathing feeds you strength. You can endure if you hate hard enough no matter what happens. I needed to hate Shaarvan. It was all I had.

I was quiet as we ate. I kept mulling over his words, trying to make sense of them in combination with the other things he'd said and done. Who was Shaarvan?

No matter how hard I tried, I couldn't understand him. Just when I thought I'd pinned him like a butterfly in a collector's display, ready for examination, he went and did something totally out of character.

After our meal, Shaarvan and I returned to our room. Could it be nighttime already? It was impossible to know. There were no variations in the lights or clocks on the wall to inform me of time.

Shaarvan brought up the bed and ordered me to lie down. I was not tired, and I doubted I could sleep, but I lay down. He stretched out beside me, tossing his leg carelessly over mine, another example of his ownership. My body, which he pulled tightly against his chest, ached from the closeness and the hard lump against my back.

I wanted to toss and turn and throw my thoughts about like the balls in a bingo game where they could flutter on the currents of the air, but I found myself thinking only of Shaarvan's body, all warmly wrapped around me. His sword no longer pointed at me accusingly. It lay limp and unthreatening. But, his body's proximity was enough to scatter my wits.

Shaarvan's breathing grew slow and steady. The warmth of his breath against my neck calmed me. It was hard to believe this slumbering giant was the man who'd made me tremble with fear and lust. Lying there, quiet and peaceful in his arms, I suddenly felt protected and safe. How strange.

My eyes grew heavy. I closed them. Then, the exhaustion of my body and mind washed over me. I wanted to think about the day, to sort and categorize, to study who I was becoming, but darkness descended, and I slept.

I woke when Shaarvan shifted me. He was wide awake. I recognized the change in his breathing, the energy of his alertness. I knew then it must be morning.

I yawned, but I felt refreshed. I stretched — as much as possible while being held in two strong arms. Shaarvan didn't loosen his hold. His eyes examined me as if recording through a video camera.

"What?" I asked crossly. His silent staring disturbed me; it made me feel twitchy and restless. It made me want to touch my lips to his and feel the strength of his power over me.

As he continued watching me, my heart began to thump — chu-chu —— chu-chu, it said, making noises like a child's train sounds. I stared into Shaarvan's eyes, waiting for his words, but he didn't offer any. He only smiled his mocking smile, rubbed my face with his hand, and slid off the bed to begin the day.

Would I ever understand him? I knew he'd lusted for me. Why hadn't he forced me again? Was it because he'd told me I had the day off?

Shaarvan didn't allow me to linger in the bed, pondering. He tossed me a dress and said, "Get up, Shaara. It is time."

The darn dress was always the same. Didn't Altar ever vary in style or color? I thought about asking if I could change it to purple or redesign it, but Shaarvan seemed strangely distant again. I slipped the dress on quickly, nervous about what the new day might bring.

When I came out of the bathroom, Shaarvan handed me a granola-like bar from the machine with all the buttons. I nibbled at it. It wasn't bad, but I doubted if anyone on Earth would want its recipe. The table in the middle of the room ascended, and then two chairs. Shaarvan placed cups of drink on the table for us.

I sat down, leery as a frightened bunny. Were all men this unpredictable, or was it just Shaarvan?

He held out my daily pill and ordered me to take it. I swallowed it down before it could dissolve and then drank from the cup to wash away the taste.

"My mother was Terran," Shaarvan said.

I almost choked. I swallowed quickly and looked up. Shaarvan was communicating.

Shaarvan ignored my cough and continued the strange dialogue. "My father was the trader who captured her. He was well-pleased with his choice of wife, which is why I determined to take a Terran wife. You Terrans are stubborn but adaptable. You breed well. You appear to make good mothers."

I took a deep breath. This sharing was suddenly not going as well. *Stubborn, adaptable, good mothers?* I skipped over good breeders, which sounded like Shaarvan was buying a horse, not talking about a wife. What great reasons to marry someone.

Shaarvan took a sip from his cup. "There were many candidates at your college. You students urgently need money."

"Money is hard to get," I said.

Shaarvan ignored me and continued. "It was difficult to settle on one girl. None of them seemed special." He took a bite of his granola bar like he wasn't in the middle of a story and about to hit the punch line.

"I knew from the moment you started talking that I would take you. Still, I tested your skin. There was no doubt you were a virgin. It was written on every pore of your palm, yet you responded with the depth of a *Shapechanger* to the touch of my lips. It was then I knew you would make a fitting wife."

"What does that mean . . . 'the depth of a *Shapechanger*'?"

Shaarvan smiled. "You ask more questions than any girl I have known.

"My father said my mother, Teea, asked many questions. You are like her, not in looks, but in spirit."

He'd ignored my question, but I didn't want to irritate him by persisting. "Your mother was from Earth . . .? Was she kidnapped, too? Is she happy on Altar?"

"Of course. Why would she not be? It is why I took you, Shaara. You are much like my mother. I think you will adapt well. We will raise fine sons."

Was I supposed to respond to such words? First of all, I wasn't sure adaptability was a compliment. I knew stubbornness wasn't.

I wished wholeheartedly that Shaarvan had chosen someone else. I wished I'd kept my mouth shut at the interview. I wished I hadn't applied for the scholarship, and I most definitely wished I hadn't reminded Shaarvan of his mother.

Freud. I hadn't read Freud yet. I *really* needed to finish my education.

Shaarvan watched me. His eyes had a way of studying me like he knew just what I was thinking. Could he read my thoughts? I hadn't asked, but he responded as if I had.

"Your mind is full of regrets, Shaara. It will take time, my wife, but you will adapt. Most girls do."

I bit my lip. I inhaled and held it a moment, then asked, "What do you do with the girls who don't?"

Again, he smiled. "You listen to every word, another difference from the others. It is a useful characteristic."

I didn't like the way Shaarvan ignored my questions. What is it? He only answers every third one?

He took my hand from the coffee mug and brought my palm to his lips. The feel of his mouth against my skin gave me goosebumps. I wet my lips and breathed in deeply. Why did Shaarvan have such power over me? How could such a brief touch make me yearn?

Still holding my hand in his, he continued. "You will like Altar. It is much like Earth. Many plants and trees are similar. There are forests and mountain ranges. You will say Altar is pleasing."

Shaarvan studied my hand, turning it over to trace the lines on my palm. "I have a house in the forest. It is small but comfortable. You will bear our son there."

What an exciting thought. Like, I really wanted an alien brat. Besides, I didn't think two aliens could make a child. Then I remembered Shaarvan was supposedly half-Terran.

I sighed loudly as I considered that. "Shaarvan, you said that Altar needs women. Do you mean that Altarians can't have *daughters*?"

He nodded. For a moment, he didn't explain. Once more, he moved his thumb across the skin of my palm. I thought he was starting a pattern, but then he stopped and examined me again.

"A long time ago in our ancient history, bio-chemists made us disease-resistant. It was effective, but it accidentally placed an inhibitor on the female marker. Fertilization when there are two x chromosomes is impossible."

I only got about half of the explanation, but I understood baby girls couldn't happen.

"So you have to go to other planets for women . . . Okay, but why can't you just ask? There must be women who'd be willing."

He laughed. "Why should we accept the inferior?"

Volunteers would be inferior? I sighed. "Right," I said after a moment, swallowing what I'd like to add. Yet something still puzzled me. "Shaarvan, how can two entirely different species . . . I mean, we are different species, right?"

He nodded. His eyes studied mine.

I noticed he'd finished his food bar. His cup was empty, too.

I had to say it quickly. I had to blurt it before he rushed me off somewhere. "Shaarvan, how can two different species make babies together?"

Shaarvan smiled as if he'd been waiting for just that question. Nodding his head, he stood up and removed our empty drink cups. "The bio-chemists solved the problem," he said.

His face had closed in. He was no longer smiling at me. His eyes had grown serious, watchful.

"But how, Shaarvan? If something isn't possible . . ." My question just hung there.

He shook his head, flashed a sign, and said, "Too much time talking. Your computer drills await."

It was obvious he didn't feel like explaining. He led me to the computer, and my torture began.

Shaarvan

She is such a curious one and with a mind quick to grasp ideas, even though I give her no more than a sprinkling of information. She sorts and then probes for more. I must go slowly. She is unstable. Her mind flashes from despair to interest and back again. She has not accepted that her adaptation is permanent, nor has she resigned herself that her future lies at my side.

My mother, Teea, made the transition smoothly, but my uncle has a Terran wife who did not. Biologically speaking, there was no reason for the failure. Terran genes meld well with Shapechanger. I have researched it. The data studies are irrefutable. Where, then, is the fault in Temina's adaptation? Does *Gregor's mutant gene theory* explain it?

Shaara continues to show no chemical aberrations. Her body is accepting the changes excellently. It is only her mind that still resists — like Temina.

Susan

I got my day and night of grace period, but by the time the evening arrived, I had made a vow to myself not to become Shaarvan's slave. I feared telling him. I suspected he might even kill me for the disobedience, but I also knew I couldn't go back two hundred years in the history of women.

When his slippy-slidy hands started traveling across my body, I yelled, "Leave me alone." and pulled away from him.

I know — stupid line, totally lacking in diplomacy or tact. All day long, I'd been trying to figure out what to say and how to deliver it, but the guy scared me to death. The way his eyes and his touch cast me in some kind of spell, I was lucky to even get that out.

"Leave me alone." got the message across all right. His hands dropped to my wrists. I felt like I'd been cuffed with a one-size-too-small handcuff on each wrist.

But that didn't bother me nearly as much as when his gray eyes turned green. It's one thing when someone glares at you. You know more or less what to expect — but their eyes don't change. Yet Shaarvan's did.

His metallic gray went from slate to forest green and on to lime, with a touch of yellow. I couldn't look away. It was horrible. His eyes no longer looked human. They were alien eyes with pupils like black triangles, large and eerie.

Shivers ran up and down my spine. My legs got all shaky and trembly. You know how the heroine in a book gets pale and cold when she hears someone she loves just died? Well, I wasn't a heroine, but I knew the feeling. I understood at that moment completely. My blood got so scared it all ran down to my feet, and it must have left me looking dead without a mortician's beauty treatment.

I'm normally really brave, but there was something about Shaarvan, with those alien eyes . . . it was like confronting a demon — a demon whose powers were beyond all-knowing.

So there we were, alien to Terran, eye-to-eye, and Shaarvan finally decided to speak. "I shall ignore your words this time, Shaara, but think well. Do you truly wish to see my anger?"

I knew Shaarvan's strength. He had proven it already with a half-broken wrist, but something in me couldn't back down. "I won't give in to you, Shaarvan," I said. "You'll have to kill me."

Those brave words were spoken by someone who'd known very little physical pain in her life. I guess I thought death was a bullet wound, with everyone you loved hovering over you to bid you a fond farewell. You smiled as you slipped quietly away. Gracefully. Peacefully. It worked in the movies and in all the books I'd read, but Shaarvan had different ideas about life and death and pain. He nodded as if accepting a challenge, and then the pain began.

I thought my wrists had already been cut off from feeling; his clasp was so tight, but I discovered as Shaarvan pressed down on them that the pain grew so intense I couldn't stand. I collapsed onto my knees, my wrists still held high above my head.

I couldn't block out the pain. It attacked me from everywhere. My head ached. My knees were on fire. Agony stabbed, pricked, and bit at my wrists. My eyes burned. The tears blistered as they slid down my face.

I was suddenly doubtful I'd made the right choice. Shaarvan wasn't acting like he was in any hurry to kill me, and the pain was incredibly uncomfortable to endure — but it was like the time I'd climbed a cliff with a friend.

"It'll be great," she'd told me. "The view from the top is fantastic. You'll love it."

About halfway up that rock-hewn stretch, I'd decided climbing was about as much fun as taking a geometry test unprepared. I hated it.

Then Barbara said, "It's too dangerous to go back now. You have to keep going. When we reach the top, we'll tie a rope and rappel down. That's fun and fast."

So there I was, halfway up a cliff and no way to retreat.

That's the way I felt with Shaarvan. Either way was a bad deal. All I wanted was to be somewhere else.

I think Shaarvan knew how I felt, but he wasn't about to relent. For a moment, I had hopes when he let go of my wrists, but just as quickly, his right hand encircled both of mine. And I was still held rigid while he had one hand dangerously free.

I suppose I should have guessed the first thing he'd do. But I didn't know much about men, and I knew nothing about aliens. With his free hand, he tore off my dress. I fought him as he tried to remove it, but although he didn't have the leverage to apply the pressure on my wrists, I didn't keep my dress on. In another minute, he'd ripped it all the way off and tossed it to the other side of the room.

I knew I was losing then. Every female knows when her armor's off — even when the armor is only a dress — she knows the war is over. But I was stubborn, and I had vowed to fight Shaarvan every inch.

I think, even then, Shaarvan would have let me off easy if I'd given in, but my teeth were clenched, and I was still glaring needles.

He let go of my wrists so suddenly it stunned me into a second of immobility, but only a second. I leaped up to rush to the bathroom, not as if the bathroom would have stopped Shaarvan — but I never got that far, anyway.

His hands gripped my waist, and he swung me over his shoulder. I tried to kick him, of course, but his arms held my legs down.

"No," I cried.

"What?" he said. "I didn't hear you."

"No." I repeated with even more vehemence.

"I thought I heard you say that. Today will be the last time you ever say 'no' to my demands, wife."

There was so much warning in his voice. I heard it, and a part of me shivered, but I was in battle rage. Again, I shouted, "No."

He slammed me down on his lap, but I didn't feel the full force of it. I was too busy trying to wiggle free, even if it meant plunging down to the floor. I was that determined to get away.

He used one hand to hold me still, and the other came down full force against my bottom. Now, I know I'd been spanked as a child. I remember it hurt, but not like Shaarvan's hand. His hand stung. It singed like fire on naked skin. The pain took my breath away. My eyes burned with fresh tears.

"No," I cried again, but I meant *no more*. Shaarvan slapped me again — full force. The delicate skin of my bottom was a wreath of pain.

"No. Please stop." I cried. "Please."

There was no longer any challenge in my voice then. I was humbled. I was down. I was ready to freely admit to having been conquered. But like a child, all I could do was cry.

Once more, Shaarvan's heavy hand came down, and I cried out again, but there were no words this time, only my moans and my sobs.

"Shall I continue, my wife?"

I shook my head from side to side. I was frantic that he wouldn't see.

"You have learned your lesson?"

I nodded emphatically.

"Please," I pleaded.

"Stand up."

I scrambled up, but he grabbed my wrists before I could back away.

"Look at me."

I lifted my eyes and trembled like the coward I'd become.

"You fear me *now*?"

I nodded vigorously. I was sobbing almost hysterically. I tried to slow my breathing. I couldn't take in enough air. My tears refused to stop.

"Lie down," Shaarvan ordered, standing up to let me by.

I threw myself onto the bed, but I pushed over against the wall and hugged it with my back.

"No. Lie in the middle of the bed, on your back."

I almost sputtered a protest, but no words dared come out. I moved quickly to the place he'd told me to go. I closed my eyes. Whatever he was going to do to me, I didn't want to know. I'd shut it out. I'd pretend I was somewhere else — even on the cliff with Barbara.

For a moment, there was silence. Then Shaarvan lay down beside me.

I cringed when I felt his body. He was naked. His hands began to travel me. I writhed beneath his touch. I tried to shut him out, but his hands played a melody I was forced to heed. This time, he didn't touch my face or my breasts. He stroked my belly and my chest over and over. His hands roved down toward my hair below, but he didn't linger there. He rose upwards again, playing with me, time after time, a series of patterns across my body.

I couldn't stop my eyes from opening, but then it was worse, for I couldn't look away. The way he was looking at me taunted me, teased me. His tongue soon lashed out to add torment to his touch.

Every place he licked was cold yet burning. Hot shivers followed his touch. Once more, he began to descend my body. I couldn't take it. I moaned. I barely stopped the 'no' I'd almost said. Shaarvan, if he heard it, ignored the sound as he continued his travels down my thighs. He followed on each limb, kissing and licking, then climbed back to my center. His hands pressured me to separate my legs.

"No," I cried, but again, I tried to squelch the word.

Gray eyes peered upward at my face. "What, my wife? Did you say something?"

I shook my head back and forth, swinging my hair with the truth of my sincerity.

"Good, then open to me, Shaara. Open."

I gasped. Then I met his eyes. Only a moment could I hold his look. His hands pressured. His eyes demanded. I didn't want to obey his summons, but I couldn't cross him again. I spread my legs as he desired.

Still, his hands traveled my body. His tongue once again tasted the road and journeyed on.

I was confused. Why hadn't he taken me? Why did he play this game?

Shaarvan lifted up his eyes and stared into mine.

"Your body must know its owner, Shaara. I shall not have a battle each time I wish to pleasure myself with you."

Had he read my thoughts? I was even more frightened then. I swallowed hard. Tears sprang afresh. I shuddered.

"I shall do your arms, Shaara, and *then* I shall take you."

I shivered at his words and at the eyes which watched me, eyes mainly gray, but also shades of green.

He began with each finger, licking it, tasting it, and running his tongue up the length. I could barely stand his touch. I wanted to scream. I wanted to run from him. I didn't move.

First my palm and then the inside of my wrist. His lips caressed my arm. His tongue bathed me until I couldn't move. His touch was driving me mad.

"Be still, Shaara," he said when I fidgeted. "I am not finished with you yet."

The torture continued on and on. He moved to the other side and repeated all he had done. My ears were ringing. My heart was thumping. I couldn't suppress the animal-like moans coming from deep within me. I was alive with feeling, yet I was almost sick from the ache of it.

"Good," Shaarvan said. His eyes hovered over me. "You are mine, Shaara. Say it."

I couldn't speak. I licked my lips, trying to obey. I tried to take in air, but I almost couldn't breathe. My inhale was shallow and half-formed. I knew I had to obey him, but how could I speak when the words wouldn't come out?

"Say it, Shaara."

His eyes glowed. Greenish. Black triangles flashed for a second.

I gasped. "I . . .I . . . I am yours."

"You will not refuse me again, Shaara. Say it."

"I . . . I . . . won't . . ." I fought for breath. I felt his hand on my chest, stroking, calming. I inhaled and felt the sudden sweetness of a full breath of air. "I won't . . . refuse you again."

Then, as he'd said he would, Shaarvan took me. I gave him no struggle. I had no will to fight. I was hungry for him. I think I even urged him on. I was desperate and crazy with desire. He took me and satisfied me until I whimpered with exhaustion, but yet, I didn't want him to stop.

When it was finished, I knew he'd once more changed me, but I didn't understand how then. It was only in the weeks following I learned what he'd done. He'd sensitized my body to his touch. From then on, there could be no refusals. Shaarvan had trained my skin so the slightest touch, his glance even, could melt me to his wishes.

He'd changed me in other ways, too. I wanted to be the person I'd been before that day, but I'd lost her. My confidence was gone. I'd discovered what a coward I was in the face of pain. I was ashamed.

There was a shift in my relationship with Shaarvan as well. I was turning into the puppet lady. He had but to flash his eyes in warning, and I scrambled to do his will. I hated my servitude and the person I was becoming, but he scared me, and I no longer had even the remnants of courage.

The days on the ship flowed together: the language program, the gym, the meals in the cafeteria, the occasional trips to the control room or garden — little varied, but for the times and whims of Shaarvan.

The nights danced by with their own rhythm. On each one of them, I was at the beck and call of Shaarvan. Every night, he led me into a wild frenzy of powerlessness. Like a master violinist, he played me in a concert of his making. Each time it ended, I knew he'd done it well. It was beautiful, and I wanted to repeat it again and again, more strongly than I'd wanted anything in life, but it was only raw desire. When our joining was over, and the night turned into day, I rediscovered I felt no contentment.

Shaarvan

It progressed well. Shaara's adaptation continued in the exceptional range of percentiles. After I disciplined her, she was far more obedient. There was more respect in her eyes when she looked at me — and there was fear as well. I had not meant to reveal my nature to her yet, but perhaps it was not a bad thing to do. Her current submissiveness was quite refreshing.

Her body accepted my dominion completely. It was receptive to my touch, and the depth of her responsiveness brought me much gratification. It was my conclusion Terrans were superior in that realm.

Yet, my senses warned me the battle to win my young wife had not yet ended. Her compliance was not inadequate, but it was false. Shaara had a look I caught at times, a stray thought, a body gesture which foretold of unstableness. I believed the passing days had merely been an interlude of calm before the explosion. When a volcano ceased to rumble, it did not necessarily mean the inner turbulence was finished.

And so it was with my Shaara. She did not openly argue with my counsel, but her mind discarded the wisdom of it. She had not yet learned the Altarian way. Perhaps a final rebellion was necessary for her evolution. Regardless, the next time, I would not be as lenient as I was before. She was not ready for full disclosure, but I would force her into the understanding of her need and of her acceptance.

Susan

In the spaces between the days and nights, I'd been thinking. I reflected on my life as it was now and pondered about who I was and who I would have been had I stayed on Earth. I was not happy with my existence. I was not content with the person I'd become.

But how could I change what had happened? How could I be who I used to be? There were no solutions. I couldn't stand up to Shaarvan. So I paced, and I paced.

I was dreadfully homesick. I missed my books, talking to people, and learning how they thought. I yearned for my friendships and the laughter of conversations with my roommates. I missed hiking on the nature trails with the blue jays squawking at me and the squirrels chattering. I wanted to feel the warm, toasty feeling of sand slipping through my toes, the smell of ocean salt brine, the wet spume spraying at my face, and the sound of the waves slapping against the pier. I wanted to see seagulls, crying their plaintive wails and watch the way they soared, gliding on drafts of wind.

I craved hamburgers, dripping with catsup and mustard, a slice of tomato, a hunk of lettuce and pickles — so sour, your mouth puckered at the thought of them. I'd die for a Rocky Road ice cream cone with nuts, marshmallows, and chocolate dripping down my hands because the sun was so hot. I could almost feel its cold, milky texture frozen on my tongue and the sweet, bittersweet taste of chocolate. And pizza. How could people live without pizza?

But most of all — I desperately missed horses with their musty smell, currying them, brushing their soft, warm bodies, stroking and petting them, and feeding them oats from my hand, having that tickly feeling as the little horse whiskers on their muzzles wiggled to get every last oat. I pined for the feel of that well-muscled body under me as we cantered through the trees, or the times when I exercised them over jump courses, and the thrill of it, the way I knew just when to lean forward as I felt the muscles bunching up, the thrust of it, and then the rejoining and pulling together to meet the next obstacle. I'd give anything to feel that high again.

There were so many things that I grieved for, and I couldn't help sighing all the time over them. Everything reminded me of home. Shaarvan and I would be walking down a hall, and I'd suddenly stop at the sight of a crewmember who reminded me of one of the guys I used to know. I'd start to call "hello" in greeting, but then reality slapped me, and I said nothing.

I'd be eating my dinner, and the tweezers would drop because I was thinking about the night I cooked spaghetti for Mom and Dad. How we'd sat there in the dark because I thought one slowly melting candle in the center of the table was more Italian than light bulbs. Dad had said, "This spaghetti probably has bugs in it. I bet that's why she won't let us see it." and we'd all laughed. I knew he was teasing me, of course, and the warmth of the feeling, the sweetness of it, tugged on me painfully.

Sometimes, something Shaarvan did set me off into reminiscing. One night, he tried to tell me about an Altarian sunset, and I lost his words because I remembered the sunset I'd seen in Malibu with Barbara and her cousin Toni. We'd been there in bikinis for the day, watching the surfers out on the point, taking in the sun, and listening to an old tape of the Beach Boys. We bought hot dogs from the street vendor and an ice bucket of drinks. We drank all the sodas and threw the ice cubes at each other in the afternoon, and then lazily packed up our stuff as the sun began to color.

The blended red, yellow, and orange all smudged across the streaky clouds pulled our eyes away from the gorgeous lifeguard. We dropped back down in the hot sand and just sat there absorbing the sky. It was a show like on the Fourth of July, just slower. No, not like that, more like when all the red and yellow crayons in the Big Pack with the 180 crayons got left in the sun too long. They spread out in splotchy streaks, all mixed up with clouds, and were still up there, melting and melding as the sun went down.

We were so busy watching the sky show we never noticed when the lifeguard climbed down off his post and left. Toni was mad about it. She'd wanted to talk to him, but I thought the sunset was worth more than any gum-chomping blond surfer.

I sighed at the memory and woke to find Shaarvan watching me. He wasn't angry, just kind of sad. His eyes, I guess, had been observing me the whole time. I wondered how much he could really read thoughts. Had he seen my memory?

I think he knew how dreadfully homesick I was. It was eating away at me. Instead of Earth being more distant, it was daily becoming more real to me. I felt panic inside me, like the feeling you got when you tried to walk on something high, and you slipped, followed by the moment of ragged terror when you grasped the fact that there was nothing underneath you. You flailed. You thought for a second you could stay up by determination alone, but then you realized you couldn't, and you were suddenly falling . . . My homesickness was like that.

The reality Shaarvan insisted on was the high wire, and I knew at any moment my foot would reach the point where there was nothing left but air, and I'd fall, and there wouldn't be any Earth to catch me.

I needed the stability of walking on the Earth's soil, of feeling the hardness beneath my feet, and knowing gravity would keep me there, safe, where I belonged.

So maybe I was feeling something more than just homesickness. Maybe it was a combination of things. In one swoop, I'd lost the Earth, my evolutionary, historical, and biological home. I'd lost my reality of the way things worked — knowing what's possible and what wasn't — and I'd lost myself, the person I'd originally planned to become.

Shaarvan knew how I was feeling. I saw it in his eyes as he watched me, but he believed kisses and pats on my head would cure me. He thought his silent patience would allow this period to pass until I was again buoyantly able to accept all the changes he kept tossing at me. But what if it couldn't?

As if to keep my mind from further processing the overload, Shaarvan increased my language learning until I was on the computer all morning. It certainly didn't decrease my unhappiness or cure my increasingly desperate homesickness. It made me even more miserable.

I felt like the old-fashioned pressure cooker my mom used for cooking purple cabbage. It needed its valve at the top to release pressure. I'd often watched the valve rocking back and forth, shooshing away all that pressure building up inside the pot. Without the valve, Mom used to tell me, the pressure inside would become so great there'd be an explosion, and purple cabbage would shoot up onto the ceiling. I had no such valve, and I knew the pressure inside me was reaching dangerous levels.

One day, while we were in the garden, I finally exploded. The tension had been piling up ever since the day Shaarvan had spanked me like a small child. I think you can only live with fear for so long. Sometimes, the body adapted so that you'd rather accept a little more pain and stress than endure another moment of imprisonment. When that day arrived, when you finally said enough, no matter how great your fear was, you acted on it.

That day, Shaarvan was doing his best to take my mind off my homesickness rebellion, or whatever it was, but I couldn't focus. I was pacing restlessly, filled with an inner tension fast approaching at critical level.

"Shaara, sit down," Shaarvan ordered.

"I can't, Shaarvan. I just can't," I told him, darting a look into his eyes, trying to tell him I didn't mean it as a challenge to him, only as a restless inability to stop.

Shaarvan's eyes weren't angry. They were full of understanding. His mind was focused on me, analyzing, examining, assessing. I was glad I hadn't angered him, but his constant attentiveness irritated me. I reeled around and took off in the opposite direction.

Shaarvan stood up and walked toward me. "Shaara, come here," he said from behind me.

I looked back. His eyes were staring at me as if he were trying to peer into my head.

"No, I won't let you read my mind," I said angrily, turning my back to him.

His swift reflexes caught my wrists. He swung me around. "Enough of this, Shaara. You are full of tension. The anger is boiling inside you."

"Tell me something I don't know." I yelled, trying to pull away. "I hate it when you read me. You won't even let me have the privacy of my brain."

"All husbands need to know what is bothering their wives."

I had just been given the light for my fuse. I couldn't be silent a moment longer. "You want to know what's bothering me, Shaarvan? Then ask me. I'll tell you."

He pulled me closer. His eyes cautioned. "Careful, Shaara. You are backing yourself into the corner again."

I understood what he was telling me, but I ignored it. I didn't care anymore. He could beat me if that's what turned him on, but it wouldn't stop this pressure, this wild, unpredictable madness.

"I want off this ship, Shaarvan. You have to take me home. I'm going crazy. Can't you see?"

Shaarvan's eyes continued to examine me like I was an amoeba under his microscope, yet he couldn't understand me any more than I could understand the stupid amoeba. Yet, so far, he hadn't silenced me. So far.

"I need friends, Shaarvan. I need books. I need my life back, where I can talk to people and go to the movies and walk on the beach and swim."

I didn't dare look at him now. My eyes had filled with tears. I kept babbling on. "I want to learn about life by going to classes, and to ride my bike and go shopping. I want to wear jeans — and anything else I feel like wearing — instead of this stupid dress that's always the same ridiculous mellow yellow and the same exact style, day after day after day."

"Calm down, Shaara," Shaarvan said, and he tried to wrap his arms around me, but I was too into my rage.

I ducked away. "No, I'm not Shaara. I'm Susan, and I'm not your wife. You can force me every night, and you can make me learn your unintelligible language, but I'm me, and I'm not going to listen anymore, and I'm not going to watch for your dog signals, and I'm not . . ."

Shaarvan's hand darted behind my head. It gripped me on the back of my neck. I couldn't move without it causing excruciating pain. I tried to bob down and twist under, but the grip only tightened. I yelped from the agony, but then I stood still. The pain seemed to have cleared my head. My anger, like a whipped dog, fled.

Shaarvan's eyes on me were not angry, as much as concerned. "You are overtired, Shaara. I shall allow you to rest."

Of course, I tried to argue with his statements. I tried to explain, but every word was met with a new round of pain in the back of my neck.

Shaarvan's eyes were unbending. "Come," he said.

What choice did I have when every word I spoke was an assault of pain? Shaarvan, with the neck grip still in place, walked me back, not to our room, but to the horrible place where I'd first wakened to find myself on the ship. Without a word of comfort, Shaarvan released his hold on my neck and turned to walk away. The door opened for him, and he left me. I watched, too stunned to speak, as the door whooshed shut.

I tested it, of course. It was still electrified. I wouldn't dare attempt to open it. I remembered the pain of its shock.

There was nothing in the room to do. There were no buttons on the wall, no computers, nothing. It was stark white, like a room for the criminally insane, like a prison isolation cell for the troublesome.

There was the usual bathroom, this one without a shower, but there was no food or drink. Even the chest of drawers was empty.

I sat on the couch and thought about the unjustness of it all. Why me? Why did I have to be taken away from my home, from my life, from even my planet? It wasn't fair.

I hated Shaarvan, and I ranted about my hate, but the empty walls didn't care. They didn't listen, didn't respond. They were part of it all — alien, distant, unfeeling, and harsh. They were just like Shaarvan and all his crewmen, ignoring my needs and desires.

I paced back and forth in the tiny room. There wasn't even adequate space to walk properly, but I thought of the pressure cooker valve — so little, yet the shooshing noises relieved all of its pressure. Back and forth, I strode, angry and bottled up with inner tension. I wanted to hit something. I hit the walls. I beat them with my fists and kicked them repeatedly. They didn't give. No dent appeared, and no hole in the plaster displayed my anger. They were impenetrable walls. I'd caused no damage, but my fist and feet hurt from the attack. Just like with Shaarvan — my rebellion only caused **me** pain.

I screamed like I'd done so long ago. I knew no one would come, but I screamed anyway. I screamed at the injustice. I screamed because I wanted to. I screamed for the pressure valve. But this particular swoosh, swoosh just didn't do it for me. Again, the walls didn't accept my abuse. They bounced the sounds back at me. Again, the only pain was mine.

Winded from my violence but somehow calmer, I corralled my anger. I made up wild stories about alien pirates who would set me free from my torture. "Take Shaarvan and make him walk the plank into the void," I said. "No, send him in a capsule to the closest star and let him feel the heat of a thousand rays, burning him as my revenge.

I planned escapes. I'd take the escape pod and fly away into the night. I'd search for a comet — no, too hot. I'd find a black hole and . . . What a stupid idea — I'd be dead if I did that, dead, dead, dead. And even if a black hole didn't kill me, why would it take me back to Earth? I didn't even know where Earth was. I got lost trying to find the movie theatre, which used to be only two miles away. How many billions of miles from Earth was I now?

OK — next strategy. Get one of the crew to stage a mutiny. Right. They wouldn't even talk to me. They wouldn't look at me. And what would I offer them? They already had their valuable cargo. Why would they want to go back to Earth?

There had to be some way to outmaneuver Shaarvan . . . except there wasn't. My brain was stressing out. I felt a horrendous headache coming on. I lay down and tried hard not to think.

Turning off the brain was harder than stopping a horse with the bit in its teeth. I pulled right and left, but it still kept on running. "Shaarvan, Shaarvan," it said.

What was the poem I'd once read about change? I remembered only some things could be changed. That was the part about yourself. You could change yourself, but when you couldn't change something . . . Change what you can . . . Accept what you can't change and have the courage to know the difference. I knew I didn't have it perfectly right, but the essence was there. The acceptance and the courage to know the difference — that part was right.

No matter how many fantasies I constructed, there was going to be no *Deus ex Machina*. Nothing was going to swoop in and change my situation. No pirates, no black holes, nothing. Did I have the courage to accept it?

My headache was pounding. I closed my eyes and thought about Shaarvan. Shaarvan's eyes when he'd told me about Altar's sunset, Shaarvan's knuckles on my face, gently stroking me. I knew the way he looked when he desired sex, the way his eyes darkened and glowed slightly green, green as emeralds, glowing orbs of desire.

I fell asleep, but in my dreams, there was still always Shaarvan. Shaarvan was there in Malibu, watching the sunset with me. His arm was around me, warming me against the cooling beach air. His eyes were watching me as much as the sunset, and when it was over and the last streaks of crimson had faded into the dusk, his lips joined with mine. In the middle of the crowded Malibu beach, we were making love, and there was no one but the two of us.

Another dream pierced through my sleep. Shaarvan and I were hiking up a cliff. Barbara wasn't there, and when I reached the point where I'd lost my courage, it was Shaarvan who helped me climb the cliff. Shaarvan was underneath me, urging me upward, telling me we were almost at the top. We reached the lookout point, and Shaarvan's arms encircled me. His eyes glowed golden-green, and his mouth dropped to mine.

I sprang up off the couch and yelled, "Get out of my mind."

There was only silence from the walls and the echo of my desperate cry. Shaarvan wasn't there. He was in me, buried at the heart of me, fastened to my soul.

"You can't love an alien," I said over and over, like a litany. "You can't, you can't, you can't."

The walls beat the rhythm of it. They seemed to like it and echoed longer in the refrain. It sounded like a Native American song. All I needed was a tom-tom. I laughed at the silliness of it, but my heart was strangely still. I put my hand over my chest to make sure my heart was still beating. Dumb. Of course, it was still beating. I'd be dead if it weren't.

I lay back down and drifted off. I dreamed of Shaarvan, but I'd gone into a deeper sleep cycle, and when I woke up, I couldn't remember the dream. Only my heart could tell the storyline. It recalled how, in my dream, I'd loved Shaarvan.

I fell asleep again. When I woke, I knew the night was over. I was fully rested. My stomach growled low and angry. It demanded food. It reminded me of how yesterday I hadn't fed it lunch or dinner. I couldn't feed it breakfast either. I had no food. My throat complained of dryness, but I had no water to appease its thirst.

Where was Shaarvan? How long would he punish me? What if he left me another day all alone without food or water? I could do nothing. I could starve in here or die of thirst. There was no one else who would know or care. The crew would never interfere, not if Shaarvan forbade it. Only Shaarvan could rescue me. Only Shaarvan.

Again, I paced, restless now. The pressure was gone from me. My rage had departed. Anger seemed to be a good emotion to get me in trouble, but when I needed it to sustain me, it always disappeared.

I had to focus on something. If I didn't, the white, sterile walls would drive me crazy. I began to talk to myself. I was like the crazy lady I'd seen in a fast food joint who'd had a whole conversation with herself. She'd been a street person, dirty and disheveled, sipping away at her coffee, which overflowed with sugar and cream, and still, she kept dumping in the packets, adding to the overflow. My friends and I stared at her, snickering behind our hands, pretending she wasn't a person with feelings.

One of the guys had gotten up to get another order of fries. He'd walked by the crazy lady on his return and seen our eyes on him.

"Hey, lady," he'd said. "Who are you talking to?"

"I'm talking to nobody," she'd said, "and I ain't bothering nobody, so go away."

Ken had come strolling back to us, looking for our praise. The others thought it was a riot. The guys clapped Ken on the back for his courage. I sat watching the woman sip her coffee and wondered how she'd come to be where she was. And all the while, she talked crazy-like to the person beside her — the one who wasn't there.

We left the restaurant soon after, as if we were afraid the craziness was contagious, but I told my friends I had to go to the bathroom. They jeered at me for not going earlier, but they waited.

I returned to the restaurant and ordered the biggest hamburger the place had. Nervously, I shoved it onto the crazy lady's table. "Please take this," I said to her. "I apologize for my friends. We didn't mean to be rude."

"Yes, you did, but I'm used to it. Now, get out of here," she said. "You're taking up my time."

I don't know whether the woman ate the hamburger or left it sitting there. I've always wondered. I rejoined my friends, and the woman was temporarily forgotten, but sometimes I still thought about her, and certain questions kept bothering me. What did it take to drive a person into such a state of mind? Why had she been like that? Who had she been once?

Now I knew what it took: isolation, deprivation, losing your identity . . . it didn't take nearly as much as I'd thought it would before you found yourself talking to someone who wasn't there.

When my throat became so parched I could no longer talk to the walls or to imaginary people, and the silence began to press in on me, I lay down again. On the solitary couch where no arms comforted me, I felt so alone. I began to cry. I cried because life was rotten. I cried because I was hungry, thirsty, and miserable. I cried at my loneliness, and I cried because I had nobody who cared. I was just like the street lady, except . . . I had Shaarvan. Somewhere on the ship, there was somebody who cared, and I knew he'd return. I didn't know when, but I knew he would return, and I knew he'd feed me and give me water. I knew he'd take care of me.

My tears dried. I lay there scratchy-eyed and wretched, and I stared at the ceiling. It still looked the same. What had I said before, an albino with acne? No, the bumps were not inward. They were pebbly like cottage cheese spread out to dry. I lay there wishing it were smooth like water, or Kool-Aid, or ice cubes. A single dripping ice cube I could suck on would be heaven.

I closed my eyes to stop the stinging of my salty tears, and I listened. I could hear the motor of the ship now. It was familiar, like the beat of my heart, a part of me.

I pictured the way the ship was speeding through space, intent on nothing but distance. I could see the streaks of light flashing by amid the great dampness of darkness that hovered all around us. The ship was the arms of comfort. It enclosed me.

I could feel the faint vibration through my body, and I realized the ship was more than the arms of comfort. The ship was the womb that carried me in its belly to a place where I was to be birthed again. On its way to the destination, it kept me safe like a mother, inside the comfort of its warmth and closeness. The ship was my new mother, and its body was my protection and my life. I felt soothed by the thought, and again, I slept.

Shaarvan left me in that room most of the day. I don't know how long I waited, but I know I was beyond hunger. I also knew I'd reached the point where I was ready to do anything he asked me to do if he'd only give me a single sip of water.

When, at last, the door whooshed open, I forgot I hated Shaarvan. I flung myself into his arms. Shaarvan had once been my enemy, but on this ship, in whatever lonely galaxy we were in, he was my only friend. He was my sustenance. He was my sanity. The ship might be my mother, but Shaarvan was everything else.

Shaarvan's arms hugged me and comforted me. His lips raided my mouth. His tongue plunged into me with a violence of long denial.

"Yes," I cried out. "Take me, take me, now. Please, Shaarvan."

He took me on the floor of that heated room. He was rough, but I craved it. After the silence and the deprivation of all that was warm and alive, I needed Shaarvan's fierceness. I needed him to wipe out the coldness I felt inside me. When he had taken his pleasure, he began to play my body.

"No," I cried. "Don't, Shaarvan. That isn't what I want." My eyes pleaded.

"You want to stay here in this room?"

His eyes warned, but I didn't have to stop to think about it at all. I sat up on my knees. "No, Shaarvan. I'll obey you. I'll do anything you tell me, but please, can't you just talk to me sometimes? I am *so* lonely."

For a moment, a flash of memories streaked through my brain. How humble I sounded. I, Miss Independent, now on my knees, promising obedience and begging for drops of conversation.

"What is your name?" Shaarvan shot the question at me like I'd dared him again.

"What?" The question took me by surprise, but then I knew instantly what he wanted. There could be only one reality — Shaarvan's. I was on his ship, bound for Altar. I belonged to the man who called himself my husband. I knew those were his realities, and he would force them on me.

The ship had taught me well. It had already told me all this. Shaarvan's reality was all I had. It was my future. It was my present.

I looked at the walls of the room. Shaarvan would leave me here for as long as it took until, in the end, he would win. I had no choice. I had to have the wisdom to accept the things I couldn't change. I would say the words, and then there would be no turning back. No more English, no more Susan.

"Shaara," I said. "My name is Shaara." Tears filled my eyes, but I wouldn't shed them. They were worthless.

"Good," Shaarvan praised me for my submission. His knuckles stroked my face. His eyes were thoughtful as he stared into mine. I wished I knew what his thoughts were.

Without another word, Shaarvan led me back through the long maze of corridors. He draped his arm possessively across my shoulders and held me close. It was strange how grateful I was to feel his body next to mine.

We returned to our room. I was amazed at the rush of pleasure I felt when we entered. I felt like running to touch the computer, the buttons, even the walls. The room was so little different from where I'd been. I couldn't understand why it felt so much like home.

Shaarvan

Poor kid. I hated to leave her there in the isolation room. She had come so far, but I had to complete her understanding. She needed to release all she was clinging to. I had to force her to accept the change. Yet, I worried as I walked away. Would she be able to adapt? Or would she turn like Temina?

I was not a fool, leaving her unattended. She was watched continuously, either by myself or one of the crew. There was nothing in the room to harm her other than the isolation. There had been reports over the centuries of females who had not been able to learn from their seclusion but instead had faced insanity. It was suspected such was the cause of Temina's fragility.

Shaara had worried me at times because of her similarities with Temina. Would Shaara be strong enough to learn what she needed to learn?

She appeared calm and compliant in the monitors when her time was over, but I still did not know what to expect when I arrived to release her. I was pleasantly surprised. She had delightfully learned her lesson and was desperate for my return. Her greeting was sexually satisfying to us both. I was well content with her progress.

One note I needed to ponder was her request for more conversation. She entreated me in such a submissive manner I could not automatically reject it, but I found her plea disturbing. Had I not been generous with my dialogue? Had I not answered more of her questions than with the other girls? Yet her eyes were filled with need, and she braved much at a time when she was still fearful I would leave her again.

I shall consider her request. Perhaps for Shaara it was not only necessary for her contentment but might be a useful training device.

Shaara

"Talking, Shaarvan, is where you relate what is important to you, and I tell you what is important to me," I tried to explain to him several days later.

His eyes twinkled as he suppressed a quiver of a smile at the sides of his lips. "That would be pointless. What is important to me you could not understand. I am not interested in the other."

I sputtered, biting my lip in frustration. "Shaarvan, I don't understand you."

"My point, exactly," he said, but he was chuckling fully, having teased me into the kind of frustration he could soothe away with one touch of his finger.

His hands began to draw lazy patterns on my skin. I had only a minute before I'd lose my train of thought. "All right. At least, please, try to explain to me what *is* important to you."

He grinned, a grin which sent my heart racing. "My ship, my wife, and sex," he said, allowing me no further conversation.

Shaarvan was challenging, but I was determined. If I had to spend the rest of my life with this man, I needed to understand him.

It had been difficult enough before when he spoke more readily in English, but increasingly, Shaarvan allowed me only to speak in his language. English received the *be silent* command. He knew how much I wanted to ask him questions and understand the answers he gave me, so he made use of it, forcing me to struggle with Altarian. And, all too frequently, whether from my misuse of his tongue or my ignorance, I amused him. I hated it when he treated me like a child. It was true I was ignorant of his culture, his language, and a great deal more, but I wasn't a child. I resented his amusement.

It was for that reason I asked Shaarvan if I could work with the computer in the afternoon, minus the shocks.

"You wish additional practice?" he asked, his eyebrow lifted in surprise that I'd asked something completely unpredictable.

"Without the shocks, Shaarvan," I pleaded as I nodded my head.

His eyes studied me so long I was sure he'd say no.

"I will permit it," he said at last, but his eyes looked skeptical as if he doubted my seriousness.

But I was happier about life then, for I had a goal. Two goals, if I counted getting Shaarvan to open up to me. My homesickness was gone, and I felt more content with the package life had given me. True, it wasn't what I would have chosen, but I was learning how to accept what I couldn't change.

So I worked harder than ever to learn the language, and the computer soon shocked me less and beeped a correct response more often.

In the afternoons, I started trying to learn to read. Shaarvan helped me. He printed out some children's books for me to practice on, and although I know he was entertained by my inability to read the simplest words, I think he also was learning to respect my drive.

Each night, I could usually get Shaarvan to answer two or three questions before his patience would end. One evening, I asked him how long his family had been traders.

"Shapechanger have always been traders," he told me.

"What do you mean, Shapechanger? I thought you said you were Altarian."

"My family lives on Altar. I did not tell you I was Altarian."

"Tell me about Shapechangers, then. Does it mean you can change your shape?"

"The plural is *Shapechanger*, Shaara. And, yes, a Shapechanger will change his shape when it serves his needs or when he becomes angry."

This was more information than Shaarvan had ever given me. But changing his shape? That was from fairy tales. "You can change into anything?" I asked, smiling mischievously. "Even something tiny?"

He chuckled. Shaarvan's laughter had a musical tone to it. When I wasn't the brunt of his amusement, I loved to hear him laugh.

"My mother has told me many of your Terran tales. I can become a mouse if you like, but you could not kill me by stepping on me. My size does not change greatly."

Shaarvan looked serious as he told me, but I didn't believe him, not then. It was later I learned a Shapechanger does not lie.

The computer kept me from ever getting bored. I began to see the attraction. I could get answers to any question. But often, I couldn't understand the answer because I didn't have the necessary vocabulary. It frustrated me to use the computer's dictionary, for the definitions were usually incomprehensible, too. Often, it was only at night, with Shaarvan, I found understanding.

"Please, couldn't you hook up a language program that could translate words into English when I don't understand?" I begged him one evening.

"No," he said firmly. "I do not wish the computer to speak English to you. You are making excellent progress. You will continue as you are."

Easy enough for him to say. Nothing ever frustrated *him*. I sometimes imagined Shaarvan had been born knowing everything.

It was useless to plead. I could see that in the darkness of his eyes. Lighter hues gave me latitude. Dark gray warned me I should back away.

" But — I don't understand many of the words," I continued, watching his eyes for any warning.

"Then you will work harder," he stated, just before he turned away, the subject closed. No warning, but no leeway.

So, I struggled and persisted. Maybe Shaarvan was right about learning more in such a manner, but it sure made it more difficult for me.

I wanted to ask the computer for information about *Shapechanger*, but I couldn't find a listing for it. It was strange not to be able to pull it up. Then, I realized Shaarvan had only given me the name in English. I felt so stupid. Of course, I couldn't find it.

What I did locate was a *shapppe*, which I discovered meant a *map of the ship*. It was a great thing to pull up. I even got a printout, one I immediately hid in the bathroom behind the toilet's controls.

When Shaarvan was absent from the room, I spent weeks trying to decipher the map. I didn't understand many of the labels on it, which were especially difficult to ask about because my questions to Shaarvan had to be completely disguised. I didn't want him to know what I'd found. Camouflaging questions may sound easy, but, you see, it meant the cover-up had to be in my thoughts, not just in what I said.

I had discovered that if I thought about two things at once, it would more or less screen out what I didn't want Shaarvan to pick up. It wasn't easy to do, and it didn't work 100% of the time, but I was learning.

One day, as I was researching the items on the map, and discovered that the large chamber with streptorre meant *sleeping Terrans*. There were smaller chambers with the word *streptorre* on them, too. Eventually, I figured out from the coding that those girls were awake.

Why had Shaarvan not allowed me to talk with them? I'd be willing to practice Altarian with them if his objection was only concerning my language acquisition. And why hadn't I ever seen the women — in the dining room, in the garden, in the control room, passing by in the halls? Why were they being kept a secret from me?

I couldn't get that kind of information from the computer. But what I did find was the door system. There was an override.

I didn't try it the first day. Shaarvan was due back, and I had to hide the map. I waited until the next afternoon when I'd have plenty of time. When Shaarvan left, I immediately set to work. Once I'd figured out the system, it was surprisingly easy. I made it through the door and out into the corridor. The map was harder to follow than I'd realized, but I stuck to it and navigated the maze successfully. The chambers for the *streptorre* were right where the map said they'd be. But guess who'd forgotten to override the doors of the girls.

I figured the doors would shock me — even from the outside, and I guessed the girls, just like me, wouldn't be able to open and close their own doors. I was irritated by my lack of planning and about to head back for Shaarvan's quarters when I saw one of the cleaner robots passing by. I'd seen several of them as I followed the map. I'd kept out of their way. This one I didn't hide from.

"Help me." I cried, and I waved my arms back and forth.

It was one of the lowest and stupidest of the robots. The electronic gadget didn't ponder the situation. It merely opened the nearest door and shoved me in.

Success. An Earth girl sat on the bed in the corner. She was sleepy. I'd awakened her. When she saw me, she blinked and then stretched as if my presence were normal routine. But I was so excited. I almost ran to hug her.

"I'm Susan," I said. "I guess you know we're on a ship."

Again, she yawned. Then she sat up and looked me over as if something about me were strange or confusing. "Yeah, tell me something I don't know. Like, how come you get to wear clothes?"

That's when I noticed she had none on. The blanket covering her was everything they'd left her with.

"I don't know," I said. "I'll try to sneak you some. What's your name?"

She looked irritated I'd bothered her, not at all glad to see me.

"Laurie, but I don't see what business it is of yours. You gonna fight me for the next . . ."

"Silence." Shaarvan's voice was like a gunshot in the night. It scared us both. Laurie paled and retreated, almost blending into the background of the wall she was leaning on.

My eyes turned back to Shaarvan. How had he found me? I opened my mouth to warn him he was frightening Laurie. I didn't get the chance to speak.

"Out, Shaara," he ordered as his hand grabbed and jerked me backward.

Laurie hadn't seemed like anyone I'd want to hang around with for a long time, but she was Terran. And she was a female. Why couldn't I talk with her?

"Please, Shaarvan," I pleaded. "I need a friend. It wouldn't . . ."

The neck squeeze was on. I walked very carefully all the way back to our room because Shaarvan never released his death grip.

"Be warned. I am angry," he said as we walked through the door.

I saw the flash in his eyes, eyes so dark they were almost black, but I ignored the warnings. "So am I," I said. "It took me days to figure out how to get to Laurie's, and you wouldn't even let me have five minutes to talk with her."

His hands flashed a second warning, but I was angry now, too.

"Lock me in this room, beat me, starve me. What difference does it make? I . . ."

Then, I saw what I hadn't believed was true. Shaarvan changed. He melded into it. One moment, he was normal — angry normal, it was true, but Shaarvan, and then, suddenly, he was a beast — a horrible snarling, growling beast. Green tiger-eyes glared at me, and it roared.

I screamed and ran. It followed on tiger paws, toenails rasping the carpet as it padded after me. There was no place to run to, and the tiger was gaining on me. I darted into the bathroom and hoped the closed door behind me would keep me safe. It didn't. The tiger came right in, snarling with those dagger teeth gnawing at the air. I dashed into the shower and turned the water on. Cats hated water, didn't they?

It did no good. This one didn't seem to mind getting wet. It pounced onto the raised surface of the shower and stood there under the faucet. I screamed again as the tiger grabbed at my dress. As I moved back, the dress ripped. I knew at any moment, the animal would tear at my skin, clawing me, scratching, and biting.

Then its massive body jumped up at me, and I plummeted down onto the hard tile floor. Miraculously, the fall didn't hurt me. Somehow, I landed on one of its paws. Yet, it didn't stop the creature from attacking. It pounced again, all four legs spread out on each side of my body, trapping me. Its hot animal breath panted into my face. Its gaping mouth and its sharp teeth lowered. I closed my eyes, knowing the animal's razor sharp teeth were about to rend my throat.

But strangely, the tiger did nothing. I waited, fearing to look up at its fangs. But it stood over me, obviously hungry, ferocious, and ready to gnaw at my flesh. Yet still, I felt no pain — no piercing sharp bite, no claws ripping into my skin. At last, I had to look.

The creature was Shaarvan, Shaarvan whose eyes mocked me.

I gasped. I didn't know whether to cry out as if he were my rescuer or to tremble at his presence.

His eyes were gray again, gray with only a hint of green. The fur was gone. The tiger stripes and the markings on his face were no longer evident.

I opened my mouth to speak, but I had no voice. I'd screamed it out. I don't know what I would have said if I'd been able to verbalize it anyway.

Shaarvan stared down at me. He was still crouched over me, straddling my body. I closed my eyes and then opened them, still not knowing exactly what I'd seen. What had happened? Had I imagined the tiger? Had I hallucinated the whole thing?

Shaarvan smiled, but the smile wasn't friendly. It mocked my thoughts. "I started to take you in my animal shape, my wife. You were delectable, writhing in your fear. But we shall save it for another time, Shaara . . . if you dare to cross me again."

I closed my eyes again, this time because I couldn't bear the way he was looking at me. I was trembling again. I didn't know what to believe, but I knew his words were a threat, and my fear, that horrible fear of him . . . I couldn't take it anymore. I let the tears come, and when they did, my sobs bordered on hysterics.

Shaarvan stood up. I could feel him watching me. His body was like a tower, casting shade . . . at least it felt like that. I think I cried even harder then. A dam had burst, and a bridge had collapsed. How much more could I take?

Shaarvan bent over and picked me up. I almost panicked at his touch, almost fought him, but he said coolly, "Stop it, Shaara. Enough."

His voice breached through the chaos of my mind. Like a cold splash of water, it shocked me still. I lay limp as he carried me into the other room.

With little gentleness, he dropped me down on my feet, and, my back to his chest, he crossed his arm across me, sealing me to his body. For a moment, he stood there reprogramming the computer. His speech was so fast that I couldn't understand the words as he issued fresh commands.

"Sit down," he ordered then even more brusquely.

He'd sat on the only chair near the computer. I didn't know what he wanted. When I appeared flustered, he pulled me down into his lap.

"Key in the override now," he ordered.

I was afraid. I could feel his anger. It rose like steam coming off a hot radiator. I could hear the fury in his voice, too. It threatened me in ways I didn't understand.

How much more punishment would Shaarvan give me for my earlier disobedience? But even as I wondered, my hands began their task. I didn't dare disobey Shaarvan.

I keyed in the combination. At once, the computer jolted me. A hundred pricking needles stung each of the sensitive pads at the tips of my fingers.

I screamed with the agony of it, and I shook and blew at my fingers until I could move them freely again and until the ugly throb faded into memory. Then I turned on Shaarvan in fury. "I did what you told me. I obeyed. But you hurt me for no reason," I sobbed.

He pushed me up, turned me around to face him, and said, "Retribution for your deception, Shaara. Did you expect your punishment would be light?"

He'd caught my chin and raised my face. I was caught in the strength of his grip. My eyes looked deeply into his. I started to speak but thought better of it. Then I gnawed at my lower lip while I pondered.

The memory of the shock on my fingers still made them ache. I rubbed them and thought some more. I closed my eyes and said, "I just used the computer to . . ." I stopped, not wanting to make it worse. "I didn't mean to . . ."

Shaarvan flashed the *be silent command*, which meant I couldn't even defend myself.

He picked me up again, one hand sliding beneath my legs before I realized his intentions, but I didn't fuss. I could still feel the edge of his anger —like a sharp current, just shy of electrocution.

He carried me over to the bed and then laid me down on it. A moment later, his body followed. He wove the spells that brought my lust, teasing and tormenting me into madness. At last, I cried for mercy, and with savage clemency, he granted ecstasy.

When our desires had been slaked, and he brought me back into a more normal plane, I found myself studying his eyes. At that moment, they were gray as a wintry day. How could they change as I knew they had? How could Shaarvan become an animal? My heart beat faster, remembering.

I attempted to question him, but again he gave me the *silence command*. Then, he yawned. The teeth in his mouth were flat-topped, not feline, but still, his open mouth reminded me of the tiger. I shuddered.

Shaarvan shifted into a more comfortable position. Then he snapped his fingers, and the light went off. Sliding his right arm around my body, he scooped me closer. I knew he was done with me this round. His sword lay limp as he molded me against him.

Carelessly, he draped one heavy leg across my lower limbs. I felt smothered, but I knew it would be safer to say nothing. Still, a low half-whimper, half-sigh escaped me. Shaarvan heard it. The other hand dropped down to squeeze my breast.

I made no further objection. The hand continued to squeeze and play, but it grew languid. It stroked my nipples, seeking a response. I couldn't help quaking at his touch. My nipples, erect and eager, responded even against my will. His organ, replete a moment ago, awakened. Shaarvan shifted me slightly. The sword gallantly sought access where there was none.

Shaarvan chuckled. "You awaken the dead, my sweet wife. I know you are tired. I will not take you again."

His hand still lay wreathed on my breast, his leg held me still, and his sword still writhed at my side, but I closed my eyes. I knew I was safe then, safe from his body, but not from my thoughts. They writhed like his sword.

I had so much to ponder: Shapechanging, deceit, failure, and why sometimes our joining, even when Shaarvan pleasured me so fully, was not of love but of mastery.

Chapter Six
Transitions

Shaarvan

She was a tigress, my little wife. Her ingenuity was brilliant. If she were a male, I would hire her at once to program computers. Such a shame I had to punish her for her inventiveness. She was very clever. I would not have believed a woman capable of such a high level of resourcefulness had I not watched with my own eyes. However, it bothered me how quickly she forgot her fear of the isolation room. That was not good.

I had not meant to introduce my other nature so soon, but her defiance was foolish. She must be shown that the consequences could be even graver. I did not wish to hurt her, but if she continued to challenge me, she would leave me no choice.

Shaara

When I woke, Shaarvan was still asleep. I studied him. My thoughts raced every which way, assaulting me from all sides. How could Shaarvan have changed into a tiger? I'd seen it. I'd felt it. I'd smelled the tiger breath, but nothing like that was possible. No one could transform into an animal. No one could grow teeth like stalactites or claws inside giant furry paws.

Hadn't physics taught that change takes energy? Even converting ice to water takes energy, but to change to a totally different form . . . Wouldn't it require fusion or something?

I couldn't understand how he'd done it. Perhaps it hadn't happened. No, I know it did. I didn't dream it. But could I have hallucinated the beast?

But there was also a difference in Shaarvan's eyes. I'd seen those eyes before. No wonder I could never tell if they were gray or green. They changed colors. He had done it several times. Green eyes a tiger. Gray eyes are Shaarvan. Contacts? He hadn't had time to change them. Besides, the tiger-eyes were more than just green. They weren't human-looking . . .

Shaarvan woke as I was studying him. My stare amused him. "Ah, I see your brain is trying to puzzle it out," he said as he chuckled low and deep.

Was it my imagination, or . . . wasn't that the same sound the tiger had made when it followed me into the shower?

"Are you frowning over Shapechanging, or deceit?" Shaarvan asked, suddenly alert. His eyes opened wide as he examined me. His brow tightened.

I was pretty sure he was still amused, but his eyes held a hint of something else. I tried to ignore it.

He chuckled once again, but the nature of it was changing. I heard the growl inside him. I gasped.

"Answer," he ordered sharply and sat up. There was full warning in his eyes. I had hesitated too long.

I practiced my wounded look. I hadn't deserved a reprimand for thinking too hard, surely. Shaarvan's eyes flicked green. It was a sure sign his anger was waking.

"Shapechanging," I blurted out quickly.

So much for thinking about how best to broach a dangerous subject.

"I didn't dream you changed into a tiger, did I?"

Shaarvan shook his head slowly. He was watching my eyes. He knew I wasn't challenging him now. Slowly, he relaxed again.

Relieved, I sat up. I was careful not to pull the covers off Shaarvan's body, but I still kept myself wrapped in blankets. I had questions I wanted answers to. Unclothed, I knew where Shaarvan's mind would be.

"Shaarvan," I began, trying to sort through the meager Altarian vocabulary I had for concepts difficult enough in my own language. "Shapechanging isn't possible, but you did it." Suddenly, the English burst through. "How do you find the energy to transform?"

Shaarvan ignored my lapse. "Terran logic, huh?" he said, studying my eyes again.

As I fidgeted, his dimples tweaked, and the smile broke through. I figured he was laughing at me again. It was like I'd had the stupidity to ask Einstein about relativity when I couldn't even comprehend high school physics.

Shaarvan's smile broadened. The dimples danced.

"If sleeping and waking are two states of consciousness, does one need to plug into electricity in order to wake in the morning?"

Shaarvan just tossed that out like it answered everything. Then he got up to go to the bathroom. I was glad he didn't expect an answer. Even when he spoke in English, like he'd just done, I still didn't understand. I also knew he wasn't going to talk about it any further. He loved to make me figure out things. I stared after him. What did sleeping and waking have to do with Shapechanging?

It was only later I remembered how *Shapechanging* had also gotten me off the subject of Laurie. I knew not to bring her up until a little while had passed. Resurrecting Shaarvan's anger at what he called my "deceit" wasn't too healthy.

In the days following, I did ask about Laurie, time after time, but he wouldn't discuss her. Every time I mentioned anything about my adventure outside, he warned me to silence. And when I begged and pleaded with him about having a friend, he flashed *no* and *no argument*.

I thought I could wear Shaarvan down with my persistence, but the truth is I got tired of asking. Any mention of Laurie or the other Terrans made Shaarvan so cold and distant that he wouldn't talk to me. If your enemy is your only ally, life gets complicated.

However, I kept gnawing over the mystery of *Shapechanging*. Sleeping, waking, Shaarvan had said. How did I know what happened when one woke up? Did the brain shock the brain? Is that what he meant? Two consciousnesses. Was *Shapechanging* similar to the transition between sleeping and waking? But when Shaarvan slept, he didn't become a beast.

Shaarvan had said anger brought on the change. But he hadn't really been angry with me. I'd think I even heard the tiger laughing. In fact, even though Shaarvan said he'd been mad about the deceit, I have a suspicion he was kind of impressed I'd broken out.

Unfortunately, there was another penalty which came out of my misadventure. Shaarvan had put a lockout on a lot of the computer information I'd been accessing. Things like maps or technical information on the nature of the ship were no longer available to me.

I couldn't understand it. If I couldn't do any more overrides, how was it a threat to him for me to pull up a map?

"Because careless words of things you do not understand can do great damage," he said.

"Damage where? To whom? I never get to talk to anyone but you," I protested.

Shaarvan just smiled his hundred-volt smile and said, "Change is the only constant."

What the heck did that mean? As usual, his enigmatic statement came with no explanation.

It was annoying not to understand. And there were so many things Shaarvan wouldn't explain. He did answer my curiosity about another matter. He didn't even hesitate.

"How did you find me so quickly?" I asked him after a bed scene when he was relaxed and pleased.

He raised himself up to look into my eyes. He was chuckling when he answered. "It took you four Earth days to ask me, Shaara. I'd expected the question at least by day two."

My face heated, as much from the fact Shaarvan had pulled my blanket down with his movement, and his eyes were feasting on my breasts. His eyes mocked me as I yanked the blanket back in place. Then, chuckling, his hands slipped under the cover to play with what I'd hidden.

"My sweet little wife . . ." his eyes smiled his amusement at me. "I have a watcher on you at all times. See it there?"

He pointed, and I saw a small round hole covered with a screen. It didn't look like a camera. It looked more like a miniature speaker.

"It spies on me?"

"Of course."

"But why?"

Shaarvan just laughed. I watched him for a moment. I didn't like the idea of surveillance, but there was obviously nothing I could do about it. But something still didn't fit.

"Wait a minute," I said. "That doesn't answer how you knew where I went."

Shaarvan chuckled and rubbed his knuckles against my cheek.

"You will like my answer to that even less, my wife."

"What, there are watchers everywhere on the ship?"

"True."

I studied him. There was more. He would tell me if I wanted to know. What could be worse than constant watchers?

"Shaarvan?"

His large hands were still cupping my breasts, but the pointer finger of the right one was starting to play with the nipple. I knew my time to wrap up this mystery was quickly departing.

"Please, Shaarvan, please tell me."

He nodded. His eyes remained on my breasts. He didn't look at my face. I suppose he already knew how I'd react.

"So be it, wife. Perhaps that knowledge is good for you to have.

"While you slept in the room where I first woke you, Shaara, I placed a device beneath your skin. It is what you'd call a tracer unit."

I jerked away from his touch. "In my skin? No. No, Shaarvan, no." I started to bolt up in protest, but Shaarvan's left hand pushed me back.

"If you wish me to answer the question, Shaara, you must be silent."

His eyes had darkened. He studied my face alertly now, watchful. I drew in a breath, let it out, then inhaled again, holding it, calming myself so he wouldn't close off to me. In a moment, I nodded.

"Wisely done, Shaara. You are becoming Shapechanger."

I didn't understand that, but I realized he'd just complimented my behavior. I waited, trying not to fidget.

"All girls, all females, even wives, are required to wear the tracer implant. It is a label that states your owner and his address. Only a special light reveals this information, but all traders carry one. The implant also sends a beacon that registers your movements. Because of it, I know where you are at every moment."

I completely forgot I was naked. I dropped the blanket surrounding me, turned about to glare at him, and shouted, "You put a dog tag on me, a permanent dog tag? With the name of my owner. Are you insane?"

"Easy, Shaara." Shaarvan's voice tried to calm and caution me at the same time.

I heard the tone, the element of warning but my anger was back in control. "Where is it?" I started checking my arms. "I don't see anything."

"I told you it takes a special light to see it."

I shook my head. I stamped my foot. "Take it out, Shaarvan. Take it out, please. I'm not a dog. I can't be owned. Please."

One hand reached out for the neck grip. I froze. Shaarvan moved me slowly back down onto the bed beside him. He didn't hurt me, but then I didn't resist his powerful grip.

"Please, Shaarvan," I begged, although his hand still firmly held my neck with his fingers.

"Listen to me, Shaara. I knew you would find this hard. I told you about the *flaorth*, as it is called because I wanted you to know about it. I knew you were too difficult not to attempt an escape at some time. I wanted you to see how quickly and easily the *flaorth* works. I believe you have discovered its efficiency."

I stared at him. His fingers were still closed about my neck. I couldn't move, couldn't bolt up and run away. All I could do was stare into his eyes and ponder his words.

Couldn't Shaarvan understand how such a thing made me feel? Trapped, frozen in a Big Brother network that spied on me and planted things under my skin. I tried once more to make him comprehend its repugnancy.

"Shaarvan, I'm a person, not a thing to be owned."

The fingers tightened a moment before easing again. It was done as a warning — not painfully, but as a reminder. "But you are owned, Shaara," he said.

The hand on my neck didn't release, but his other hand began traveling in circles on the skin of my shoulder and arm. He hadn't started the patterns — not yet, but already I was finding it hard to concentrate.

"*I* own you, Shaara."

I wanted to scream *no* but the word came out like a moan. His fingers began the first circuit of patterns, and the strange fog of desire rose up inside me, swallowing my resistance and all thoughts unconnected to what he was doing to me and what I wanted him to do. When Shaarvan's lips met mine, I could speak no more. The hand on my neck dropped off. I hardly felt its departure.

Afterward, I cried. I couldn't forgive myself for allowing another episode of Shaarvan's victory march. It was I who kept giving in to him. I had no more will than a slut. I hated myself for the lust that seized me and then completely controlled me.

Shaarvan placed his arms around me. "Why do you do this?" he asked.

I didn't know what he meant. I continued my weeping, mourning my lack of principles and the stamina to resist him.

"Why do you chastise yourself and feel self-hate?" Shaarvan persisted. "I have made you my wife. I have told you I will not sell you. Why?"

How could he not understand? How could he not see me? My misery grew even stronger as I understood Shaarvan never would understand. Yet I knew I must answer him. He would demand it.

I sighed and tried to restrain my sobs. "Because you have made me a thing, Shaarvan — something owned."

He growled, not unlike the tiger. Yet this time, it was not a warning. I think he was only frustrated I was not acting in a manner he'd predicted.

"I have not called you a 'thing,' Shaara. You are a girl, a female, so of course, you are owned. All females on Altar belong to a male. It is our way."

"I'm a Terran, and it's not *our* way."

He snorted — an odd sound from him, he who was always so controlled. It stopped my tears. I turned and stared at him, gaping.

"Wrong," he said. "There are many places on your Earth where women are owned. You mean, in your one little part of the world where you have convinced men you are equal. But you have not *convinced* them, Shaara. You have emasculated them. They have no power because you have made laws, so they cannot prove what you say is false."

Of course, I started to give him my opinion about it, but Shaarvan immediately flashed the *no argument* sign. I sighed hotly, seething because he wasn't even giving me a chance to argue.

"It is a waste of time discussing Terran philosophy," Shaarvan concluded as he rose up and walked away.

Shaarvan

I think I cured Shaara of asking about Laurie. I silenced her at each mention. She could not endure having her questions go unanswered, so at last, she stopped asking. I hoped she'd forget about the escapade.

I shall never discuss the ship's prostitutes with her. For one thing, as the wife of a Shapechanger, the subject was entirely unsuitable. And, with Shaara in particular, it would be especially ill-advised. It was easy to imagine she would immediately invest all her energies in attempts to save the slaves from their lives.

I informed Shaara about the *flaorth* yesterday. I must say she reacted predictably. I think if I had told her where it was located, she would have taken a knife to her skin and attempted to remove it. She was a remarkably obstinate girl. She wished to argue the Terran philosophy of male and female equality with me as well. I must remember not to allow that subject to come up again.

Kekor was only two days away. I looked forward to the visit. I have not decided whether to take my wife. She was not ready yet, but I did not like leaving her alone. She has already proven her ingenuity in getting into trouble. It would be better to keep her under my watchful eye, but Kekor would be hard for her to handle.

Of course, there was the possibility such an experience might be beneficial for her. I shall consider it.

Shaara

Shaarvan told me the ship was approaching its first planetary stop since Earth. When I heard we would be landing, hope grew. Was it possible someone there would help me? Surely, other aliens wouldn't condone kidnapping. Someone might even be willing to return me to Earth. If only Shaarvan would let me visit the planet with him.

"Please, please, may I go with you?" I begged when Shaarvan was in a very good mood.

His eyebrows raised in amusement. "I doubt you are ready for Kekor yet," he replied with a knowing smirk.

Yet his eyes were still smiling, so I explained how well-behaved I'd be if he'd let me go.

He watched me a moment, then raised his hand. I stopped. The hand opened flat was a warning. The higher the hand, the greater the warning. This one wasn't high, but I wouldn't push it. My eyes dropped to the floor.

Shaarvan nodded his approval. I was learning, he was thinking. He stroked my cheek briefly with his knuckles, and then he lifted up my chin with his hand. His eyes studied mine. I gave no challenge. I knew the danger all too well. I concentrated hard on looking placid (and only slightly hopeful).

"Well done," he said. "Perhaps I *will* take you."

When I started to say something, he moved his finger to cover my lips. I knew that sign, too. I was willing to keep my mouth shut if it meant a chance for freedom.

"I shall schedule your training session today to include the conduct of Kekor women. Your answers will determine your readiness to go."

It wasn't thrilling, hearing the list of do's and don'ts of Kekor. As I listened and read, I discovered slavery was not only present but flourishing, at least for the female half. It began to look like this wouldn't be the planet of my freedom. Escape would probably worsen my situation, not improve it.

Still, a visit planet side would get me off the ship, and I'd see something new and different. Imagine an alien planet. What would it be like? What would I see there?

I had the computer issue a printout so I could study. It didn't provide an English translation, of course, so I had a lot of figuring out to do. I was glad Altarian reading was like Spanish, with one vowel sound for each vowel. And there were no irregularities at all. (I wished French had been so easy.) But my vocabulary was so limited. Every sentence of the printout used words I didn't understand.

Yet, I figured out the key parts: *Always be accompanied by a man. Speak only with permission and then quietly. Carry nothing in public. Never meet the eyes of any man but your mate . . .*

It had to be a joke. Didn't it? Yet I knew it wasn't. It was too similar to the behavior Shaarvan demanded of me, and ridiculous or not, I knew I'd have to learn the stupid rules so he would take me with him.

Yet when Shaarvan returned later, he didn't ask me about the Rules of Kekor but for something called the *Code of Femininity*. I hadn't come across that yet, so I tried to tell Shaarvan about the rules I'd spent hours figuring out.

He shook his head at me, and when I tried to explain, his hand flashed a sign I figured meant *desist*. Then, he began to advance towards me with a familiar look in his eyes, and I forgot about the *Code*, the planet, and everything but Shaarvan.

Shaarvan never gave me any choice when he desired me, but I admit he did a good job of satisfying me. Whenever he left, I was warm and fuzzy with contentment and much less inclined to argue. Argue — what a laugh. I'd float for hours on a high of *yes* and *anything you want, Shaarvan*. Sometimes, it would take me an hour or so before I felt like me again.

That day, as the warm, fuzzy finally slipped away, I continued my computer research, and I found the *Code of Femininity: A woman must look to her husband for all things. She must obey and cherish his every spoken thought. In him, alone, will she find her happiness.*

It took me twenty minutes to translate the *Code*, and then I was rushed for time to memorize it. Not only was it a repulsive statement of male dominance, but I had to learn it in Altarian. The computer corrected my pronunciation time after time. The vowels were easy, conjugations a cinch, but which syllable received the stress — that was the killer. Finally, a beep from the computer said I had it.

Yet, what I worried most about was not the recitation but the drilling Shaarvan would give me about the content. Could I lie successfully enough to fool him? Lying had its own dangers.

I found later I'd worried without need. Shaarvan listened to my recital, asked me to explain it in English, and then dropped the subject. I was home free. Or so I thought. Shaarvan hadn't told me yet whether or not I could go.

I wanted to let Shaarvan be the one to bring up the topic, but he didn't. He started talking about other things. Why, of all nights, did he want to talk about Altar when I needed him to talk about Kekor.

Finally, I couldn't be still. "Shaarvan," I blurted out. He waited for me to continue. "Shaarvan, do I get to go?" I didn't want to beg, but I was so worried he'd say *no*.

He smiled at me. I could tell he'd been playing with me, teasing me to see how long before I'd ask. His eyes assessed mine. They searched for anger or rebellion; I sure wasn't feeling any. I felt like a teenager being offered car keys for the first time. I'd promise him anything.

"I think so," he said after the longest pause in my life. "I think it will be good for you."

I thanked Shaarvan with kisses and hugs. I don't think if I'd thought about it ahead of time, I would have thrown my arms around him so bravely. I never knew for sure how he'd react to things, but when I did it, he only laughed and hugged me back.

When the day finally arrived, I was allowed to watch our approach to Kekor in the control room. From a tiny brown pea, it grew into a mega-basketball. Even so, it took us hours to get close enough to see anything interesting. I thought I'd see large blue seas like on Earth, but Kekor didn't have any oceans, only huge, perfectly- round lakes. Kekor, from a distance, looked like a golf course, with big blue holes dispersed at even distances.

Kekor was a rather large planet with several moons, one of which Shaarvan told me still had active volcanoes. For a while, I watched for eruptions, but apparently, it was the off-season for them. Shaarvan had laughed when he told me, so I wasn't sure if that was true or not. Did some volcanoes erupt only seasonally?

We were still orbiting Kekor when Shaarvan said it was time to return to our room for sleep. I was disappointed. I'd thought our landing was imminent, but Shaarvan said sometimes a ship had to wait for several days until the officials granted permission for it to land. "Bureaucratic paperwork," Shaarvan said, but he later explained that everyone on board the ship must be distantly screened before Kekor deemed us safe to land. I guess when you considered some terrible virus that could be brought onto the planet from outer space, it made sense.

However, the very next day, the announcement came that Shaarvan's ship had received permission to set down. The man who delivered the news got a hearty slap on the back. I'd be apprehensive if Shaarvan did that to me, but the crewman just grinned.

I'd thought things would speed up then, but they didn't. The planet remained at the same distance. All the round lakes I could see from the ship's window panel grew not one iota bigger.

The crew multiplied. Men came on deck I'd never seen before — not in the cafeteria or in the control room. A couple of them glanced at me, but mainly, they set right to work, taking up stations without a word to anyone. They immediately pushed flashing buttons, did an analysis of things, slid out triangular slips of paper, and checked off circles on their printouts. Of course, I couldn't get close enough to see the details, but it appeared that everyone was working furiously to get us ready for touchdown.

Meanwhile, Shaarvan strode about like a harried general, touching shoulders, bending down to look in monitors, or taking up the triangular slips of paper to read them and return them to their owners. Every so often, Shaarvan glanced over at me and then away. I hoped he'd continue being so busy he failed to recall I hadn't done my computer drills that day.

Just about the time my stomach was growling loud enough to catch the eye of a nearby crewman, a man came in carrying a pile of small white boxes. He handed two of them to Shaarvan, then moved off to pass them to the others.

The smells emanating from inside the packages told me they contained food. When Shaarvan, sitting down beside me, handed me one of the boxes, I discovered, as I peeked inside, that the box held a drink and a rectangular piece of pie — something that smelled and even tasted a lot like lasagna. The pie was shaped like a bar and was encapsulated in a sturdy, crumb-free bread. When you bit into the pie, nothing dripped since it congealed immediately. What I liked most about it was that no matter how long it took to eat, the lasagna bar remained hot.

I ate about half of mine then drank some of the fruity drink. Shaarvan gave me one of the pills I always took and then insisted I finish the rest of my beverage. When I'd done so, he bussed the boxes and went back to his pacing, inspecting, and, in general, breathing down everyone's neck.

I sat back in the fuzzy chair, which seemed to be solely mine and thought about the planet we would soon be dropping in on. I wondered if the people would be like Shaarvan and the crew. Were all aliens universally the same physically?

I think, at some point, the ship's orbit must have dropped lower. Finally, I could see something besides faraway lakes and sandy-looking dirt. Several greenish areas, mottled with dark brown, came into sight as we drifted closer to the landing site. Shaarvan had earlier told me Kekor had pleasant forest reserves. I was pretty sure I was seeing one. I wished we could journey to it and walk under what I imagined to be pine-smelling trees, but Shaarvan had already warned me that our planet side time would be brief. No scenic routes, no forest hikes.

I stared out into the blackness above and around us. One of the moons sat in the corner of the ship's screen. It wasn't the volcanic one, and it frankly wasn't all that exciting. It looked like it had paint splotches across its surface — white on a dull gray background. No one lived there, but Shaarvan had said there might be robotic mining machines.

Down below, Kekor looked almost lifeless and dull. Yet, I didn't care if Kekor was as dreary as its lonely moon, just as long as I could get out and walk on real dirt for a while. What a difference it would be . . . just to touch the ground and breathe air that wasn't recycled. I couldn't wait!

Shaarvan looked up and met my eyes. The paper in his hand went limp as he smiled across the room. I suppose he'd picked up my excitement. I would have dropped my eyes, but Shaarvan didn't seem annoyed. In fact, he winked at me. I'd never seen him do that before. My mouth dropped open, and I stared.

The man standing beside Shaarvan turned to follow Shaarvan's gaze. When he perceived the object of Shaarvan's perusal was only me, he twisted back around and speedily backed away. Shaarvan didn't seem to notice. He took a step toward me and kept coming, still holding the unread triangle of paper.

"Come, Shaara," Shaarvan ordered, booming the command as if I were hard of hearing.

I rose and met him halfway. He stretched out his hands, placed them on my arms to turn me about, and then, taking my hand, led me toward the room's exit.

Had I done something wrong? Worriedly, I peeked up at Shaarvan's face, but he appeared to have lost interest in me. In fact, he'd slowed to read the paper in his hand. He let go of my hand, stopped, and, still concentrating on whatever he was reading, called out. The man who'd turned to look at me came scurrying over. Shaarvan spoke with him, handed him the data, and then again steered me toward the door.

I should have guessed what Shaarvan wanted. He'd just remembered I hadn't used the computer yet. He hooked me up, kissed me on the cheek, then left. It wasn't fair. I hadn't disturbed him. I hadn't made any bad slipups either. But, perhaps Shaarvan thought otherwise. He hadn't said.

Hours later, when he returned, he was no more talkative than before. "We shall eat in the dining room now. Our approach to Kekor progresses slowly," he said.

I certainly agreed. "It was exactly what I'd been thinking — well, as much as the computer allowed me to think of anything while I was being drilled.

"Why does it take so long?" I asked. "I thought you got permission to land."

Shaarvan smiled. I could see he was in a good mood, but he took my hand, led me out of the room, and issued one of his quiet commands.

In the dining room, as our choices for the meal slid down into the center of the table, Shaarvan occupied himself with playing with my hair. I wore it long, and it had a tendency to curl into ringlets, which drove me nuts. I used to comb them out, trying to look like everyone else, but not only did I not have a blow dryer and the fancy brush I needed, but Shaarvan wouldn't allow me to do much of anything with it. I'd tried braiding and even tying it back, but he demanded its freedom. He said he liked the curls, liked to fondle them, and see them bounce back into shape when he let them go. I found it irritating, but I'd learned not to pull away — especially not when I was waiting for answers. Besides, a playful cat is always more comfortable to be around than a pouncing predator whose sharp claws are extended for the kill.

Shaarvan smiled again, touched my nose with his pointer finger, and said, "We have received permission from Kekor, my wife, but now we await our turn." He took my meal from the table's center, and pulled back the cover, then slid it over to me.

I wanted to discuss the situation more, but Shaarvan didn't approve of talking while we were eating. I sighed and picked up the tweezers while glancing at him, hoping he'd forget his rules and, for once, explain something thoroughly, but even when he did speak, Kekor wasn't his topic.

Shaarvan was once more discussing protocol on his home world, Altar, and my behavior when his brothers were in attendance. Although they were family, according to Shaarvan, he warned me I must be careful with each of them. The older one was a doctor. He would try to convert me to his thinking, which would steer me into trouble if I listened.

Discussing the younger brother brought even less warmth to Shaarvan's eyes. "I will not leave you alone with him," Shaarvan told me. "He is dangerous, Shaara. Do not trust him."

Although I'd wanted to discuss Kekor and the approaching visit, the information Shaarvan was giving me about his brothers was equally intriguing. I bubbled with questions, but Shaarvan only shook his head and retreated back into silence. His good mood seemed to have evaporated.

The next morning was the day we expected to make landfall. I was so excited I could scarcely draw adequate breath. I slipped on my dress — a pale blue one. (Shaarvan had finally allowed me to vary my wardrobe —— but in color only.)

"On Altar, you will wear the family hue," he'd lectured. "Here on the ship, I shall grant you this small freedom. You are young. It is to be expected you would amuse yourself with such silliness."

He'd insulted me, but I didn't care. Variety — childish or not — was something I enjoyed. I would savor my days of free will.

That morning, we ate a bar of hard-packed food and drank the usual liquid. I was never hungry at the start of a day, but I knew from experience I must make an attempt. Shaarvan had no tolerance for lack of appetite. So I gnawed a bit and drank my hot beverage, and of course, took another of Shaarvan's chalky pills.

The control room was even more crowded than the day before. It seemed excessive — far more men than stations. Some of the crew were even sitting on the floor. After I sat down in my doggy chair, I watched them gather about Shaarvan. They didn't crowd him, though, and at one point, Shaarvan gestured to me. They backed away slightly then, leaving a space so I could see, or more likely, so Shaarvan could view me.

Shaarvan gave a brief speech in which, if I'm not mistaken, he was detailing our arrival. One of the men handed him what I think was a weapon. Shaarvan checked it over and displayed it to the men. I think he was showing them how to load it, maybe, but I couldn't see clearly. When he handed it back, he accepted a long pole from another of the group. Shaarvan demonstrated its use on the man who'd handed it to him. I think I was observing a mock fight.

Nobody started cheering or egging the men on, like the kids used to in high school when such a thing happened. The crew just stood back and watched, their eyes fixed on Shaarvan's hands and feet. Shaarvan used the pole to hit his combatant right in the stomach. The man grunted, but he didn't otherwise react.

Then Shaarvan struck the poor man's legs and back. Each time, I covered my mouth in horror, afraid I'd make a noise that would distract them. I cringed at their violence, ashamed Shaarvan could be so mean to someone completely defenseless. Unfortunately, Shaarvan's last act of violence was the worst — a blow to the man's neck, which felled his opponent. The man dropped to the ground like a heap of laundry.

I half rose from my spot wondering if my Girl Scout first aid badge would help me take care of a wounded Altarian, then remembered I wasn't allowed to move. I fidgeted back into position but continued watching, hoping the man was okay.

As my chair readjusted to the shifted weight, Shaarvan's opponent popped back up and bowed to the crowd. Shaarvan laughed and slapped the man on his back. The man beamed as if Shaarvan had done something wonderful. The crewman looked proud of the beating he'd just taken. With the weapon at his side, the man gestured to the other men and then led them out of the control room. They were all laughing by then. I shook my head in wonder.

Shaarvan shot a glance at me, then looked away to scan the room as he did so often. I thought he'd make his circuit of paper-reading and monitor checks then, but instead, he walked toward me.

"You project, Shaara," Shaarvan said.

Was that a bad thing? I studied his face, trying to understand what he was talking about.

Shaarvan lifted me up and drew me close to his body. "*They* do not feel you, Shaara. It does not matter with them, but on Altar, you must learn control."

I hadn't moved from the chair before he'd stood me up — not really. What did he mean? What had I done?

He laughed. "No, I am not angry with you, my wife. I am proud. You are Shapechanger already. You grow strong with it. Our sons will be powerful."

He pushed me away slightly so he could stare at me. "But your eyes remain . . . Never mind. It is too soon. I confuse you, I see. Never mind, my little wife. You need only to know that you please me." Then he stroked my hair, not as he did sometimes, for his own amusement, but as if he were bent on reassuring me.

"What were you . . ," I started to ask about what I'd just seen, but one of the crew interrupted, calling out something.

Shaarvan whirled about, barked a couple of words I didn't understand, and then shoved me back into the chair. "Sit," he ordered.

So many puzzles. Would I ever understand him?

I could feel the sudden excitement all around me. I didn't know what was going on, but I found out later we'd just been approved to go into the lineup. I thought it meant we were finally going to land, but although we took up a lower orbit, we still didn't have the official okay to land. It was so annoying. The spaceport couldn't be that busy. We hadn't seen a single ship. At least, such was my reasoning. Later, I found out how mistaken I was.

"Shaara, imagine looking at a dartboard from ten miles away. If everyone around you were at an equal circumference from the dartboard, you wouldn't believe they were there because you couldn't see them, but each of you would be heading for the same bull's-eye — do you understand?"

When he put it that way, it made sense, but it seemed strange to picture a group of spaceships all wanting to land at the same time, especially when we couldn't see any of them.

It was amazing how nice Shaarvan could be — sometimes. He'd even be nicer if he didn't spend so much time acting like he knew everything — even if he did. What surprised me almost as much as his occasional kindness was the fact he knew so much about things like dartboards and fairy tales. I figured his mother must have told him, but why would Shaarvan's father have permitted such tales? I thought Earth was something we women were supposed to put aside and forget. Did Shaarvan ever think about his human heritage?

Of course I didn't understand then what I learned later. Shaarvan had no human blood. He wasn't really half-human.

When we finally got permission to actually set down, I saw the proof of what Shaarvan had told me. The spaceport was huge. It made the LAX International Airport look like a watermelon patch, and the biggest amusement park look like a child's playground. Shaarvan told me this one was the smallest of the five spaceports on Kekor. Boy, was Earth behind.

There were ships everywhere. Each of them looked different. It wasn't like at an airport where planes had been fashioned to look more or less the same. This place had ships the size of a Volkswagen bug all the way up to the mass of a skyscraper. One ship looked like a robotic spider. Another was the spitting image of a snowplow. Some had wings, some were cones, and some resembled giant pyramids.

We landed on our own spot, but out close to the edge. There were lights everywhere and parking spots with glowing dials of color. Our zone, as Shaarvan called it, had green flashing lights all around its circumference. It would probably be very dangerous to be colorblind at a spaceport. Can you imagine parking in the wrong spot, and then some alien ship drops down on top of you?

I'd thought the landing would be more exciting than it actually was. Our touchdown was so smooth you could hardly feel it. I'd imagined it would feel like descending in an elevator except at four times the normal speed. I'd assumed we'd have to buckle our seatbelts and be crushed against our seats, but there was none of that. Shaarvan never even sat down. The landing was like a car coasting to a stop. (My ears didn't even pop.)

Once we were down, all the windows halfway around the front of the ship cleared so we could see out. It was great. Lots of activity was taking place outside the ship. I saw robots, long chains of them, carrying cartons and silver boxes and bundles of machinery along paths of blinking white lights. People marched by all boringly alike. Most of them wore suits similar to Shaarvan's crew, and they looked just like people everywhere.

But I did see one of the men with an animal on a leash. His pet (I assume it was a pet.) looked like an orange-hoofed octopus. The thing galloped next to him on its little brown horse-shaped hooves, hopping up and down like it was on pep pills. Its orange coat rippled, and you could see little fur balls at the end where the coat hung down to the ground. The creature had no tail, and its head didn't seem to have any eyes, but it kept twisting around like it was looking at everything.

Shaarvan got kind of mad about it, though — just because I got in the way of one of the crew. I didn't mean to. I was just standing at the window, trying to see where the octopus went, and Shaarvan grabbed me up, threw me over his shoulder, walloped my rear end hard, and tossed me back into the chair. It scared me to death, and he almost knocked the air out of my lungs. And oh, how the crew stared. They, who never, ever noticed me — gawked.

Of course, Shaarvan's actions were followed by a hand sign that said, *don't move.* He didn't have to bother with the gesture. The look in his eyes told me that if I moved again, I'd be sorry. I kept my head down for a couple of minutes and sulked, I guess you could call it, but too much was happening for me to remain subdued for long. When I thought Shaarvan was no longer watching me with that stern gaze of his, I raised my head and resumed my fascination with the spaceport.

I'd thought that immediately after we docked, we'd leave the ship and go visiting, but Shaarvan continued to work with the crew. The computer printout kept spitting out papers, the guys with the earphones kept calling out numbers, and everyone was acting like there was lots of stuff still to do.

I had to sit there, half-bored to death (because absolutely nothing new was happening outside), but although I may have fidgeted a bit, shifting in the seat with impatience, I sure didn't move again. As time passed, fewer and fewer robots drifted by. No other groups with interesting pets entered our area, and the butterscotch dust of the planet's dirt had all repositioned itself after our arrival. There was nothing on the horizon to see — no mountains off in the distance, nothing but flat, dull-colored dirt. The sky was a pale gray-orange, and the primary sun looked almost like Earth's. The other one floated off to the left, a faint bluish orb with no other interesting properties that I could see — other than the fact that it was blue.

Then, finally, I saw one of the ships lifting off. I thought there'd be a loud noise and smoke and fire, like when Earth rockets did their count-down, but this ship, one of the huge pyramids, didn't make a sound, and I never saw any smoke. It merely lifted straight up, like a rocket, and then shot sideways to the right.

I watched its process, delighted by the chance to observe something exciting, but the ship didn't take off and journey into the stars. It just stopped and hung there. For the whole time I waited for Shaarvan, that ship didn't move again— 400 feet off the ground and frozen. As I started searching the sky, I saw two others, ships that looked like mushrooms with plates at the bottom, both of them hanging in the sky. It was sure some cool magic trick. But how could they achieve blast-off from there? How could they just hang in one spot?

Eventually, Shaarvan returned to my side and said, "Come, wife. We must prepare." His hand gripped my arm, but I was eager to go. I walked back to our room, obediently silent but almost prancing in excitement. Shaarvan remained in his thoughts, pondering something heavy, I suppose.

I was afraid that when we returned to the room, Shaarvan might punish me for being difficult, but he didn't bring it up. He walked over to the button panel, adjusted the machine, and then dialed. Something dropped. He handed me the resulting outfit.

Packages that came from the machine arrived flat and about the size of a mailed letter. Yet the moment one shook them out, all the folds and wrinkles smoothed out. It was kind of miraculous. This time, the miracle didn't help the appearance of my dress. Despite the fact that it appeared neatly pressed and new, the gown was so incredibly ugly — puke-brown, with gold braid spiraling down the sleeves. It could only be compared with someone's bad seventh grade sewing project. To wear the thing would have brought death to a junior high girl — death or excommunication, which amounted to about the same thing.

I slipped it on anyway, not wishing to antagonize Shaarvan. I figured that once he got a good look at the horrid thing, he'd override the machine and let me choose what to wear.

It wasn't just the ugliness of the cloth. The sleeves were full length, with a strange cuff-like covering that flowed over each hand. It was uneven, too, dropping down into a V-shaped excess at the front, narrowed at the back. On the collar, there were a series of rings of gold braid, starting at the bottom of my neck up to my chin — all part of the dress, which made the neckline stiff. It also made the collar look like a heavy Egyptian gold necklace — at least five inches thick. I could barely move my neck when I fastened the dress completely. The braid was completely stiff and restrictive.

The dress reached to the ground and *dragged*. I was sure the clothes machine had made a mistake because the gown was obviously far too large for me. Yet when I complained, Shaarvan informed me that was the way dresses were worn in Kekor. I stared at him in dismay before sweeping my eyes over the dress again. Women wore this every day?

I was doubtful I'd be able to walk in the thing. There was so much material dangling from the bodice it was like wearing a tent. I lifted up the side and held the material up like I'd seen done in period movies. No wonder no one jogged back in the age of Queen Victoria.

"Shaarvan, please, tell me you won't force me to wear this monstrosity," I pleaded. "I can program something much, much nicer. I'd even wear that boring yellow color you were so fond of."

"Only if you wish not to go with me, wife," he said. His eyes surveyed me in the outfit, then shrugged. I guess he thought I looked okay, but what horrid taste Kekoreans had — at least the men, since I supposed they were the ones who'd designed it.

I really, really wanted to go down to the planet, but the dress was so ugly . . .

Of course, I acquiesced. How could I pass up the opportunity to visit an alien planet? How could I let vanity interfere with adventure? Still I hoped that Shaarvan was correct, that all the women on Kekor were wearing dresses just as hideous. That would be the only way I'd feel okay about this fashion sacrifice.

Just about the time I'd become resigned to looking like a trick-o-treater, Shaarvan ordered up my headpiece. The hat was like a golden daisy, but at each point, a long gold-colored braid hung down. When he set it on my head, I almost cried. Despite my pleas, again, he refused to let me accompany him without the full regalia.

However, what I'd thought was shockingly grotesque got even worse, for Shaarvan had to wrap each dangling petal of the hat around a strand of my hair. When he was finished, each and every curl had been entirely enclosed in a braid. I had no mirror to see the effect, but I could well imagine. Medusa, here I come.

Having finished my accessories, Shaarvan put on his own outfit. His was fashioned in the same dreary color as mine, but he didn't have the braid at his neck. His shirt had long sleeves with gold trim at the wrists. His top opened in a long, slender V down to the hairs on his chest. (I thought that was kind of sexy, but I didn't tell him so.) His pants had braid at the sides, too, a little like military pants, but flared slightly in a kind of bell-shape. His pants and shirt were snug instead of tent-like, and although the color reminded me of two-day old garbage, he definitely looked a lot better than I did.

"Where's your hat?" I teased, but Shaarvan didn't smile.

"Not another word about the clothing, Shaara. I shall not allow you to mock Kekor."

I met his eyes with my most innocent look. "I will speak only with permission," I quoted. Then I curtseyed saucily.

Shaarvan eyed me a moment, looking rather suspicious. I don't know if he knew what curtseys were supposed to mean, but I'm sure he realized I was being cheeky. For a moment, his eyes glinted like he was about to give me another lecture. I kept my head down, staring at the fake leather boots I'd donned, which perfectly matched the putrid mustard-brown dress and concentrated on the words I'd just said.

The silence between us was tense for a moment, and then I felt rather than saw the easing of it. I glanced up, still maintaining my humble-downcast look, but I saw the sides of his mouth curve up. The steel had dropped out of his voice when he said, "Remember that, Shaara."

In spite of his brief smile, I knew he'd given me a warning. I nodded and continued my eyes-lowered stance. After a moment, Shaarvan took my hand and led me out.

Shaarvan

I sincerely hoped I was not making a mistake in taking Shaara. In spite of my bedding her daily, she was still sassy and full of mischief. Outwardly, she pretended to be compliant, but her mind was as full of rebellion as ever. She was bold, a fact that amused me, but she was foolishly impulsive, a fact that did not. Would she be able to learn the difference? Was she capable of adapting?

At first, my wife envisioned that she would attempt an escape on Kekor. Thankfully, her research into Kekor's customs disillusioned her of that. I did not believe she would be foolish enough to attempt it now, but with Shaara, I could not be certain of anything. Of course, I assigned three guards for her protection, and I would not take my eyes off her for a second. I would not lose her nor risk her to Kekorian protocol.

Earlier in the control room, I dealt with my wife's disobedience rather lightly. Perhaps I should have been more forceful, but I could read no thought of challenge in her demeanor. I was constantly reminded by her thoughts that she was young and rash.

She disturbed the crew, something I could not allow. Perhaps it would have been better to reprimand her more decorously, but a swiftly administered swat seemed the quickest and most appropriate reminder of her failure.

Regrettably, several of the crewmen reacted. They lost their concentration. I shall address it with them when I return from Kekor. They must allow no interruption to their focus.

My father warned me that commoners did not have the skills of the Shapechanger. I have observed this over the years, but it reminded me that the responsibility for shipboard success required my continued leadership. I must train the crew with as much diligence as I train my wife, the first because they are not Shapechanger, and the latter because she will be.

Besides, I suspected that when it came to Shaara, there would be many future disruptions. She was troublesome, yet I would not give her up. *By my pledge to the Somber Tree and the Stars*, it was true that the girl pleased me.

Shaara

When we reached the control room, Shaarvan immediately began ordering everyone around. His words were too fast for me to follow. Watching him and listening to his discourse with others always reminded me of how much effort Shaarvan took to talk slowly with me and to limit his words to my inadequate vocabulary. I drowned in Altarian when he didn't.

A group of about twenty of his crew surrounded us. They were armed with pole weapons and looked deadly serious. All were wearing outfits similar to Shaarvan's, although theirs didn't dip in the front as much nor stretch about the upper arms with the bulky muscles that Shaarvan's body displayed — not that the crew displayed any fat or weakness in strength. I doubt that Shaarvan would have allowed that.

The faces of the crew displayed no excitement. I supposed to them this was merely another stop. Were these men homesick for Altar as I was for Earth?

Although it had been months since we'd left Earth, the lights in the exercise room provided sufficient tanning and sunlight exposure, so the men's faces glowed with good health. None of them ever looked pale or sickly. It was only beside Shaarvan that they seemed weak and small. (Of course, they still towered above me, but even on my planet, most people were taller than I was.)

I bit my lip and reminded myself to remember to keep my eyes lowered, but it was terribly difficult with all the excitement of our approaching departure — the men, the weapons, the costumes, and . . .

Over their heads and in between the crews' bodies, I suddenly saw that another group was entering the control room. Everyone turned to look. New guards were leading a group of women. Earth girls!

I started to rise, wanting to see more clearly. A sudden glance from Shaarvan changed my mind. Instead, I adjusted my body, stretching taller for a moment, then crouching lower when a space appeared between the elbows of two crewmen.

The women were all wearing the same awful dress I had on. Theirs lacked the ridiculous gold braiding, but it was the same putrid color. Still, removing the braid helped to lessen the vileness of the gown, and I noticed that they were free to move their heads about. I felt like I had armor plating growing up the sides of my neck. The unfairness of that freedom almost made me comment, but another fleeting look from Shaarvan stilled any thoughts in that direction.

The women's dresses dragged on the ground, just like mine did. They'd have the same problem with tripping if they weren't careful. I hoped none of us would take a fall over the hem.

My eyes were busy scanning the women, looking at their faces, trying to see if I knew any of them. That's when it finally hit me, the big difference between our outfits. None of the women were wearing the stupid hat I had on. Why did they escape being *snake women?*

That outrage made me completely forget to drop my eyes. I didn't even notice when Shaarvan drew near me. He suddenly jerked me up and yanked my chin towards him; "You will not attempt to communicate in any manner with the females. Acknowledged?"

I nodded. I was relieved I wasn't in trouble again. Besides, I'd already observed that it wouldn't do any good to try to talk to any of them. They'd all been drugged. It was like looking at sleepwalkers or dope heads.

Right after that, we began our march down the ramp of the ship. It must have resembled the start of a big Christmas parade. Of course, there was no band playing and no Santa Claus, but we were marching all the same — Shaarvan and I in the front, and all the others streaming behind us, stretching clear from the back of the control room down the ramp toward Kekor's dirt pathway.

Almost immediately (Well, no, we were almost halfway down the ramp.) I forgot about my promise to be quiet. I was still burning about the awfulness of my outfit and the fact that the others were hat free. I tugged at Shaarvan's hand and asked, "Why are the women coming, and why don't they have to wear snake bonnets?"

Shaarvan halted abruptly. So did the entire crowd behind us. I looked back and then up at Shaarvan. His eyes had darkened — no more than a breath away from changing into the black triangles of his tiger image. I gulped hard.

"I don't recall giving you permission to talk," Shaarvan said, with a voice that could have frozen a boiling cup of cocoa — instantly.

I stilled my racing heart and sighed, mostly to give me a chance to calm down so I could offer him my most guiltless look. Batting my eyes like a Southern bell, I replied, "Shaarvan, we're still on the ramp. I didn't think it counted until we set foot on Kekor."

I'd amused him. A smile cracked the corners of his mouth. His eyes took on a moment's twinkle. Unfortunately, in no more than two seconds, he grew serious again. The instant he did, he started in on his signals. His finger tapped my mouth for silence. I got *first warning* and *no talking* all at once.

It was overkill. I'd already figured I was out of line. I guess I was pretty lucky he'd thought I was cute. My whole trip had been in jeopardy just because I'd forgotten to keep my mouth shut.

Shaarvan glanced around for the first time since he'd stopped. Everything checked out. The guards were standing stiffly, almost at attention. The women had stopped, too. Most of them were staring at the planet's caramel-colored sand in a robotic kind of glassy-eyed stupor. They seemed completely oblivious to the fact they were about to step onto an alien planet.

Shaarvan decided that all was well and started forward without any explanation. It's as if he didn't need to communicate with them. Perhaps they were mind-linked somehow, but I didn't think so. Yet no one had asked about Shaarvan's reason for stopping or said anything else, for that matter.

We continued our march down the ramp, Shaarvan eyeing the horizon suspiciously as if he feared some kind of attack. Men carrying the pole-like arms Shaarvan had demonstrated earlier followed us. Each guard held their weapon in a defensive position, their eyes, like Shaarvan's watchful and leery.

As we reached the bottom and were about to step onto the soil, two of the men passed us and stood in front. I looked up at Shaarvan, surprised that he'd allow them to do so, but then I realized that, of course, he'd ordered it. As we stopped to wait for the others to catch up a bit, Shaarvan, still scanning the area with his eyes, seemed to relent a bit from his harshness.

"Shaara," he said quietly, "Be grateful you wear the *bonekay* on your head. It means you are *not* for sale."

That stunned me. For sale? My mouth dropped open. I prepared to launch a thousand words.

Shaarvan, noting my look, met my eyes and said gruffly, "You wish to return to the ship?" His eyes had turned glacial. I swear the coldness burned me. I swallowed my outrage and lowered my head.

But my ears were still ringing with the echo of Shaarvan's words. I suddenly realized what was about to happen to all the women who accompanied us. How had I ignored the facts? How had I not assembled what I'd begun to piece together? Had I been blind? Shaarvan and his crew had landed on Kekor for the purpose of selling the women. Women like me — slaves.

Whether my dress was ugly or not — whether the hat I had to wear suited me or looked like something from a Halloween store — neither of those things was important any longer. My face burned from my stupidity. I chanced to look back at the women, hoping things might change. A miracle would happen. The women would suddenly fight. But they were still too drugged to know. There wasn't going to be any miracle, not unless I performed it.

I wanted to. I desperately wanted to save them, to rush over and attack their guards, to kick and scream and beat at someone's chest. But I didn't. Shaarvan's hand was on my arm, and even as I'd thought such things, his fingers squeezed and tightened.

A single tear slid down my face. I hunted for control. It would do the women no good if I were sent back. I needed to stay with them. Maybe I could do something later. Maybe I . . .

"You will not interfere, Shaara."

I looked up, but Shaarvan wasn't looking at me. His eyes were still inspecting and checking off details in his mind. Shaarvan was scarcely aware of my presence, yet he knew my mind. How could I fight someone who could read minds? How could I do anything for the others when I was just as much a slave as they? I mused over the problem as we continued on.

We'd left the ramp by then. I wanted to ponder freeing the women, but I was walking on an alien planet for the first time — on Kekor's dusty, caramel-colored, well-packed dirt. How could I concentrate on the unsolvable?

I stared down at my feet. They were lifting and setting down with no more resistance than in the halls and chambers of Shaarvan's ship. I figured that meant the gravity must be very similar to Earth's and to the ship's. But how could that be? Shaarvan had said that Kekor was bigger than Earth.

I had so much to learn, so much to question and attempt to figure out. I wished for the hundredth time that Shaarvan was more talkative.

The air of the planet was thick with odd smells — unidentifiable odors, not bad or unpleasant, just strange. At first my nose had picked up something that reminded me of coffee grounds, but I quickly decided it had only been the smell of the inky-black, rubbery-textured surface of the ramp. Apparently, at least in the spaceport, Kekor smelled more like Earth deserts — of heat-cooked rock and powdery sand.

The dust stirred up by our countless shoes only rose an inch or so, yet even so, the air, which I'd expected to greet us with freshness, was as dusty and tasteless as some of the meals I'd sampled in the dining room. Oh, there was an abundance of air, all right, but not noticeably richer than the ship's. It was dull and lacked flavor. It wasn't at all like the sweet scent of flowery, grassy Earth.

Despite my disappointment at the dreariness of Kekor, I still wanted to take in everything. There might be a rock, a creature, a flower, or a plant — anything that could strike my eyes as being special. After all, I wasn't on Earth anymore. Something had to look alien.

But even though my eyes were flitting about like a hummingbird in search of nectar, I was also conscious of Shaarvan's occasional gaze and trying to remember to keep my eyes down. And all the while, I tried to shut out my worry over the fate of the women, so Shaarvan wouldn't pick up on it. I had a lot to cope with.

I had so much looked forward to visiting Kekor. But the women behind me, the women marching off to slavery, kept stealing my pleasure. I kept picturing the faces I'd seen in passing, wondering if any of them had shared a class at the college with me. Had any of them lived in my dorm? Had they sat in a seat behind me? Had we passed in the hall, the school cafeteria, the school quad? And now they were about to be delivered to an alien buyer. What would happen to them? How would they be treated?

"Shaara . . ." The sharpness in Shaarvan's voice reminded me again that I, too, was in the same situation. I'd forgotten for a moment. Turning about to look at the women, I'd forgotten Shaarvan's rules.

I looked down at the ground, watched my feet propel me forward, and sighed. The women behind me were for sale, but I'd already been bought. There was no difference between us. Yet I felt guilty. I should be doing something about it. I should be helping them to escape . . .

But there was Shaarvan — Shaarvan, ready to pounce, ready to scold, ready to turn into a ferocious beast . . .

I sighed again and tried to think of other things, things that wouldn't get me in trouble. I kicked a small rock, angry and despondent. The rock traveled a couple of feet. Shaarvan's grip on my arm dug in until I whimpered. He shot me another glance but didn't say anything.

Shaarvan's world had space ships and technologically advanced toilets, yet it was barbaric. Chauvinistically backward — socially or was it culturally? Whatever . . . it was most definitely dark age backward.

Angry, I wanted to kick another rock, but I didn't. I let one pass and then another. Kicking rocks wouldn't help the situation. It would only get me in trouble again. Shaarvan's hand on my arm was once again light, but I knew how swiftly it would bring pain — with a stray thought or a kicked rock. I groaned, but silently, inwardly, and I kept on walking, head down, eyes scanning for something, something that would take my mind off what we were there for, why we had come to Kekor.

Shaarvan and I, and the long line of guards and women, were walking down a beautiful, white-lighted path. On other paths, robots whizzed by us, wheels fastened to their bodies like skateboards. Their blinking green-lighted eyes stared after us as they slid by. What did robots think? How did their eyes see the world?

We reached a moving pathway and stepped onto it. It was an escalator that didn't go up or down, just straight across the sands. The moving pathway rolled on and on as far as you could see, reminding me of drawings in perspective that grew narrower and higher off in the distance. It wound around several gigantic ships, those so high, as we passed by, it was as if we stood beside the Matterhorn. We saw no one near them. The ships stood forlorn, inactive, almost dead-like.

At one point, Shaarvan led us off the escalator, and we walked again down another lighted path. In the distance, one of the mushroom ships took off. Like the one I'd seen from inside Shaarvan's ship, this one rose vertically, zoomed to the left, and then shot across the sky. It didn't attach itself to whatever web the others rested on at 400 feet but continued upwards, passing the three moons of Kekor, the yellow sun, and the blue, and then soared off into the blackness. As I watched, it was soon only a gleaming, metallic star.

It took a moment before I realized I'd stopped, and Shaarvan and all the guards and girls were waiting for me. I was embarrassed. I wondered why Shaarvan hadn't yelled at me or pulled me forward. I looked up at him, afraid. Would he send me back to the ship? Would he bellow, or lecture, or worse, punish me in front of everyone?

But Shaarvan's eyes and his mouth were laughing. He wasn't irritated in the least. He brushed his knuckles gently against my face. "That was a Westlan Shapechanger ship," he said, and his voice rang with pride.

We continued on then, without speaking. I wished I could have asked Shaarvan questions. Why did Shaarvan's ship look so different than the Westlan Shapechanger one? Weren't all Shapechanger Altarian? What was Westlan?

I didn't understand about the Shapechanger. They fascinated me yet repelled me, too. I had knots in my brain from trying to figure out the sleeping/waking analogy with its change in energy, and I still wondered how Shaarvan could be both a man *and* a beast. I knew he was different than his crew. I felt that difference. I saw it in the eyes of the others as they watched him. I was pretty sure that most of the crew weren't Shapechanger. Could there be two species on Altar?

I wondered if I'd ever learn about Shapechanger. If I did, who would tell me? It wouldn't be Shaarvan. He just kept confusing me.

Another treadmill, another walk, and still, the enormous spaceport stretched out before us. The city seemed like a mirage we would walk toward forever and never reach. Its towers sparkled under the giant, now slightly orangish sun. Shaarvan had said we wouldn't visit the city this time. I wished we could. A city of aliens — how interesting that would be.

We'd been walking for at least an hour and were far from the ship by that time. I marveled at how Shaarvan remembered which way to go. He had no maps in his hand. There were no beacons or signs or billboards to guide our way, yet his step was certain. He never faltered or stopped to check his bearings. It was a good thing that Shaarvan didn't need to ask directions, for the spaceport in this direction seemed deserted. The ships we passed were no more than silent sentinels with their masters elsewhere.

I wondered how different all the ships would be inside. Were they all housed by men? Wasn't there at least some with a female crew? Then, I recalled Kekor's laws. I supposed if such a crew existed, they would never land on this planet.

We reached a kind of tram where we all got to sit. Shaarvan and I had a unit with three of the crewmen. I think they were our guards. Each one of them fingered the long pipe-like weapon, and their eyes darted about apprehensively.

The men made me nervous. I was afraid if I shifted in my seat, they might pepper me with whatever their pipes contained. Shaarvan ignored their presence except when he caught me watching them. Then I received the eyes-down sign. Sometimes, I was glad there was no *stop-breathing sign*. Shaarvan probably would have been tempted to use that, too.

The cars behind us contained all the Earth girls. I found I could look down and still peek at them from under my eyelashes. It gave me the chance to examine their faces. I discovered, to my relief, that none of them looked familiar. That made me feel better, although I couldn't have done anything regardless. Still, it gave me a small degree of relief. Selling strangers was probably easier than selling friends.

Shaarvan had carried water for himself and me. He ordered me to drink, and I did. I started to pass the flask to a guard, but Shaarvan shook his head. I should have known, but I hadn't thought. Still, Shaarvan didn't rage at me. He merely shook his head and gently tapped my nose with his finger. I didn't know if that was a signal I was supposed to understand, which I didn't, but at least he wasn't upset.

Personally I thought it was rude of Shaarvan not to offer the guards a drink, but I noticed later they had their own. I was glad. I didn't dispute Shaarvan at the time, but it was nice not to feel guilty about hoarding water.

The scenery outside the windows of the tram was not much different than what we'd seen so far — miles and miles of caramel-colored dust and sand. We passed a few boulders, some rather odd-shaped as if they'd been sat on and squished half-flat. Others were more rounded — quite normal-looking, except they shone with something black and glittery. Shaarvan warned me that if I drew near one, I was not to touch it because the part that glittered was sharp as glass.

All too quickly, our ride ended, and we were on foot again. We were quite far away from the spaceport and could no longer see the faraway city. It was then that the men took a *necessary* stop. They didn't hide what they were doing. They just slipped their uniforms down and had at it. It didn't seem to bother them in the least that it was a communal event or that there were women present. They just pointed, shot, and watered the ground, jerking a bit as they ended the process. I tried to look away, to pretend I wasn't aware of what they were doing, but it was hard to find somewhere to look since men were all around me.

Unfortunately, the fact that they were urinating reminded me that I needed to go, but when I turned to ask Shaarvan, I found that he'd left me with the guards to join in the action. It was kind of scary having three strangers watching me without Shaarvan by my side. I'd never thought about what would happen if he weren't present. Shaarvan was the only person I knew on this distant, alien planet — a very chilling thought.

He returned almost immediately and urged me away from the others, telling me I was to follow suit. Regrettably, the three guards followed us. Shaarvan expected me to piddle with an audience?

"I expect your obedience, wife," was his sharp response, which didn't sound the least bit sympathetic.

I attempted to step away, but Shaarvan's hand on my arm tightened. His eyes flashed. I squatted where I was, concentrating on the matter at hand.

Kekorian dresses were not made for "roughing it." Between my struggle with the excess material and staying upright, I'm sure the guards were able to see more than I intended. But one does one's best and ignores the rest. When Shaarvan handed me a rag to clean myself, I was grateful for that at least.

We rejoined the others and then continued walking. At the end of maybe an hour or so, we stepped on another of the flat escalators and rode standing up.

We were on that one much longer than we'd been on the others, and the scenery slowly changed from the desert into rolling grassland and finally into a forest with trees tall as skyscrapers — lush and plump with green.

At one point, Shaarvan dropped my hand and pushed me down into a sitting position. He stood over me, his legs on both sides of me, his pipe gun pointed outwards. I looked back and saw that all the guards had done the same. It was beginning to look like *shoot-out at the OK Corral*. Who were we, Bat Masterson? I couldn't remember which were the good guys or why.

We traveled on at the same steady chug-a-chug, the escalator taking us off into nowhere. The forest shadowed the tram and made the sky appear dark. I shivered, and Shaarvan unpacked a blanket and wrapped it around me.

I heard the sound of an animal, something like a cougar or wolf. I know the call of both is quite different, but although I heard the howl/roar many times, I still wasn't sure about the species. I didn't see it either, but I was glad that Shaarvan had the pipe ready. We were exposed on the tram. Whatever it was could have leaped up onto the escalator and happily munched away.

Shaarvan and his crew continued to guard, surveying the distance like we were a wagon train and attack was imminent. I felt a new tension in the air. I wasn't sure if Shaarvan feared whatever animal was prowling about or if it was something even worse. I found myself peering out into the forest, expecting at any moment that something horrible might snap and crunch our bones. For the first time, I thought it might not be a good idea to visit alien planets.

Off to the right, I glimpsed a series of spires. Like stalagmites in a cave, they poked upwards towards the sky. With something to measure distance by, I could see we were steadily advancing toward them. I watched the structures as we came closer. Strangely, some of the fear building up inside me began to dissipate. I didn't understand, but somehow, looking at those jagged-edged towers brought me tranquility. I could feel a shift in the men, too. The nearer we came to the spires, the less tension I felt.

The structures I saw as we came in among them were like giant Stonehenge columns. Some still pointed upwards, but most had fallen. It looked like an enormous giant had tilted them into archways. We traveled underneath these stony shelters. It was strange how it all should have been eerie, but there was a feeling of peace and safety within their midst. There were miles and miles of the columns and upside down v's, stretching further into the distance than the eye could see.

As we had entered under them, Shaarvan and the guards behind us sat down. Only the three guards, who clung to us, remained standing, pipes ready and outward. Shaarvan was resting behind me, his legs and arms surrounding me. He pulled me closer so my back lay against his chest. His chin leaned on the top of my head. I could feel his lips in my hair.

I had a thousand questions, and I thought this would be a great time to ask. I made the gesture for permission to speak. Shaarvan gave an emphatic *no sign* followed by *no argument.*

I sighed dramatically but quietly, just to let him know how difficult this silence bit was. Shaarvan chuckled soundlessly and picked up my hand. He kneaded it like it was bread dough and then raised it to his lips. The tip of his tongue delicately licked at my wrist. Chills went up and down my spine. I shivered. How did he do that?

Shaarvan moved me sideways onto his leg so he could watch my eyes. His lips met mine briefly, and his eyes teased me until my face heated. Then he laughed. I saw the laugh, but no sound escaped his mouth.

I was miserable. There were three guards in our car and a hundred more behind us. Shaarvan's intimacies embarrassed me. He saw it in my eyes, and again he laughed. Then he pulled my hair back and whispered in my ear, "A Shapechanger wife will make love whenever and wherever her husband demands it."

I sought Shaarvan's eyes. Was he serious? I couldn't tell, but he was frightening me. No spires could give me tranquility with Shaarvan near.

Gently, Shaarvan pulled me back against his body again. Once more, his arms enveloped me. One hand moved to find my breast, and I think he felt me trembling. He brushed my hair aside and whispered into my ear. "Rest easy, Shaara. I shall not take you here. The lesson would not be worth the risk."

Then, for a short period, I was content. My head fit perfectly under Shaarvan's chin. I felt cocooned and safe. Despite his frightening threat, he didn't tease me again.

All too soon, the stone tunnel ended. The men stood and took up their protective stance. Tension re-entered their faces and posture, but the gremlins, whoever or whatever they were, never attacked.

When we arrived at our destination, Shaarvan and I were the first off, then came our three guards and, finally, all the others. There was a long, narrow pathway to follow on foot. It felt like dirt, but we raised no dust as we walked.

For at least an hour we walked toward a stone building, one surrounded by the same stark stone pillars of our earlier passage. As we came closer, I realized that these pillars had been used in the building's construction. The house, if that's what it was, rose up a good three stories high and was capped with slabs of the pillars, askew and at different heights.

I thought, at first, that it was carelessly constructed in a hodgepodge manner, but it wasn't. It was alien, and although it didn't look like any kind of architectural design I'd ever seen, there was an eerie, cold unity to it. Something in it made me shiver.

We walked under another of the stone tunnels. The fork where the two slabs met must have been at least twenty feet above us. The cold, damp feeling we got walking under those forked pillars made me think of England's pea soup fogs, but there was no reduction in visibility, just a feeling of dread like I'd gotten from a movie I'd once watched about Jack the Ripper. That same feeling, that shivering tension, was the same as the moment before Jack sliced a young girl with his long, thin knife. Once more, I shuddered.

At the end of the tunnel, we came to a giant door. One of our guards laid his hand on it, and a deep, low rumble came from inside. One by one, each of us had to touch it. Even the girls' hands were lifted up to the stone. I hesitated when my turn came, not wanting to feel the door for some reason, but I knew I had no choice. Just as I'd imagined, the touch of it was cold and slimy, like the inside of an aquarium nobody had cleaned in a while.

When we finished greeting the door, the first guard placed his hand on it again, and the door disappeared. I don't mean it slid up or down or sideways. That slab of concrete, the one we'd just touched — solid and slimy — was suddenly gone.

We walked through the hole of the door's disappearance and into a huge chamber with no walls or windows. I turned to view the space we'd just passed through. It had closed up. From this side, it appeared as if there'd never been any door. Four stonewalls surrounded us. As if that were not a claustrophobic nightmare, a glance upwards and down showed that even the floor and ceiling were fashioned of solid granite. We'd entered an exitless box of concrete-like rock.

Chapter Seven
Surprise!

Shaarvan

I almost didn't take my wife with us when she spoke on the ramp, but then her quick rejoinder and the flirtation in her eyes made me laugh. She was a wayward child at times, yet she was good for me. She amused me with her playfulness. I had not once found her boring, quite to the contrary. Her company, in general, pleased me. It was for that reason I allowed her to accompany us.

I had not been sorry. Shaara had behaved amazingly well. The long stretches of walking she bore with no complaint. How different she was from the girls I'd brought with me before. None of them endured the trip without airing objections — most of them held attitudes that bordered on insolence. Two of them I had to drug to keep them from becoming overly tedious. I was prepared for that possibility with Shaara, but she did not require it. She was quite the opposite. Not only had she not complained of anything, but she seemed delighted by it all. Her eyes, still blue as the morning sky, darted here and there as if she wished to absorb and memorize each scene she saw.

Our respite under the *tombs of the ancestors* was made far more pleasant because of her presence. The warmth of her small body pressed against mine, the touch and smell of her, and the way her eyes expressed her every thought restored my energy. And, even there, amidst the threat of the "hordes" on every side of us, their eyes a constant reminder of our trespass on their valuable property, Shaara gave me laughter. I shall double her guard in the future. I shall not risk her at any venture.

Shaara

Shaarvan lowered his pipe weapon. His body grew less rigid, his face less stern. His eyes remained focused on the far wall, the one opposite where we'd entered, but it was obvious that whatever he expected held no threat. He must have felt my appraisal. He shot a glance down at me and gave me a nod of approval. His hand squeezed mine gently, and then his mind drifted off, his eyes watching the wall again.

Sure enough, the cement slab started to move. I was no longer worried. I'd seen this set at the Haunted House in a local amusement park. Yet, here, no one promised what followed would be pleasant. Perhaps I should have fretted, yet I trusted Shaarvan. I don't know how that was possible, but I did.

The wall retreated. I thought for a moment the room was growing larger. It wasn't. The opposite wall was closing in parallel to the first. I scanned the room again. It was a good thing nobody had decided to lie down and take a nap. They would have been crushed.

None of the men seemed concerned about the traveling walls, and the girls were still zombies with frozen eyes. I placed my hands over my ears, but the noise was more vibration than sound. The teeth-gritting throb pierced my jaw, quivered my flesh, and made my feet feel as if I were on roller skates. We continued walking forward and sideways — whichever way the wall led us. Then, with one final grinding moan, the walls stopped moving. All the men sat down.

I started to sit, too, but Shaarvan pulled me forward – closer to the wall on the left.

"Touch the stone, Shaara," he ordered me, and then he did the same.

A hole-like door appeared, and we walked through it. As we continued, I looked back and saw the wall behind us was once more solid.

"Why are we leaving the others?" I whispered.

Shaarvan touched my lips for silence but answered. "We will meet with the owner, and then the others will follow. You, Shaara, must remember what we discussed. There will be no speaking without my permission."

I nodded, but I didn't understand what the big deal was. There was nobody around.

We continued on, turning and twisting in a maze as complex as the ship's. At last, we reached a dead end. Shaarvan turned to the right and placed his hand up on the wall. The wall slid open.

Inside was a vast chamber, bigger than the room we'd first entered. A thick green, grass-like carpet spread across the floor, and the walls held moving murals. On one panel, I saw the guards and girls we'd left. They were all still sitting with relaxed faces, outstretched legs, and weapons laid down at their sides.

I hoped the floor wasn't as cold as the walls I'd touched. I wouldn't want to be sitting on that hard stone if it were.

Shaarvan moved forward, and I had to walk swiftly so as not to get tugged along. Towards one side of the room, there were several raised stone pillars of various heights, covered with the same grass carpeting as the floor. Shaarvan and I walked towards the highest one.

He lifted me up onto it. The broad-topped post was about five feet off the ground, not scary high, just slightly strange, like sitting on the back of a horse in someone's living room. Shaarvan sat on a lower pillar. His feet touched the ground. I wondered why I got the highchair.

About the time I was set to ask for permission to speak, in came a man wearing the most ridiculous suit I'd ever seen. He looked like a circus performer gone fat. His orange and yellow shirt had no expansive V-neck like Shaarvan's. His was merely a vest, and the two sides couldn't possibly meet with his watermelon belly bulging outwards. The man's stomach hung out and cascaded down over his tight orange pants. The yellow braid at the sides swelled out like a bothersome growth, except one could tell the expansion of it was only due to the man's extreme excess of flesh.

The man had a friendly, big grin on his round, fat face as he glanced at Shaarvan. Bushy, thick eyebrows spread all the way across his brow. Under his round bubble of a nose, whiskers perched — like those of a cat. His eyes twinkled when he took note of my presence. My first thought was that one couldn't help but like the guy. I found myself grinning like a fool until I remembered to look down before Shaarvan caught me.

The man sat down on one of the columns just a slight bit lower than Shaarvan's. He started talking right away, but I couldn't understand what he was saying. His words were pitched almost musically, so it sounded like he was singing rather than speaking. But when Shaarvan answered, he, too, sang.

The man turned to regard me. A few more songs were sung as both men stared at me. It was most uncomfortable. I kept my eyes down and tried not to fidget.

Shaarvan stood up and walked toward me. His hands went up to my waist, and he lifted me down.

"Turn around slowly," he ordered.

Both men watched as I obeyed. I felt like I'd turned into a robotic doll.

"Walk to that wall and return," Shaarvan added. I did as I was told, but I was getting very nervous. If I was not for sale, why was Shaarvan forcing me to perform?

I attempted to disconnect all thoughts. It was safer that way. If I really started thinking about this, I knew I'd explode. I wondered what the point of the men's conversation was. I was pretty sure they were discussing me while they sang to each other. Was I for sale? Had I irritated Shaarvan to the point that he was going back on his word about keeping me?

When I returned to his side, Shaarvan placed me back up on the pillar and went to the screen where you could see the guards and the girls. I heard him telling them to come forward. All the guards and zombie women stood up. They assembled into a more organized group and walked forward through the first of several invisible doors.

As they traveled towards us, the funny fat man in his orange and yellow costume edged closer. Shaarvan and he exchanged more songs, and the man peered up at my face.

"He wishes to see your eyes, Shaara. Look up," Shaarvan ordered.

I obeyed, but my eyes sought Shaarvan's. I'm sure they looked frightened because Shaarvan sang to the fat man, and the guy backed up two steps. Then, the two continued to sing to each other. Why did Shaarvan look uneasy?

Again, Shaarvan took me down from the giant stool. "I have given him permission to touch you," Shaarvan told me.

My body was shaking by then. I didn't have the courage to look into Shaarvan's eyes. I was afraid of what I'd see. Had I proven too difficult, as Shaarvan was always telling me? Had Shaarvan grown tired of my questions and my tirades? Only his arm across my shoulders kept me from bolting. I don't know where I could have run to, but anywhere would have been better than where I was.

The fat man reached out to touch my hair. He held a lock in his hand and stroked it as he examined it. He seemed pleased. I could have told him I didn't have lice, or was he checking for dandruff? His eyes, when they met mine, still seemed kind, but I was so scared I thought I'd pee my pants.

The door slid open, and the zombies and their guards joined us. The fat man dropped my lock of hair and turned to watch as the girls entered the room. He seemed to lose all interest in me as his fat, short legs waddled towards the girls.

Shaarvan put me back up on my post. His arms lingered a moment, and he nodded I'd done well. I searched his eyes for answers, but he flashed "silence." I was too drained to argue. I looked down. My eyes were welling with tears, and I had the shakes so bad I knew I couldn't have stood. I was so thankful to be out of the spotlight, I was staring down at my hand and wasn't focusing on what was going on in the center stage.

When I finally pulled myself together, I wished I hadn't. The fat man, who I'd thought was kind of nice, had removed one of the girl's dresses and was feeling her all over. He did it in a clinical sort of way, but it was in front of everyone. Meantime, all the guards and Shaarvan watched without protest.

The girls were all still zombies, and the one who was getting all the attention was oblivious, so maybe I was the only one who cared, but I cared a lot. Yet, I didn't move or say anything, purely in self-defense. I was afraid if I drew their attention, it would be me down on the floor with no clothes on.

The fat man seemed pleased. He laughed and sang/chattered with Shaarvan. Then, wiping his finger on the side of his pants, he stood up, walked over to the wall, and pushed. I suppose there must have been a button there, but I didn't see it. Yet almost immediately, his own men walked out. They herded up the girls and led them out of the room. Shaarvan dismissed our guards. They left. Soon, it was just the three of us again.

Again, the fat man came to stand near me. I resumed my human earthquake tremors. He wasn't the friendly doughboy I'd thought he was. I was terrified he'd touch me again. If he did, I knew I'd scream.

Luckily, this time, the fat man wasn't allowed close. I was glad when Shaarvan removed me from the pillar. His proximity helped stop my trembling. Possessively, Shaarvan draped his arm down over my shoulder and across my body. His hand fell right at my breast, and he began stroking me. My face grew hot. I wanted to wiggle away, but I didn't. I kept my face lowered and waited for Shaarvan to stop. Besides, his possessive mauling did have the effect of reassuring me. I figured it meant that the fat man had not bought me. It was obvious I still belonged to Shaarvan.

The fat man and Shaarvan sang to each other several times, and the tension in the room dissipated. The fat man laughed. He waddled over to the wall on our left and touched it with his hand. As it opened, I could see a huge cupboard with sectioned drawers. The man fumbled inside and came back with a square metal box. He reached out with it to touch my stomach. I flinched and would have stepped back, but Shaarvan was behind me.

"Be still, Shaara," Shaarvan snapped.

A second time, the man reached out and held the box below my stomach. It touched me for no more than half a minute and then was withdrawn. The man peered down at it and laughed. His laughter echoed in the empty room. It ricocheted from wall to wall, and still, the fat man laughed.

I tried to turn so I could see Shaarvan's face, but his arms around me allowed no movement. Still, he must have felt my urge. He kissed the back of my neck as if that would answer my questions. His arms squeezed me gently, but his lips remained silent.

I watched the fat man return the box he'd touched me with, and the cupboard once again disappeared. Then, he began to sing to Shaarvan. I felt Shaarvan nod, and the doughboy began to talk to me in Altarian. I heard some of the words I'd learned, but the accent was so different I couldn't connect the words. I didn't know what he wanted.

Shaarvan once more kissed me — this time on my cheek and explained. "He's congratulating you on being pregnant, Shaara. The proper response is 'Quip'."

"What?" I yelped. I totally forgot about not speaking. I searched Shaarvan's eyes, hoping he was teasing me. "No!" I cried out in English when I saw in his eyes that there was no joke.

Shaarvan flashed his signs of warning. I didn't wait to read them. I'd seen the look in his eyes, the hardening of his cheek muscles as he grew angry. I examined the grassy carpet, yet my thoughts were whirling in a tornado of horror.

Shaarvan lifted me back up onto the perch. I was limp from my shock. Pregnant? I couldn't be. It wasn't possible. I was too young. He was an alien. Having a kid wasn't supposed to happen for a good ten years. All in all, it wasn't fair. In fact, it was horrible news.

Shaarvan lifted up my chin and pounced his finger off my lips in the "silence" command. I just stared at him. What words would change anything? He'd wounded me. I was bleeding out my future, and he was telling me to be silent? Oh, heartless one.

Shaarvan walked away without a single glance back. What had I expected? That he would treat me suddenly like a person with feelings? I watched the two of them pour drinks and sit talking. I was the one who needed a drink. I was nineteen, not old enough to drink in California, it was true, but I didn't think the laws were the same in Kekor. Yet neither man offered me even a sip. I was just a wind-up toy — a pregnant wind-up toy without feelings.

I sat on the highchair and watched them, getting more and more depressed. True, the fat man wouldn't get me, but now I was stuck in this nightmare. Pregnant! I hadn't even finished college. I'd never gone to Paris to see the Louvre or the Eiffel Tower or those cute little cafes on the corners where you could sit and speak French with all the Parisians. I'd never gone to see Big Ben or Buckingham Palace or Stratford-on-Avon, where Shakespeare was from. I'd never even gotten to ski, and now I was going to be a mother. It was unbearable, tragic, and entirely unjust.

Why hadn't Shaarvan done something to prevent my pregnancy? Surely, with all their technology, Altar must have invented birth control — unless Shaarvan wanted a kid. Did he do this to lock me into his alien insanity? A trillion or so light years from home? I think I was already trapped. Pregnancy wasn't necessary. So, that had to be it. Shaarvan wanted an heir, a son to carry on his name. Thanks for asking if I wanted a child. Of course he never asked my opinion about anything. The jerk. He had a lot of nerve planting seeds in a garden that didn't belong to him.

Shaarvan and the fat man kept drinking, and I kept getting madder. By the time they were done and had stood up, I was livid.

The fat man left. Shaarvan returned to my side, lifted me down, and took my arm. We walked down a long hall and into a private chamber. It was really kind of an elegant chamber, all in gold trim with bronze statuary, but I was so fired up I barely saw it.

To make it even worse, Shaarvan hadn't even noticed my anger. He'd shown me to the bathroom and then signaled me to sit at a table filled with dishes and bowls filled with different foods. I sat all right, but I didn't start eating. Did he care? No. He just ignored me. I don't even think he realized I hadn't eaten a thing until he was completely full. Then he frowned and studied me a moment.

"I have forgiven you for speaking in Petrov's chamber. I realize it was the shock that made you forget. Why do you not eat?"

I didn't answer Shaarvan, but I glared the full force of my wrath. He took one look at me and burst out laughing.

"I see," he said as he chuckled away with the most irritating look of complete satisfaction on his face. "Fine, you can dine later."

He reached his arm around the table, grabbed me, and threw me over his shoulders, carrying me to the bed like an old rug.

Incensed by his laughter and by his attitude, I fought him, so outraged I'd forgotten everything I'd learned.

Shaarvan only laughed harder. He held down my arms and tossed one great, heavy leg over my lower body. His tongue wove the patterns on my skin. I fought them. I gritted my teeth. I tried to focus on my rage, the injustice of his treatment of me, and how hurt I was that he'd impregnated me. I even bit my lip, but I couldn't withstand him. In a minute, I was his.

After, as we lay entwined, Shaarvan, with his nose nuzzling at my hair, resting but still interested in another round, finally asked me why I was upset.

"You don't care. Why do you bother asking me?" I snapped.

"That is probably true, but I did pose the question. You will satisfy my interest."

Despite my vexation, I could see that Shaarvan was no longer thinking about sex. His eyes were at warning level one, not to be challenged. Yet my temper was too full, too eager to spin out of my control. "You never told me I was pregnant. It was like I was the last one to know. And I don't want to be pregnant. I don't want to have a baby."

I was so angry then that the words flowed like a river raging after a storm. "I'm too young to have a baby. I wanted to see the world, to learn to ski, to get a job and . . ."

"Enough."

It was an order, but I almost couldn't stop. I took in deep breaths, striving for control. I knew he would punish me if I continued, but it was so hard to shut off the flow.

Shaarvan had pushed himself up. His mighty arms carried his weight as he stared down at me. The sight of him might have alarmed me further. I was often taken aback by the massiveness of his heavy chest and shoulders and the great strength of the muscles in his bulging arms, but this time, it was his eyes that drew mine.

His eyes mocked me. "Poor little girl," he said cruelly. "What did you think would happen when the big bad wolf captured you and carried you off down into the bowels of his cave?"

Shaarvan's face had twisted. He was suddenly so alien I couldn't bear to look at him.

"Stop it," I cried out as I lunged away from him, away from the bed, and away from his ominous words. But his arms folded around me, and he tossed me back down. His leg again trapped my lower body, so I couldn't break free. Yet still, I wrestled with him — scratching, hitting, and biting, lost to good sense and self-preservation — until one of his hands reached round my neck and cupped it in the neck grip.

Despite the temporary chaos in my mind, I knew the pain of that grip. I froze and stared up into his eyes. *I won't cry. I won't cry*, I told myself, but tears came sliding down my face. I hated them, and I hated myself for being so emotionally weak. Why couldn't I be stronger both in mind and body? Why couldn't I stand up to Shaarvan?

His eyes softened with my tears. He released my neck. His arms reached around me and held me until my sobbing stilled. Then he grabbed up his shirt and ordered me to blow my nose.

I obeyed, but I was still angry. My tears had not been the sign of surrender but of unloosened anguish. I cried out words in hardly comprehensible sobs. "You made me parade in front of that awful man, and you let him strip that girl where everybody could see and . . ."

"Enough."

I held my breath to stop the words. I'd gone too far. Shaarvan's eyes had darkened into tiger diamonds. If I pressed him, I knew he'd Shapechange.

"You take liberties you were not granted." He sat up. His eyes continued their change. I saw the tiger-green for a second before he calmed.

"The Terran girls and Petrov are none of your concern, Shaara."

He breathed in deeply. His eyes grayed back into steel as they roamed my naked body. I reached down for a cover, but he grabbed my wrist and brought it back empty.

"If you are cold, you will look forward to my warming your body."

Carelessly, his hand traveled across my stomach and down. It rested for a moment where the black box had found a new life forming. "You are my wife, Shaara. Of course, you will bear my sons. I had assumed you understood these . . . *facts of life* as you Terrans call them."

"But . . ."

"Silence."

Shaarvan's eyes held mine as his finger traced my jaw. It was making a pattern on my skin. With the recognition, my brain cried out. *No, don't give in again.* I glared. He accepted my eyes and held them. I couldn't look away. The patterns grew bolder. My brain couldn't speak then. My heart beat faster and faster. *Traitorous body.* I shivered, but it was not from the cold.

Shaarvan laughed and conquered again.

Shaarvan

The satisfaction I felt in hearing the good news Petrov brought was immeasurable. I shall soon have a son. I shall teach him the wonders of the universe, the rhythm of the ship, the power, and the grandeur of the Shapechanger. I shall share with him the lore and knowledge I have gained with the Old Ones. And when he is joined by other sons, we shall build a fleet of ships and expand our influence across the newer planets, forming ties with the Keets and Brebals.

To think that such a little one as my wife could bring me such pride made me soften towards her. I shall grant her many liberties when she delivers me a son. Yet, I shall not allow her to sleep in her own room as some do. She shall always stay by my side. I shall not accept even the birth of a son as a trade for her.

How intriguing my little wife was. That quick and ready brain of hers was constantly thinking, yet what strange thoughts and ideas I discovered within. It took me by surprise when she was angry about her pregnancy. Did not all females wish to bear a child? Was it not the avenue for their status in the realm of men? Shaara had proven herself to be highly fertile — shouldn't that cause her great joy?

Yet, she seemed unaware of the desirability of such a station. Had I neglected some part of her education? Or was she again retreating to her memories of a world that was no longer hers?

I could no longer lock her in the isolation room. She would need to be treated far more delicately now. Hopefully, it was only time she needed, time to become accustomed to her new status.

She challenged me again with her refusals in my bed, yet I shall ignore it this time. She was overwrought with shock. But when would she learn that she cannot fight me? When would her acceptance be complete? My little Shaara — how could she be the source of my contentment *and* my vexation? Was that not a paradox?

Shaara

The next day, we retraced our steps. The same escalator with high volts of tension, the pillars of stone, the long walks, another escalator, and the shuttle where we could finally sit. It was all the same. Our return to the ship was as uneventful as our arrival at the mansion.

Yet, without the girls, the guards were more relaxed. They talked among themselves. I felt their eyes on me off and on. I wasn't allowed to look around, but I could feel the creepy sensation of their curiosity. Only our personal guards, who had somehow multiplied to six, continued to be watchful and alert throughout the journey, and, of course, Shaarvan, who never seemed to let down his guard.

The part of the space station we walked through was as deserted as before. I kept looking for changes, searching for something exciting to watch. The same sleepy ships stood in their parking spaces, and still, I saw no one about them. Only the dumb robots, blinking away, riding their skateboards by us. I didn't see the strange orange octopus or any other oddities. How could an alien planet be so boring?

Liftoff was also disappointing. No noise, no shebang, not even a feeling of acceleration. We just slowly rose and lifted like helium balloons floating upward. When we arrived in orbit, we hung there for several minutes. And then, without warning, *kaboom*. The sky went crazy. Talk about fireworks. It was gorgeous. I'll say that for it. It was like flying through a three-dimensional rainbow.

On the other side of the colors, there was only blackness. I thought we'd made a mistake. There was nothing but dark. Then, a little bitty surge — nothing much, like accelerating from 50 M.P.H. to 70 M.P.H. with your foot down. Not a big deal. Yet, on the screen, you could suddenly see flashes of lights and streaks like comets. And that was that. We were once more on our way.

"Shaarvan," I said later that night. "Why didn't it feel like we blasted off? Didn't we have to fight gravity? Why didn't we feel weightless and float about inside the ship?"

Shaarvan laughed, but he did explain. "You understand about magnets, Shaara?" he asked.

"Yes, but what do they have to do with it?"

"You know that a magnet has a North and South end, right?"

I nodded.

"If you attempt to put two magnets together with the North ends coming close, they repel or push away from each other. Every planet is a magnet with North and South poles. This ship has *bipolar magnetic traction*. To leave a planet, the closer pole of the planet is focused on and intensified. The ship's magnetic polar is turned on. That pushes the ship upwards and away from the planet's pole. The stronger the repulsion, the further we go until there is little gravitational pull. Then, the magnetic attraction is reversed towards the nearest star, and we are pulled towards that in an electromagnetic field that moves us away from the planet of departure."

"You could call it the polar push?" I said, joking around.

"So you understand?"

"Shaarvan, you'd make a great teacher. I do understand." I smiled up at him to let him know how much I appreciated his taking the time to explain. "But what about gravity?"

"Magnetism is stronger than gravity. Gravity is actually one of the weaker forces of nature."

"You don't have warp speed, or anything, do you?"

Shaarvan laughed and tousled my hair. "I have given one lesson tonight on space travel. Do you not think the other mechanical systems can wait?"

I had to admit he'd been generous with his time and patience. I threw my arms around him and kissed him, and, of course, that led to other things, so science lessons were over for the night.

I saw takeoff and landing many times. It rarely varied. Kekor was only the first of many planets we visited on our way to Altar.

I discovered that, from space, the planets all looked Earthlike, with clouds, water, and generous areas of dirt and/or foliage. The colors of each were somewhat darker or lighter, the hues more intense on one, the clouds speckled or slightly yellow or orangish brown, but from space, most unsatisfactorily similar.

Shaarvan laughed when I commented on this disappointment. "Planets that are capable of supporting our needs must be similar, Shaara. An air breather's atmosphere requires such similarities."

"But couldn't the clouds be purple and the ground pink? Couldn't we see yellow water?"

Again, Shaarvan laughed. His head shook negatives while his eyes continued chuckling. "Shaara, think. I know Earth has not explored the galaxy, so you could not know from all the reading you liked to do, but logic tells you that the chemicals that would change the color of clouds, dirt, and water would also prevent humanoids from developing on the planet's surface. There is a small degree of variance that an air breather's body can accept."

It made sense, but it definitely wasn't what I'd imagined when I'd thought about landing on alien worlds.

Spaceports were also alike from planet to planet. I saw the identical flashing paths and landing strips, ships that looked exactly like the ones we'd seen before, and the same blinking robots, always carrying and moving crates and boxes here and there.

Shaarvan told me that spaceports were planned that way. "Uniformity makes for ease of commerce," he explained.

It also makes for boredom, I thought, but I was starting to learn to keep my mouth shut and not disclose every opinion.

Shaarvan allowed me to go planet side with him most of the time. He liked to show me off at the buyer's mansion. It was like I was the demonstrator model. Sometimes, I had to do really bizarre things. One dealer wanted me to sing. Boy, was he in for a disappointment. I sang *Twinkle, Twinkle, Little Star*. It was all I could think of. I thought it was rather appropriate. But an opera singer, I was not. Anyway, in spite of my singing, the buyer bought the girls.

Later, Shaarvan informed me that I must learn more appropriate songs. "A star is nothing like a diamond," he ranted. "A diamond is hard. It has a surface that cuts almost any other material. A star is a liquid-gas fusion tank. How are they similar?"

"But Shaarvan," I tried to explain. "From Earth, stars are shiny like diamonds."

"That is from the ripples of atmosphere, my silly wife," he laughed. "And stars are not small. They make planets look like a speck of dust against a giant mountain."

I sighed. "The buyer liked the song."

"He didn't like it, Shaara. He didn't speak your native language. Thankfully. He just liked the way you looked singing it."

So, guess who had to learn a Shapechanger song?

Shaarvan sang it for me that first time, and I almost cried. I didn't understand the words, but his voice was lovely, and there was a projection of meaning in the melody that haunted me.

"It's beautiful," I told him. "And you should be the one who sings for buyers, not me. Your voice is professional."

"Shaara, Shapechanger do not use words such as *beautiful*. It has no meaning."

"Of course it does. It means . . . I liked it."

"Why?"

"I'd like it better if I understood the words, but the melody speaks."

"Good, go on."

Shaarvan's eyes watched intently. Too intently. Why had he become so serious? I didn't know what he wanted to hear.

Apparently, he read my confusion. "Shaara, what does the *melody* say to you?"

"It's just a feeling . . ."

"Feel it, Shaara. Tell me."

His eyes urged and commanded at the same time. I closed my eyes and began to speak. "I think maybe there was a sadness there, and then . . . a striving towards something, Then more sadness. I think . . . There was a triumph, too . . . like a victory at the end . . . and I . . ."

"Extremely good. You are adapting to Shapechanger well."

"What do you mean, 'I'm adapting' to Shapechanger?"

"You will learn the words now," he ordered.

I wanted him to explain, but I knew he wouldn't — not when his eyes steeled into silver daggers.

I sighed heavily and thought about what he was asking me to do. "But it's too long, Shaarvan. Isn't there a children's song I could learn first — one that's easier?"

He laughed. "This is a children's song, Shaara. Adult songs have no words."

Line by line, Shaarvan translated. I was surprised by how much I *had* understood by feeling the music. The words only mirrored what the music had told me:

> *Spread among drops of soil and peat,*
> *the Somber Tree rises from tiny roots,*
> *its heavy branches stretching upwards,*
> *striving to touch the cloud-filled sky.*
>
> *From the vastness of its full-grown height*
> *boastfully, it scorns the basely ground,*
> *haughtily casting ominous shadows,*
> *it laughs into the wind at earthbound man.*
>
> *Man observes the tree touching sky,*
> *and so he climbs it and learns about fear.*
> *He scurries down from the Somber Tree,*
> *fleeing his dreams, ignoring desire.*
>
> *He plows his land and plants his crops.*
> *He lives his life at the foot of the tree,*
> *flinching at shadows, hiding his misery,*
> *ignoring conquest of the Somber Tree.*
>
> *But others are not content with the choice.*
> *A challenge is issued: take and conquer.*
> *The Somber Tree must meet its master,*
> *no matter the barrier, no matter the price.*

Even then there are those with no limit
who vow that man will be victorious.
With the weaving of strands of DNA units,
mutations are savored, examined, and tested.

From those who change when the need arises
comes a new species: the Shapechanger.
Round and round the Somber Tree roots
this new breed of men gazes at heavens.

Then, using their newly formed Powers
with tooth and nail in a tiger's shape,
upward they climb, limb by limb
ascending the heights of the Somber Tree.

Through the boughs of the haughty tree
they scale upwards, higher and higher,
claiming their rights, claiming their triumph
forging new ways like the Somber Tree.

"Victory is ours," say the people below.
"We have conquered our challenge.
We have now touched the heavens.
We are equal to the Somber Tree."

And so the Somber Tree no more is proud,
no more the victor of the cloud-strewn sky,
it hangs its branches, sobs sticky sap,
humbled before the Shapechanger.

But the altered men peer down at the others,
suddenly aware of how much they differ.
They have no wish to shame the tree,
or to flaunt their hard-earned victory.

Nor do they wish to share glory
with those who walk in the dirt,
trembling with fear of the unknown,
living their lives at the foot of a tree.

The people cry out, urging return
"Come back to the ground," they beg,
But their voices are dust strewn harsh,
and their faces are wreathed by envy.

The Shapechanger review their options.
The sky is their home for the claiming.
They are altered and new — Shapechanger.
How can they return to the others below?

They try to explain how they cannot go back
to the people who live at the foot of the tree.
But their kin throw rocks, swearing vengeance,
casting out the new species they've made.

The Shapechanger, thus set apart from the rest
Mourn the loss of their brothers and friends.
They pledge alliance with the Somber Tree
and for a while reside within its great boughs.

But their tiger claws find no food in the tree.
Neither does their man shape assist them.
Powered by Change, they form strong wings,
and take to the skies in new freedom.

Those who accept there is no more limit
fly further and explore their new realms.
They build new cities, prosper new lands,
They breed a race stronger and truer.

These ones who accept the limitless future,
Soon lift their eyes higher above them.
They trade their feathers for metallic wings
and leave the root-bound Somber Tree.

And now, forever, we ascend the stars,
leaving the deep-rooted Somber Tree.
For we are the ones who accept no limit,
this species of man, the Shapechanger.

"It is a beautiful poem," I said again, but then I saw Shaarvan's eyes mocking me. "All right. The message of . . . striving towards a goal and succeeding is uplifting. How is that?"

"You speak too much English."

"I cannot say that in Altarian."

"You must learn, Shaara."

"The song has a good lesson," I said in Altarian.

"That contains more meaning than your female word beautiful."

I thought it strange that the Altarian language had specific dialects that each of the genders used. Males rarely used contractions and were deprived of words such as "beautiful, I wasn't positive, but I suspected that males also had their own vocabulary from which females were excluded, but that wasn't a subject Shaarvan allowed me to explore, so I asked instead about the poem.

"There are things in the poem I still do not understand, Shaarvan. What good would it do for a tiger to climb a tree? And how could . . ."

"It is allegorical, Shaara."

"But I still don't understand . . . "

"It is not necessary for you to understand."

And that was the end of that, except I had to learn the song, word for word, and *then*, Shaarvan told me that I would never be allowed to sing it or say the words to anyone who *wasn't* Shapechanger. I'd thought that the whole point of learning the song was so I could sing that song instead of *Twinkle, Twinkle Little Star.*

I discovered that all children's songs were deep and allegorical like that one. Shaarvan made me learn fifteen of them. Committing them to memory was about as easy as memorizing the name of each bone in the human skeleton. Yet, since they were the teaching songs of the Shapechanger, none of them could be shared with outsiders. Shaarvan never did teach me a song I could sing for a buyer, but it didn't matter, for no one ever asked me to sing again.

Most of the buyers more or less ignored me. Often, I was put in a chair and "turned off" for the entire session. I liked it that way. I could look around the room and listen, although most frequently, the conversation was not in Altarian but in some other foreign language that Shaarvan always seemed to know. I tried to shut out the selling of the girls part. That still made me bristle, but any thought about interfering brought Shaarvan's eyes, and his eyes always silenced me, knowing it was a warning of what would come if I acted out my feelings.

Most of the buyers were more or less anonymous in my mind, but the ones who asked me weird questions or wanted me to do something strange, of course, stood out in my memory.

The buyer who insisted that I eat gloakk, I remember. He wanted to know if Terran girls would adapt to it. Gloakk tasted like dried bananas. It wasn't awful. Shaarvan made me eat many things worse, but I'd hate to make a steady diet of it.

Shaarvan was pleased that I tasted the gloakk, and he smiled and nodded at me. When we returned to the ship, he rewarded me with a free hour in the garden, which was a heavenly reward.

I wandered barefoot on the paths with flowers on both sides. I smelled the sweet fragrance and admired the beauty — a word I still thought was applicable to life. There were pink and red flowers that looked like roses, even though they didn't grow on thorned bushes but on low single-stemmed stalks. I picked a red one and enjoyed its scent, one that reminded me of ocean breezes. I lay down under the tree and closed my eyes. I pretended there was a breeze rustling the branches of the tree. I believe that birds twittered, sharing their delight in the day.

It was a delightful hour. It made me wonder if Altar would really smell and feel like the ship's garden. I hoped so.

Shaarvan

The days proceeded smoothly. The ship had no problems and would not need inspections and corrections until we returned. The crew remained attentive, and the men were both courteous and timely in their scheduled duty shifts.

Only Teban caused me concern. He coveted my wife — foolish man to yearn for the wife of a Shapechanger. Shaara was innocent of the infatuation. I observed her closely, and I read her mind frequently when she was in the control room. Her mind fluttered from subject to subject and was often thinking thoughts that were unwise, but she was unaware of Teban's interest in her. As long as the man kept his distance from Shaara, I resolved not to interfere, but should he touch her or make known his interest, I would abandon him on the next planet side visit.

My wife seemed to have forgotten her pregnancy. She hadn't referred to it since we left Kekor. I believed she was pretending it had not happened. I shall not bring it up, but I have begun teaching her the children's songs that she will need to know for our son.

Her disgust at hearing that she was carrying my child concerned me. Would she injure herself or the child? I shall, of course, allow nothing in her proximity that she could use to do harm, nor shall I permit her to stray from my sight.

Shaara wanted to work with children before she was taken. She used to have a fondness for them. Perhaps she only needed time to become accustomed to the idea of bearing a child. It was my hope that by the time our son was birthed, she would no longer resent him. I know that my mother would be happy to raise the boy, but I would much prefer my son to be with us.

The training of my wife has become easier over time. She stopped rebelling after Kekor. I did not know whether that was from her Shapechanger assimilation or her body's response to the pregnancy. Whichever the cause, I was thankful.

Taking her planet side continued to be a pleasure. Her delight in simple things: a flower she saw by the side of the path, a new food she got to sample, even a stranger's costume that was novel, gave me the most incredible sense of enjoyment. I saw those sights through her eyes. The texture of the flower became unusual, the food was reexamined in my mouth, and the costume was noticed where I would previously have passed it by.

I enjoyed Shaara's presence beside me, her tiny hand in mine, the warmth of her body as she lay her head against my chest, and her smile. I savored her smile, as I never thought I could. I found myself teasing her, saying things only to catch the flash of her teeth, to watch for the glimmer in her eyes, the way she raised up her chin and tilted it slightly to the side when something was funny to her. I discovered that her hair was a different color in the sunlight than on the ship. Why should these things have become important to me? Why was I distracted from my thoughts in order to catch the sight of the softened hue of a stray curl? This never happened to me with the others.

Shaara

I fell asleep in the garden. I dreamed I found a shell with the sound of the ocean. Its appearance was that of an abalone shell, in rainbows of pearly colors that blended. It was shiny on the inside, yet subdued, an Impressionist painting of a rainy day. What does such a dream represent? Was it my new life? My roommate at college, who liked to study dream meanings, would probably have claimed that a shell signified fertility. I had to giggle at that one.

Shaarvan's hand upon my face awakened me from my musing. He was on his knees, smiling at me when I opened my eyes. I reached my hand out to him, and he took it. He sat down beside me on the grass and leaned his back against the tree.

It was strange how different places revealed different images of people. Shaarvan in the control room was autocratic. In our excursions, he was both autocratic with the guards and me, but also in warrior mode, ready to attack anyone that eyed us funny. I supposed that autocratic, superior, and all-knowing was his formal, public image. Yet, in our room or here in the garden, he was kinder and gentler — a teacher, a lover, and sometimes, even a friend.

Shaarvan must have caught my thought. His eyes were mocking me in his amused manner, but he gently pulled me closer. His lips met mine briefly. Then his eyes closed, and he rested.

I stayed quiet, hoping he would take a nap, hoping I would be permitted to stay longer in this restful place. Sure enough, he fell asleep. I was glad. I let my mind drift about, thinking about him lying there, relaxing beside me.

It was always interesting to watch Shaarvan with the buyers. He was cordial and charismatic. I think that Shaarvan had the ability to sell the proverbial refrigerator to an Eskimo. He was usually laid back with the buyers, listening, talking, and drinking some kind of cordial when they offered it.

The only time I'd seen him angered by a buyer's request was on Strefa when a buyer asked to check my blood. It had made Shaarvan furious. The guy had only wanted to make sure I didn't have some horrible disease brought from Earth. Shaarvan had told him that the lab onboard the ship had purified all the girls, but the buyer kept insisting on having his own medical examiner double-check. I thought the guy had a point. I was surprised to see Shaarvan enraged over it.

Shaarvan finally allowed the man to take blood from one of the girls who was for sale. The buyer had been really pleased by the results, but Shaarvan had been cold and distant with him afterwards.

Later, when I'd been permitted, I'd questioned Shaarvan about his anger. I'd even mentioned that the buyer could have tested my blood and that it wouldn't have hurt me that much.

"You do not understand, Shaara," Shaarvan had said. "Necplor questioned the integrity of a Shapechanger. It was an insult. I shall never sell to him again."

I should have accepted Shaarvan's answer and not persisted, but I was always trying to understand what made Shaarvan mad. "I don't think he intended to insult you," I said.

Shaarvan's eyes had flared, and he'd flashed the *no argument* sign. I'd been really surprised. I hadn't meant it as a challenge. But, when Shaarvan's eyes grew hard and glaring, it was always best to inspect the floor.

I started biting at my lip nervously, a habit that Shaarvan wasn't fond of. He stopped me, raised up my chin, and sighed. "I am not angry with you, Shaara. It is only that you still do not understand. Girls, even wives, may not interfere in Shapechanger business."

I signaled a request to talk, and, unbelievably, Shaarvan granted it. "I did not mean to interfere . . ."

"Understood. That is why I am not annoyed."

Conversations like that left me very puzzled, but I figured I just had to keep putting all the confusing pieces together. Then, someday, maybe I'd understand Shaarvan.

Gray eyes with the most incredibly full lashes were staring at me. I could see the hint of a dimple on Shaarvan's right cheek. It was a great relief to see the dimple. I was never in trouble when his cheek dent, as he called it, was showing. I lay my head on his chest and listened to the steady beat of his heart. An arm wrapped around me and pulled me closer. I closed my eyes and felt the finger of his right hand building a pattern on my arm. The garden was such a lovely place.

Shaarvan

Shaara asked me if Altarian mothers had to stay home or could still work. I had to explain to her that Shapechanger women never worked. She was considerably distressed about that. It was almost as bad as her reaction to the *flaorth*. She only relaxed when I told her about accompanying my parents on their travels. She had not understood I would not leave her behind when I left. She is only alone with the computer or for a brief time when I lock her in the garden as a reward for her good behavior. How could she suppose I would allow her to be separated from me for long periods of time?

I assumed from the nature of her questions that she has begun to contemplate the arrival of our son. Why else would her conversation center on motherhood?

Shaara

I had bouts of morning sickness that canceled shore leave for me the whole time we landed on Sloorum. Shaarvan wouldn't let me go anywhere.

"I only throw up in the early morning, Shaarvan," I pleaded, desperate to go see something beside the inside of our ship.

"I know," Shaarvan reminded me, and he certainly did. He was always there with me, kindly considerate during my misery. Still, he was adamant that I could not leave our room.

He ordered me soups and bread things and made me stay in bed for hours. It was so stupid. It wasn't like I was sick. I was just pregnant.

When the ship left Sloorum, Shaarvan took me to the ship's lab for medication. I wasn't crazy about going to the lab. (Forget what I said about that buyer sticking me with a needle to test my blood. I hated needles.)

Sure enough, the first thing the man in the lab did was to pull out my blood, just like the buyer on Strefa had wanted to do.

The medic, after inserting my blood cells in a couple of machines, spinning it, turning it in different colors, and then running it through some more machines, said that I was fine. He told Shaarvan that my body was having a typically Terran reaction to my pregnancy and that there was nothing to be concerned with. That's how I discovered that other species did not have morning eruptions. Thanks a lot, Earth.

The lab guy said that he would give me a shot, and I would be cured. I asked Shaarvan what kind of drug they were going to give me. "My dear husband," said I wouldn't understand. He started to hold me still for the approaching needle, but I ducked away from him, risking his anger. I told the medic that he wasn't going to poke me with a needle unless he promised it wouldn't hurt my baby. I said it right directly to the lab tech. (in Altarian, I am proud to say) and waited for him to respond.

Of course, he didn't. The big coward. He stood there with his mouth dropped open five inches and waited to find out what Shaarvan would do about my insurrection.

Shaarvan broke out with a big smile and began to laugh.

Then, both the lab tech and I had pelican mouths. Shaarvan — laughing when I was being disobedient? Had the world gone nuts?

I must have been in shock. Shaarvan's arm went around my shoulders. He pulled me towards him and kissed me.

"My silly wife," he said. "Do you know how much I want this son of ours to be born healthy? How could you think that I would allow anyone to harm him or you?"

He kissed me seriously then, right in front of that poor tech. When I came up for air, the injection was already happening. It was a cruel trick, but after what I'd done, I knew I was very lucky to have avoided punishment.

Anyway, my morning sickness disappeared, and I was no longer confined to my boring room, and the planet visits began again.

I hated and loved the planet visits. I always feared seeing a face I knew in a girl being sold. I think Shaarvan tried to prevent my doing so by his constant harping, "Turn around, Shaara. Face the front, Shaara. Behave, Shaara."

The part I did love about planet visiting was getting off the ship to see everything. I never knew what I'd get to observe, and it was an adventure each time, even if the planets and landing ports were more or less identical.

There was one other part I dreaded about going planet side, though. I hated the buyers who were touchy-feelies. Most of them wanted to feel my hair like it was unique or something. They all had hair, so I didn't understand the difference. Of course, mine was long and curly, but hair is hair.

Some of the touchies wanted to feel the skin on my hands, and some the skin on my face. Shaarvan never allowed them to touch me anywhere else. I wish he'd told me that on Kekor. I wouldn't have been so scared.

When my pregnancy advanced beyond bulge to bloated projection, Shaarvan's tune changed. He let nobody touch my hands or face, and then almost all the buyers wanted to touch my growing watermelon. Shaarvan would stand there shaking his head for the longest time as they talked, emphatically negative about whatever they were asking. Then, I'd see him sigh and give his permission. He was reluctant even then, but it seemed that touching a pregnant woman was like rubbing Buddha's fat tummy — it brought them luck.

Shaarvan was becoming more and more possessive. Not a mansion did we visit that he didn't throw his arm around my shoulder, pulling me close. Maybe it was good for business. Maybe it made every man want a girl so he could prove ownership. I don't know why Shaarvan did it, and questions about why Shaarvan did anything mostly went unanswered. Sometimes, my probing why questions even annoyed him. I kept trying to keep the whys to myself.

Only one buyer (that I know about) was denied touching me anywhere. It was on Standor. Shaarvan wouldn't allow that buyer anywhere near me.

I only knew about it because Shaarvan raised his voice and yelled at the buyer when the guy walked towards me. I thought I was in trouble. The buyer almost made a scene over it, but Shaarvan had been firm.

Later, Shaarvan apologized for taking me there.

Shaarvan apologizing to me? "Why?" I asked, having no idea what it was all about.

"I have worked with that buyer before," Shaarvan told me, "but I will never sell to him again. He has become a polluter."

"You mean he dumps garbage?"

I could tell there was a real communication problem here. We were staring at each other like one of us had gone crazy.

"What is a polluter, Shaarvan?"

"One who injects drugs under his fingernails."

"Oooh," I cried, making a face. "That's awful." But then it hit me that I still didn't understand something. "Shaarvan, what does that have to do with me?"

"A polluter can scratch someone on purpose or accidentally, and the drug can go into their system."

"Then why didn't you worry about him touching you?"

"*I* am Shapechanger, Shaara. I was not sure how much your immunity has built up yet. I would not have taken you there if I had suspected."

Were Shapechanger the Supermen of the Galaxy? Was there anything they couldn't do? It made me feel very inferior around Shaarvan at times. He sometimes seemed close to invincible.

He must have read my thoughts. His arms went around me, and his lips comforted me.

Shaarvan

I was elated that Shaara did not want the baby harmed. She disobeyed me in the lab yesterday for fear that the shot the tech was about to give her would injure the child. She flouted several commands, but I did not have the heart to censure her severely. I was very relieved that she had finally accepted the child.

The tests the lab administered indicated Shaara's absorption of the new DNA is still running above schedule. She has been a good candidate, as most Terrans have proven to be. Her Terran genes are collapsing, with little resistance and no damage to her body. Her adaptation is presently at 56.3 %.

Shaara

Whenever we were approaching a planet, if I had done my computer time, Shaarvan would let me watch in the control room. Landings and takeoffs were the only time I liked to be there. On rare occasions, I saw other ships dropping down or heading up into space, but the best part about the approach was hoping I might see someone or something new. A pet like the orange octopus, a plant, a trinket, or anything else I'd never seen before.

On each planet, we were sure to see peculiar, unearthly, and curious architecture. The designers seemed to have little reason for the abutments, arches, and curly cues they placed on buildings. All of the planets we visited had weather control (Shaarvan said it only rained at night, even on Altar), so flat roofs, pointed roofs, and even round roofs were never done for stress reasons, like accommodating for a pile of heavy snow. I wondered, sometimes, if the architects just built each mansion more strangely than the next to outdo each other with their weirdness.

Architects traveled a great deal. They seemed to get bored with a planet quickly, so often, we'd see buildings and mansions done by Prefren or Chalaw on seven or eight different planets. Although the constructions would each be unique, once you knew the architect's characteristic flavor, you could identify his work anywhere. I enjoyed the challenge of noting such details, and, as usual, Shaarvan was an excellent teacher.

Sculptures of creatures that looked bizarre, the way I'd once believed that aliens would look, often decorated the buyer's yards and entrees. These sculptures had tentacles or beaks or distortions of what people usually looked like. I thought that maybe the sculptures were modeled after gods or goddesses of long ago, but I couldn't understand why the buyers would want them in their homes.

Many of them were so ugly they were nightmare visions and horror book portrayals of evil incarnations. I kept wishing for a camera so I could take pictures and compare, but Shaarvan said that photography was a concept not found anywhere but on Earth.

"The buyers want a one-of-a-kind, Shaara. If you were able to take a picture, you would steal a statue's uniqueness."

"A picture doesn't steal anything. It just records."

"It takes away an image. To take away without permission is to steal."

"Then I'd get permission."

Shaarvan sighed, shut his eyes, and opened them to stare at the ceiling. "Shaara, you have no camera, but you have a brain to remember anything you choose to recall. You need no more."

I couldn't understand why an advanced civilization had no photography. It was strange.

Shaarvan got tired of this particular issue because I guess I kept bringing it up. Again, he attempted to explain. "Shaara, listen for once without a word." His eyes held enough warning to seal my lips for an hour. Maybe.

"People emote energy and emotions. Do you understand?"

No, I didn't understand the "emote" part at all, not even in English. I shook my head.

"When you are angry, even before you speak or show me with your body movements, I can read the anger emoting from you. All Shapechanger can read emotions. Your television and pictures cannot emote. They are empty and without interest to us. Now, do you understand?"

I asked permission to talk. "I don't understand how you read me."

Shaarvan stared into my eyes. I could see he was trying to put his ability into words, but finally, he just shook his head. "Shaara, I can't explain that one. Shapechanger just can."

For every answer, another puzzle. That one really bothered me, too.

One of the things I most enjoyed seeing on the planets was the animals. We saw a variety of pets from planets we never got to visit. We saw pets more plant-like than animal. The Wofy was a plant/pet like that. It often made noises through its leaves as people approached. Its whistle sounds were sharp-pitched, and if you came too near, the sound hurt your ears. This particular plant-animal didn't move at all, so I told Shaarvan that it shouldn't be classified as a pet.

"It grows attached to its owner and purrs when in close proximity. What would *you* call that, my wife?"

"I'd call that weird."

Shaarvan laughed. It was the good kind of laugh (when he wasn't mocking my ignorance), and his dimples showed deliciously.

Some of the mansions we visited had other pets as strange as the orange octopus with hooves. On Sandorf, there were rainbow fish. They came when you called to them and actually took pellets of food from your hand. They had whiskers like a catfish, and the whiskers tickled.

The Sandorf buyer gave Shaarvan food so I could feed the fish. I thought that the buyer was really nice. He hadn't been touchy-feely either, and he had told Shaarvan that I had a nice smile.

My favorite animals were the laffy pets. I loved them. I thought of them as puppies. Their dainty pink tongues lapped at my fingers and face. They were tiny, no bigger than dwarf bunnies, and roly-poly and fluffy soft. Shaarvan and the owner allowed me to cuddle them, and I discovered they would play when I dragged my hair. I laughed like I hadn't since Earth. I knew Shaarvan was watching me, but he didn't say a word about my sitting down on the floor with them.

Playing with the laffy pets, I realized how much I missed all the animals on Earth. It would be so nice to have a kitten or a puppy, and I really, really missed horses. The exercise machine might offer movements like a horse, but it didn't smell like one or neigh when you came to feed it.

When we left, I begged Shaarvan for a laffy pet or any kind of pet, but you can guess what he said.

"You will soon have a son to care for. You will have no time for frivolous things like pets."

Jerk.

Most of the time, Shaarvan was a pretty tolerant slave owner. I wanted to see all the weird, different alien stuff I could see, and Shaarvan permitted me to see a lot of it. He let me touch sticky plants, and pet boofpaws, taste all kinds of weird dishes, and hear the crabela, which you could only hear if you climbed down into a cavern to do so. Sometimes, I thought maybe Shaarvan even cared about me. He was sweet about some things.

I mean, some guys wouldn't take the time to show you all that stuff. And I really don't think he was wild about climbing down into that cavern. He spent the whole time worrying that I'd get hurt just because I was a little pregnant.

Shaarvan usually took the time to introduce me to the whole spectrum of the new and fascinating, but I wanted to collect it, too. And that he would not allow — no pets, no souvenirs. He wouldn't even let me keep a pretty stone I found on Caliper, and that wouldn't have cost him a penny.

That's not fair. I make Shaarvan sound like a tightwad. Money wasn't the problem. He'd buy me anything I wanted if I'd eat it. He carried a piece of super thick plastic, which he used just like a credit card. He could buy things with it. He just wouldn't let me take anything back onto the ship.

"Shapechanger do not possess things," he repeated every time I begged.

When I'd try to explain that I wasn't Shapechanger, he'd give me the *no argument* sign, a hand jerk from chest outward. I couldn't bat my eyes, beg, kiss, promise, give him puppy dog eyes — nada. He wouldn't relent.

One time, I vowed I wouldn't talk to him anymore if I couldn't take just one little souvenir from Renka. I think Shaarvan thought that was a great idea. I lasted two days without speaking a word. During that time, he didn't have to answer any questions. He didn't have to hear any arguments or complaints. I think he was, quite frankly, enjoying it too much. I had to start talking again before he backslid into the non-communicator he'd been at the beginning, or so I rationalized.

"Shaarvan," I said on day three.

"What happened to the quiet zone?"

"You don't care if I don't talk, do you?"

He laughed like the idea amused him. "No," he said at last.

"You didn't suffer at all?"

"No, actually, I think it was good practice for you."

"Shaarvan."

He looked down at me as if *seeing me* for the first time in three days, and then he really began to chuckle.

"Why are you laughing?" I asked, frustrated almost beyond words.

"I just realized that was supposed to be a Terran punishment," he said, and he kept right on laughing.

Sometimes, Shaarvan was enough to send a person into violence. What would Gandhi have done if nobody noticed? So much for waging war about souvenirs.

If I ever got back to Earth, I would have not one single proof of my trip through outer space. No one would ever believe I was more than a nutcase who wrote for the supermarket rags. "Sure, aliens swept you up in their spaceship," people would say, and their hands would be making loco circles around their heads.

It probably didn't matter too much. We were going in the opposite direction from Earth, but I think it's a Terran attribute to establish proof of visitation. It seemed so unreasonable that Shapechanger traveled more than any other species and never collected anything to show for it. What did they hang on their walls? What collected dust on their shelves?

Shaarvan

Teban has not learned from my warning several Tides ago. He still cannot take his eyes off Shaara when she visits the Control Room. I have spoken to him a second time. I am aware that he is young, but he is also foolish. This time, I relieved him from duty.

After Teban left, I turned and viewed my wife. It was still true that the first thing one saw was her size. Even my crew, most of them commoners, men who rarely grew as large as Shapechanger, all tower over her. I have become accustomed to her smallness. I rarely think of it anymore. Her spirit more than makes up for it.

Was it her size that drew Teban's eyes? Or was it her hair flaring down her back like a pennant of her femininity? The colors in it did entice the eye. Even onboard the ship, the light caught many golden strands. Were those what pulled Teban's eyes away from his common sense? I understood, but still, I could not allow his attention on my wife. I shall leave Teban on Cloister.

It was strange how different Shaara appeared to me as I looked at her now. Her eyes had changed little from their Terran blue. Her cheekbones were only slightly higher. Yet I was positive that she already had the look of Shapechanger. Each day, she became more pleasing to me. It was hard to blame young Teban for his good taste. I could barely take my eyes off Shaara, either.

My son proclaimed himself now. Yet, Shaara remained undaunted by his growing prominence. The child had not slowed her down in the least. Still, she strode forward without complaint, courageous as ever. She seemed to have boundless energy, and that uncontrollable curiosity of hers never dimmed.

Even the sickness that had plagued her mornings left her undaunted. She rallied amazingly and protested when I left her on the ship to unload girls on Sloorum. And the day when I allowed her to walk down to the crabela's cavern, it was I who was concerned that the steepness of the path would prove difficult for her passage. I think she would have jogged down if I had permitted it. She had little fear for her safety at such times. I had to watch her vigilantly.

My wife was close to acceptance of her new life. She resisted the rules less and seemed calmer over my governance, but still, her old life impinged on her thinking too much. She often became obsessed with trivia and of late had waged minor battles over such silliness as souvenirs and cameras.

For several days, she even *punished* me with a regimen of silence. I supposed I should be harsher with her at such times, but the truth is that I savored her peculiarities. I shall never grow tired of the outlandish thoughts that flash across her brain. I find my wife extremely pleasing in all ways.

Chapter Eight
Adaptation

Shaara

I have been disappointed that all the aliens we've seen have looked humanoid. Where were the two-headed Martians and the bug men or giant rock people of science fiction? Everywhere we've been, the aliens vary only in color, hair type, and size. I might as well be on Earth for all the variety of people I've seen. Of course, I asked Shaarvan about it.

"Scientists are divided about that issue," he told me. "Some say that all humanoids were seeded from the same original genes by some God-like race that came before us. Those pillars on Kekor were an example of some of the evidence for that theory."

The pillars certainly had been eerie, and I remembered the feeling of tranquility they projected. Surely, only the wisest of ancestors could have built them.

"The other scientists," Shaarvan continued, "believe that humanoids are just the top of evolution in an oxygen/water environment. Stages of growth from single-celled life seem to evolve upwards into biped, symmetrical, single-headed individuals. Hands seem to be essential for survival among the top species of a planet, and two eyed vision provides the best vehicle for an advanced brain stem."

I understood about half of that. I think if Shaarvan hadn't kept rubbing his foot against my leg and pushing my dress higher with it, I might have understood more. I kept tugging the hem back down, and Shaarvan kept popping out complex words.

"I always thought aliens would look different . . . like all those statues I keep seeing in the gardens and entrees of the mansions," I said wistfully.

"Some of them do. That's where the models of those statues come from."

Shaarvan's eyes were focused on how high he'd managed to raise up my skirt, but I didn't want to be distracted.

I moved away, wanting to hear more. I forgot about getting too near Shaarvan's hands. He reached over and pulled me in front of him.

"Tell me, please, tell me about the aliens," I begged. I tried to hold onto Shaarvan's hands so they wouldn't keep wandering.

"Those aliens need a totally different environment, Shaara," he said as his lips began attacking my neck.

"Shaarvan." I moved my neck away. "Why don't we ever see them?"

"They stay on their own planets." He nuzzled my neck again. I tried hard to ignore it. "I think they find humanoids ugly," he added.

I moaned. Shaarvan turned slightly to find my lips. I gave up. I was silenced.

I was surprised when Shaarvan returned to the subject later in the cafeteria.

"One day, you will meet Tem," he promised. "He is the current head of the Shapechanger on Westla. He has seen the nonhumanoids."

I dropped my tweezers in my plate of klust. I left them there. This was a lot more interesting. "He saw them? He went to their planet?"

Shaarvan picked up the tweezers and wiped them off on a cloth. "Eat, Shaara," he demanded, "or I shall tell you no more."

I already felt like *El Blimpo*, with my kangaroo pouch growing bigger and bigger, but I took the tweezers and poked around in the klust.

Shaarvan continued, "Tem went to many planets, Shaara, and he still did not see all the different species of non-air breathers."

"Why did they let him visit?" I asked, puzzled.

"Are you eating?"

I tweezed in a pile and started chewing. I was on choice number 124 in the food machine. Klust was about as thrilling as eating kindergarten paste.

Shaarvan went on. "Tem changed his shape to that of the planet dwellers. He thought he could establish trade with them, but there was no commerce that was shared by our different bodies."

I swallowed. It was better than chewing the stuff, anyway. "But it would be fascinating to talk with those aliens. You could share ideas and all the research done everywhere."

"Do I gather that you would like to go visiting?"

"Oh, Shaarvan, I wish."

"Talk to Tem. When you hear what non-air breathers are like, you might prefer your nightmares." He smiled teasingly. "You Terrans were all raised as xenophobes anyway."

I protested. "I'm not. And I think meeting aliens with different experiences and ideas would be fascinating."

Shaarvan laughed so hard I thought I must have said something incorrectly. "You have not been eager to meet the divergent thinking of Altarians and Kekorians."

I had no response to that one. I guess he had a point. It was one more thing to occupy space in my poor, overworked brain.

Later, I decided that my answer should have been that hearing non-air breather's ideas didn't mean I had to accept their way. That was the difference. Kekorian and Altarians gave me no other options. Why is it that brilliant answers only come afterwards when you're not having the conversation?

Shaarvan

My wife is deeply interested in the non-humanoids. Who would have thought it — a Terran eager to see the ones who drive the brave to cowardice. She has the heart of a Shapechanger. How could I have chosen such a girl? Was my computer program so exceptional, or is it true that the *Saberey* guard our lineage? And if that tale is true, why did they forsake Tem and look the other way with my brother?

We were approaching the planet Pastondon. Of course, I would not take my wife there. If not for the fact that Stev was an old and good friend, I would not land there at all. What kind of life did I give to the girls I took to him? I asked myself that, and I did not like the answer. I shuddered to think that had I not chosen my Shaara, she might be fated for such a place. It was not good for a trader to dwell on such things, but I could not stop my thoughts of her being sold into a harmful environment. She would be dead in a five-Tide. Her courage, her curiosity, and her babbling tongue would bring her much suffering. Could there be another such as she in the group I was leaving behind?

What kind of wife weakened her mate until he doubted himself so greatly? Was Shaara to blame, or was the doubt in me? Was my brother, Pathe, correct that we were responsible for the fate of these girls and must bear the guilt if their future was not secured in safety and contentment? Yet, I followed in my father's place, guided by the traditions of my forebears. I have not doubted the rightness of their course before. I must give this thought.

My wife has grown big with the child. Her health was good. She glowed with an inner vitality and spoke of our son with an eagerness she failed to hide from me. Shaarac, as I shall call him, has enhanced some of Shaara's adaptation, which was to be expected. She was only at 66.1% absorption in her latest test, and yet the signs of her alteration were steadily becoming more pronounced. Her eyes were not as blue as a quarterTide ago. Her clarity of thought has developed, and her thoughts are projected with a force that promises great ability.

When she bears the child, I shall take them both to Westla for testing. I shall be proud to present my wife to Tem. She honors me.

Shaara

Sometimes, there were planets we landed on that I never got to step foot on. Shaarvan told me that women were not safe there. I wondered why Shaarvan was leaving the girls there then. When I asked, he just shook his head at me and gave me the *no argument* sign. That didn't mean that I stopped wondering about it.

Pastondon was one of those planets that Shaarvan said I couldn't visit. It was a desert environment, and Shaarvan left wearing a short, lacy football jersey and very short shorts. Boy, does he have great legs. I hoped that the women had to keep their eyes down on Pastondon. I didn't want them checking out Shaarvan's legs.

That was the first time I had to spend so long by myself. I was lonely. I cried all night. I couldn't believe how moon struck I'd become, or maybe it was just because I was six months pregnant. Shaarvan told me that's why everything made me cry.

And it was awful. I cried when I couldn't have the laffy pet that had the cutest purple eyes in a roly-poly squeezy-squishy body. I cried when he wouldn't let me ride the horse exerciser anymore because he said it was too rough for my condition. I even cried, sometimes, when he told me I'd done well or he praised my increasing language abilities. Sometimes, I cried when he just looked at me with that cocky attitude of his and the little half-smile that told me he was thinking about me.

I think every drink of water ended up being stored in my tear ducts. I had the cleanest eyes on the ship. If the robots ever needed help washing the floor, I'd be the water faucet.

Luckily, Postodon was the last planet stop before Shaarvan's home world. Luckily — because Shaarvan told me it wasn't safe for me to go tramping around planet side anymore. I didn't see why not. The exercise would be good for me, but you know about the "no argument" sign.

I have started thinking a lot about what Altar will be like. Shaarvan always said it looked like Earth in the places where we hadn't yet destroyed our planet with pollutants and concrete. But it wasn't Altar's geography I worried about.

Shaarvan had a mother, a father, two brothers, and a sister-in-law. It was what *they* were like that concerned me. Would the women be conditioned zombies, obedient to their husband's every whim? Would the men act like the crew, not seeing me or worse, perceiving me like the buyers did as a broodmare? What if his family didn't like me? Was I there on approval? Shaarvan had said he wouldn't sell me, but maybe after the baby was born, he'd give me away if I didn't work out well. I worried about it a lot when Shaarvan wasn't around. Who wouldn't have?

Shaarvan returned from his desert adventure sex-starved, as usual, so I guess none of the planet's women got a good look at his legs. I wished I'd gotten to go. I pestered him with questions, but Shaarvan wouldn't talk about it. He was grouchy when I asked him as if I'd done something wrong, even though I hadn't. He caught me biting my lip when he flashed his signs, and he mellowed out, but he ordered me not to discuss Postodon again.

It had been boring without Shaarvan. I'd been locked inside the room, with only the computer to keep me company. Shaarvan had wired the buttons with meals that were delivered through the granola bar drop. I don't know why one of the crew couldn't have taken me to the cafeteria. It would have been a relief to leave the room, but when I'd suggested that, Shaarvan had almost bitten off my head.

Was there no one he trusted onboard? Did he think that someone would attempt to seduce a halfPass pregnant wife? Or, was it me that he didn't trust to behave while he was absent? Did he think I'd attempt to escape or try to release all the girls locked up in those individual rooms?

After Postodon, we had almost a full thirtyTide in space to travel before Altar. I had only that long to become bi-lingual and to get bigger — talk about making a great first impression. Walrus lady meets alien mother-in-law. And only a thirtyTide to focus on a whole new set of rules and codes of conduct. It was hard not to panic.

Shaarvan was more careful of how he took me now, but my big belly never seemed to dull his appetite. If anything, Shaarvan seemed kinder, warmer, and a whole lot more tolerant. In our room, he talked to me openly about Altar and most of the planets he had visited. Sometimes, he'd even let me ask more than three questions before his appetite kicked in.

However, even if he were more lenient with my crying jags and my many questions, the hand signals still flashed, pain followed disobedience, and he was still the teacher-master, and I, the obedient pupil-puppet. That was the one constant that never changed.

I began to sense when I had the latitude to speak or must keep my mouth shut tight. I learned to watch Shaarvan's eyes and posture for feedback. I learned to listen more than speak, and I discovered that information was always easiest to get after sex.

One day, Shaarvan started referring to my stomach as Shaarac. I thought, at first, it was a new vocabulary word for pregnant. It took a while before he let me know it was our son's name. So much for baby books and discussing whether the boy would be Eric, John, or . . .

It was strange to think of having a son. You can't argue it's not true that you're pregnant when the morning sickness hits, and it becomes a definite fact when you feel the first fluttery butterfly kick. By a halfPass, Shaarac was as real as my fingers and toes. (Shaarvan assured me that my toes were still there.) Little Shaarac, alien or not, was a part of me, and I knew I'd love him when he was born.

I did worry, sometimes, that Shaarac might be deformed. All the scientists would tell you that two people from different planets couldn't produce a child, but it was obvious we had. What would Shaarac look like? A kitty cat?

If these bio-medics were so expert that they'd solved the problem of interspecies co-mingling different genes, why couldn't they have solved the problem they had created in the first place?

It was researching in the computer banks that made me understand about the pills Shaarvan had given me. I couldn't begin to figure out all the technical stuff, but I could understand the part that said that two different species could not reproduce. It was there, right on the computer.

That night's questions were all about what I couldn't understand on the computer printout. Shaarvan told me I didn't need to. He made me so mad sometimes.

I persisted, night after night. Repeatedly, he ignored me or flashed the "no argument" sign. One night, I began to blubber about aliens and deformed babies, and "Why couldn't he tell me?"

At last, he relented. "Shaara," he said through gritted teeth. "You know how difficult you are?"

I nodded my head. I'd heard something about that before. (Like about 3,499 times)

Shaarvan shook his head and called me his *stubborn Terran.* "There is no need for these tears or your agonizing," he said. "I have told you that I shall always take care of you. If you would learn to trust me, you would not upset yourself so senselessly."

I opened my mouth to argue, but his finger flashed the *silence command.*

"All right, Shaara. You will not like this, but I will give you the information, only so you can stop worrying about Shaarac's safety. Shaarac is fine. You are fine."

Shaarvan was quiet a moment, perhaps translating the words in his mind since he was speaking to me in English, a thing he had not done in a quarterPass.

When he started explaining, it was exactly what I'd feared. In the time after my kidnapping, while I'd slept, the process had begun, and the pills had finished it. You could almost say those little white disks were anti-birth control pills.

It hurt when I finally understood. I'd thought, when Shaarvan had told me I was Shapechanger that it was an ownership thing. It wasn't ownership. It was a propagational necessity. The biomedics, the ship's lab, and Shaarvan had changed me. I no longer had Terran chromosomes, or not that many. I had Shapechanger's.

Of course, I cried. I cried at everything, but if you were to lose your heritage, you'd be upset, too. Shaarvan used my body for his desires. I guess I'd gotten used to that. There wasn't anything I could do about it, and I must admit it was a part of my life I did enjoy. But, to find out that he'd used the inside of me, too, and not in the way it came, naturally, but in the way he'd altered it, was like . . . like, not having any core that belonged to me. Devastating.

Somewhere in the back of my mind, this trip had been an interlude. Somehow, I'd planned to return to Earth, and I thought that when I finally did, life would continue like before. I know that didn't make a lot of sense. "Shapechanger mate for life when they plant their seed," Shaarvan had told me once, and another time, he'd said, "You are mine forever. There are no divorces in Altar." But, on some level, I had still pictured returning to Earth . . . someday.

But my stay in the Altarian lab had transformed me into a *nonhuman*. It had made my ticket to Altar a one-way trip.

Just like in those science fiction movies where the nasty aliens try to change Earth's history to achieve whatever horrible aim they have . . . well, Altar had done that to me. They had stolen my biological history, and I didn't like it one bit.

"In order for you to have Shaarac, your DNA *had* to be cellularly altered, Shaara."

Shaarvan was still trying to tell me about the two groups of chromosomes, but I didn't care if I had a hundred groups. My chromosomes were mine.

"Shaara, pay attention. I do not wish to repeat this."

I was angry but not stupid. I listened.

"One is a sex-linked chromosome group, and one is a genetic makeup, your identity. The lab gave you Shapechanger genes in both groups so you have the ability to conceive and so you will never get sick."

Sure, it was nice not to have cavities or cancer or any of the other bad stuff, but . . . a good medical health plan was not an even trade for my humanity.

Shaarvan kept talking. "It took a twentyTide for your cells to divide enough to start changing your chromosomes."

I'd never even known. There I was, having a video game war inside my body, all those Shapechanger genes taking over while my Earth genes died, and I had slept through it all.

Then, Shaarvan told me about those stupid little white pills. *No wonder my Terran genes hadn't had a chance. I'd massacred their defenses.*

"When you deliver Shaarac, it will give you a double jolt," Shaarvan said. "You will be fully of the blood."

Great, Shapechanger in me and within me.

"When a Shapechanger woman gives birth, her blood is as much Shapechanger as mine," Shaarvan told me proudly.

All I could think about was how I'd never be Terran again. In fact, according to Shaarvan, I wasn't even Terran *now*.

Shaarvan was amused that it mattered. "I said you would not like it." He stood up and came closer. "I have noticed you are always resistant to change."

Resistant to change. That was a laugh. He rewires my insides, and I'm guilty of being resistant to change. I gave him my strongest glare.

Shaarvan ignored the look. He came up behind me and dropped his hands down on my shoulders. His hands began to massage my back and shoulders. Was that supposed to relax me, make me say, *oh, well?*

The massage was spreading. Shaarvan's hands had begun to dip lower in the front. I squirmed in my chair. If Shaarvan touched me there or demanded sex, I'd scream.

I breathed a sigh when the hands returned to my back. It was hard not to relax into the massage. His hands were so good.

Shaarvan's voice, when he spoke, was low and husky. His thoughts were moving beyond chromosomes. "Actually, I do not understand why this concerns you at all." He paused to kiss the side of my neck. I shook him off.

He moved to the other side. "Why worry about what is inside your blood? You cannot see it."

Darn. The lips on my neck had made me forget Shaarvan's hands. They were crawling up the sides. No one massaged there. I stiffened and pushed my arms down rigidly. His hands continued massaging my skin. In a minute, he was massaging my breasts. But I was too angry to give in that easily. Shaarvan had promised me those pills would not harm me. "They are for your own good," he'd told me.

Changing my chromosomes was for my own good? So far, I hadn't seen any benefits. I'd gotten a fat stomach, which made Shaarvan happy, lost my heritage, and become a cat woman.

The only area that was a plus was that Shaarac would be OK. So he'd be part cat. Cats were always easy to potty train — no diapers, just sand. Shaarac might not learn to talk Altarian right off, but he'd be able to meow and hiss.

I whirled around, freeing Shaarvan's hands from their possessive groping. Then I backed away and let him have it.

"Maybe I don't want to be a cat woman. It's OK for you to have teeth and fur. Men are supposed to be hairy. But I'd rather be human."

I stamped my foot in emphasis. It felt good. "Too many people are allergic to cats. Everywhere I go, people will be sneezing, and I don't want to respond to 'here, kitty, kitty.'"

I was just warming up now. I had lots more to say. "Maybe you like Shapechanging into a cat, but being *catty* is an insult to a woman."

Shaarvan wasn't even trying to turn me on now. He was too busy laughing.

"Think it's funny? Well, maybe men can prowl around at night, but I don't think you'll like it when I do. And a *cat house* is not a place most men want their wives to end up."

I was getting pretty good at reading Shaarvan's eyes, watching the shifts in his expression, noting the degrees of tension. Captives who are dependent on the goodwill of their owner learn that quickly. It's necessary for survival.

I knew Shaarvan was laughing, but I also knew he was dangerous. Yet, I was so bitter about what the Shapechanger had done to me that I couldn't stop my words.

Shaarvan could easily have revenged himself by becoming a wasp or a flea, even a full-sized amoeba chasing me around the room would have been frightening. But he was gentler now, and I guess he didn't want to scare me too badly.

When he Shapechanged, it was at first almost funny. It certainly didn't scare me. But if being attacked by a horny rabbit doesn't sound that bad, you have to remember — a Shapechanger is always his same size.

Let's just say that after the horny rabbit incident, I stopped talking about cat woman, and for the longest time, if I mentioned *chromosomes* or *DNA*, Shaarvan would start wiggling his nose at me. It was enough to keep me silent.

Shaarvan

My wife was incorrigible. She was in such a state about understanding the DNA process that I finally told her. Then she was appalled. She fought against it, as she had every step of her training. This time, she began to deliver a stream of wisecracks.

I have noticed that when she was the most fearful, she made fun of a situation. I believed it was her attempt at lightening the horror she felt. If that was so, it was a healthy activity for her. However, I still needed to remind her of her place.

I allowed her several minutes to flare up in that manner. I must admit she was funny, but I knew I had to reprove her for it. I think I found a suitable punishment. I took the stories of the Easter bunny that Teea had told me and turned myself into its living caricature. My Shapechange did not frighten her, but she was warned of the danger of her disrespect. I must admit I very much enjoyed the circumstances, but Shaara did not share in my enthusiasm. I think she will be more cautious with her words in the future.

Footnote: I have decided to permit Shaara to talk with certain members of my crew. There are a few older men who can be trusted with her innocence. I shall educate them as to the protocol of such discourse. I shall not permit them, of course, to discipline or correct her. Shaara is a member of the highest-ranking family of Shapechanger. She may be unaware of her new status, but the crew cannot be. They must give her the utmost courtesy.

In this manner, my wife will be prepared to meet my father and other Altarians of rank. Even though she is new, she must be ready for her role on Altar.

Shaara

As we neared his home planet, Shaarvan started making me talk with the crew. There would be three of us at a table, and Shaarvan would sit there listening as I tried to make what I thought was small talk with a stranger.

I was very intimidated. Not only did Shaarvan expect me to respond immediately when I didn't know what to say or how, but I must constantly remember to keep my eyes down. (I never realized how much I depended on gestures and eye contact for communication.)

And when I forgot, especially when I met the eyes of the man in front of me, Shaarvan would be coldly cruel in his tone with me. And, once, when I refused to speak, too frustrated with the difficulty, Shaarvan used the neck hold and humiliated me in front of the other man. It was unfair, and I hated it.

I suppose it was almost as bad for the men. They were as nervous as I was. They had always had to pretend that I wasn't there, and then suddenly, they were required to talk to me. It must have been a difficult adjustment to make for them. Their words were as stilted and stiff as mine, and they knew the language.

The crew were not good about talking slowly either and they didn't enunciate as clearly as Shaarvan. I was not allowed to read their faces or lips, and so sometimes, a question would be completely incomprehensible to me. From time to time, they'd also use words I didn't know. That was not so bad. I was allowed to ask for elaboration, and then most of the men found a way to simplify their words. Still, it was an exasperating time, made worse by Shaarvan's constant presence and my fear of his reprisals. There were just too many laws or courtesies I was required to remember. And, in the process of dredging my poor worn-out brain, I forgot most of the rules.

To be fair, I suppose Shaarvan was lenient with me. He never seemed to mind my failure to speak correctly. Sometimes, I thought he was even a little bit proud of my successes. Yet, when I made one little mistake, like the time I interrupted a man because I suddenly remembered the word I'd been trying to use and wanted to clarify my answer, Shaarvan's rage was so pronounced that his eyes changed their color, and the shadow of a tiger's variegated fur was visible. The crewman almost leaped away. At the last second, the man checked his lurch and broke into a sweat instead. I don't know why he trembled. The tiger had come for me.

Most of the time, I remembered the correct procedure. The crewman would say, for example: "Tell me about Kekor. What architecture did you observe?"

I'd try to give the crewman a logical answer using my limited knowledge of what men wanted to know. Emotional responses were never acceptable. I couldn't say, "I liked it, or it was pretty." I had to give a fact, like, "The architecture utilized stone and glass, etc." Do you know how difficult that was with a limited vocabulary? Getting out any kind of sentence that made sense was a challenge.

And, as if all that weren't obstacle enough, baby Shaarac kept delivering kicks at random moments, and Shaarvan continually toyed with my hair, twirling it around his finger. Occasionally, he stroked my leg with his hand or ran his tongue across my palm. And I was never permitted to pull away. The first session taught me that.

A crewman had asked me to describe the *crabela's* call. I had begun trying to assemble an acceptable response when Shaarvan's finger stroked the inside of my arm. Intent on my answer, I glared at Shaarvan and jerked my arm away. Bad move.

Shaarvan turned alien green tiger-eyes towards me. "Leave us, Sten," he said to the man. "Wait outside the door."

The crewman had taken off without a word, and I'd wished desperately that I could follow. I hadn't meant to anger Shaarvan. He stood up, pulling me in front of him. His hands on my arms felt like claws. I hadn't been brave enough to check to see if they were.

My hands had not been free to plead for liberty to speak. I'd opened my mouth and said, "I'm . . . " I'd gotten no further in my apology. Shaarvan's *Silence* had beaten me to it.

The tiger-eyes faded quickly. I think Shaarvan realized that I'd meant no challenge.

"Shaara, you have much to learn," he said. "I think you try, *sometimes*. But remember this above all else. No matter what else transpires, you must always consider the *Primary.*"

I know there'd been a Primary somewhere in all those lessons about Altar. I remembered hearing the word, but I couldn't remember what the Primary said. Shaarvan must have read it in my eyes. He sighed, shook his head at me, and continued the lecture.

"Shaara, the Primary is that you must always *please* your husband."

His hands no longer gripped my arms with sharp, pointed daggers. I freed one arm and flashed permission to speak. Perhaps Shaarvan saw the confusion in my eyes. He nodded his consent.

"Shaarvan, I *was* trying to please you. I thought you wanted me to speak Altarian. I'm sorry, but I can't concentrate when you start touching me."

"Silence is better than rebellion."

It didn't matter that Shaarvan then flashed the *no argument* sign. I was so frustrated; I was beyond words. I sighed in exasperation and dropped my eyes, but Shaarvan immediately lifted my chin for examination.

"I shall give you no punishment this time," he said in an unemotional manner. My legs started trembling with the threat.

"But do not forget again, no matter where you are or what you do — you have only to remember this, Shaara — that it is I, your husband, that you must please."

For a moment, his eyes flashed green, and the words — "It is I, your husband, you must please —" hung, shimmery like the image of a bright light that lingers long after your eyes are closed. It was frightening, but Shaarvan scared me a lot anyway. He was always so dangerously unpredictable.

I thought that practicing the language was the main lesson I'd been working on. There had been so much more to learn in those trainings.

When Sten returned, I felt terribly embarrassed. Immediately, I tried to answer the question he'd asked me before.

"No," Shaarvan barked out. "Never initiate."

The renewal of Shaarvan's anger was more than I could bear. I started to cry right there in front of both of them.

The crewman and Shaarvan just waited, not saying a word. When I controlled my tears, Shaarvan handed me a cloth and then nodded for Sten to continue.

Every conversation was more or less like that. Sometimes, Shaarvan was even harsher with me. I cried many times. On occasion, I couldn't respond at all, and I broke down because I just couldn't take it anymore. I hated those times the worst, but Shaarvan was the most forbearing then. My mistakes never upset him; only my rebellion brought forth the tiger.

The sessions made me appreciate Shaarvan's patience with me during my months onboard the ship. I realized how aware Shaarvan had always been of my limited vocabulary. He had known which words I knew, and he had tried to limit his sentences to those. His conversations with me made me feel successful and encouraged. The crewmen had no idea how to do that. Thirty minutes with them, even when Shaarvan wasn't distracting me, was almost as bad as the computer's idea of painful language instruction. At least with the computer, I didn't feel disheartened and stupid when class ended.

The conversations and the interactions did help me, though. I received practice not only in the language but also in responding to men in Altarian society. Learning not to initiate conversation and to respond without verbosity were both difficult concepts for me. Under Shaarvan's highly punitive tutelage, I think I learned quickly.

My sittings made me realize that, on Earth, my training had been almost the reverse. We Terrans use small talk to fill our dead air. Whenever I'd felt a silence become too prolonged, I'd thought it was my job to plug it. Altarians never used unnecessary filler, and as Shaarvan continued to work with me, I learned that lags in a conversation were not my responsibility. Actually, when I gained the proper vocabulary, I supposed that conversation with a man would be a lot easier on Altar than it had been on Earth. Because, there, I wouldn't have to pretend to be interested in sports or try to learn the names of all the football and basketball teams just to fill in those spaces.

I was beginning to understand intellectually how conversations were supposed to be carried out in Altar, but my instincts were still all in the reverse. It was those Terran instincts, I was afraid, that were going to get me into trouble. But, after weeks of training, I did begin to feel a little more prepared to meet Shaarvan's family. I prayed that I would remember all the lessons. Even though, on bad days, all the rules swam around in circles in my brain, like liquid in a blender, and whatever was being made inside me, I knew the blending wasn't finished yet.

I fretted about it. I worried that it would be harder to practice a controlled mouth when not in a training situation. I was scared to death I'd forget and initiate a conversation with one of those questions that kept bursting out of me without warning. And, if I did, I knew Shaarvan's punishment would be swift and painful. I hoped he'd keep trying to be patient with me, but it was very difficult learning to be a Shapechanger's wife.

That wasn't all I was anxious about. I still kept agonizing over meeting his family. I so much wanted to know all about them, but Shaarvan rarely spoke of them. He'd mention his parents, but if I asked about the brothers or the sister-in-law, he'd change the subject. And, unlike finding out about my genes, persistence never clarified anything.

The most frustrating thing in the world had to be that hand outward from the chest — the "no argument" sign. I could tell the level of Shaarvan's displeasure by the abruptness of the ending. Sometimes, he made the sign look like a horizontal karate chop. Then it reminded me of our Earth gesture of "cut," which I was sure came from the guillotine's cutting off of someone's head. The way Shaarvan used it, when I asked him about his brothers, looked just like a guillotine cut.

When I asked Shaarvan a question about Tevor, his father, Shaarvan's posture became rigid. He sat up taller and became solemn. I don't think Shaarvan realized his change of position. I think it was just an automatic thing. Was his father a military man? Yet, when I asked him, Shaarvan only laughed at me, and told me that there was no need for an army on Altar because no one would ever dare to attack the Shapechanger.

"My father is the head of the Traders on Altar," Shaarvan told me. "He owns forty-three ships, and those ships have traveled throughout all known worlds."

That was interesting, but it wasn't the kind of thing I wanted to know. I didn't care **who** his father was. I wanted to know what he was like. Shaarvan didn't seem able to tell me that kind of information. All he could tell me was that his father was Shapechanger — like that answered all my questions.

"Why did Tevor choose Teea as his wife?" I hedged, trying another angle.

"Because he started getting older and realized he had no heirs."

"But why Teea?"

Shaarvan smiled into my eyes. "Maybe because she was *difficult*, Shaara."

Shaarvan rubbed his knuckles against my cheek and then placed his hand squarely on my belly. Shaarac moved, and Shaarvan's eyes again smiled into mine. "I think you will need to talk with Tevor about that question," he said after a moment.

"Shaarvan, if I can't converse with a male, I mean, more than responding to questions asked, how can I *talk* to your father?"

Shaarvan continued to smile at me despite the degree of frustration that had entered my voice. "That is between the two of you," he chuckled. "You may never be allowed to, Shaara, but then again, Tevor *may* give you permission. If he finds you deserving, he will grant you the freedom to talk."

"But . . ."

"There are exceptions to meeting a male's eyes and talking with one, Shaara. You already know that sometimes I consent to your doing so when it serves a purpose in my business, but that is only because I am at your side. I am there to protect you, so it is safe."

"Protect me from what?"

"From big, bad wolves like me, Shaara."

I had to smile; Shaarvan was undeniably adorable when he teased and smiled like that. His dimples made my heart do flip-flops, but still, I wished he'd answered the question.

The dimples disappeared as he became serious again. "The other exception to the rule is a close member of the family, like my father. If he does permit you that freedom, Shaara, I shall not forbid it."

I had a feeling that Tevor would never grant me any special favors. I was sure from the things Shaarvan had said and from his body language in talking about his father that Tevor must be a stickler for obedience. I doubted I'd ever be *deserving.* I sighed and changed the subject.

It was interesting how different Shaarvan was when I asked a question about his mother, Teea. His eyes softened. He'd sit slightly forward, relaxed, and he'd tell me stories about how Teea had tried to protect his brothers, Pathe and Thenos, from their father's wrath. She'd never succeeded, but that she had tried seemed important.

"Why couldn't she ever get away with it?"

"Lies are the strongest emoters of all," Shaarvan told me. "They smell like sulfur."

I knew what sulfur smelled like — rotten eggs. No wonder Shaarvan knew that time in the control room when I'd fibbed.

"I've never been able to smell a lie," I said.

"It will come, Shaara."

"You mean after Shaarac is born?"

"Yes, when you are fully Shapechanger."

I didn't want to think about that. I pressed on. "But didn't Teea know about that . . . ? Hadn't she been told that lies smelled?"

"Of course, but she kept thinking her Shapechanger blood would let her get better at it. She would never out-and-out lie. No Shapechanger can do that. She would simply try to evade, but Father caught her every time."

I guess I was looking a little puzzled, trying to make sense of all Shaarvan was telling me. He smiled at me, brushed a lock of hair back, and continued.

"Some women get very good at Shapechanger magic, Shaara. Teea is strong, but she can never be as strong as my father."

"What do you mean — Shapechanger magic?"

It was the wrong question. Shaarvan's eyes shuttered like someone had pulled the blinds down. "Tell me about the laws for Altarian women," he demanded.

It wasn't like we hadn't reviewed this ad nauseum. I heaved another sigh, but I started reciting. "Women must be accompanied by their husbands or guards in public. They may not speak to a male without permission. They may not initiate a conversation with a male. They must not look into a male's eyes without permission. They may not carry a weapon. They may not interfere in business. They must obey their husband in all things. They must obey any male who does not dispute their husband's wishes. They may not be verbose . . . "

I couldn't remember any others, but I knew there were more. I was afraid Shaarvan would be angry that I'd left some out, but I don't think he noticed. I wasn't sure he'd even listened. I think he'd just required me to recite the laws so that I'd know that my question about the Shapechanger was unacceptable. But why, and why didn't he just tell me so, if it was?

Shaarvan

My wife has worn me down with her questions. I should treat her more sternly, but she gazed at me with those soft blue-gray eyes, and I had not the heart to be sharp with her. Yet, what could I tell her about my family? Should I describe my father, whose coldness was only lessened when he looked at Teea? How could my wife understand that? There was no coldness in Shaara.

Nor could I attempt to explain Pathe and his sour, barren *non-wife*. I supposed that Shaara would have sympathy for Pathe. Perhaps my wife would find my role in the matter unforgivable. I did not look forward to seeing the look in her eyes, then. I would not discuss Pathe with her. She will learn the sordid details of the story soon enough.

And then, of course, there was my younger brother, Thenos. I will keep Shaara far from him. Not a finger of his perverted body will ever come in contact with my innocent wife. I would kill him if he even thought of touching my Shaara.

How could I explain such a family to my naïve, young wife? She is worried that they will not accept her. I think she fosters hope that they will be a loving Terran family. My mother will love her, it is true. There will be warmth there between them but from my father and the others? That, I do not believe.

Still, I must take Shaara to the heart of my family. She must be introduced to the blood to learn to know her own. She must be given her title. *Shaara of Shaarvan.* The Shapechanger will record her name on the Somber Tree. And my son, Shaarac, must also be grounded with his lineage. His name will soon be placed at the side of mine. Thus, must it be, for it is the way of the Shapechanger.

Chapter Nine
Introduction to Altar

Shaara

It seemed incredibly quick. A little more than an Earth month, an Altarian fortyTide, had seemed so long to wait when Shaarvan had first told me our destination. But the day arrived, and Shaarvan permitted my presence in the control room, allowing me my first view of Altar.

He had told me that his planet was a lot like Earth, and it truly was — much more so than the other planets we'd landed on. I could look down and see the continents. They seemed scrambled and more coffee brown. The oceans glowed in sapphires, but if Shaarvan hadn't told me otherwise, I probably would have believed that we'd returned to Earth.

We were standing in front of the big picture window (Shaarvan never called it that, of course) and came in behind the two moons. Seeing Chroma, the smaller of the two, orbiting the larger Clofa was strange. That dispelled all my doubts about Altar being Earth.

"The two moons cause constant variations in the ocean tides," Shaarvan told me. His arm pulled me close, and he was nuzzling at my neck.

It made me nervous when he exhibited such public displays. I forgot the silence command and whispered. "Must be hard to surf the waves."

"Did I give you permission to speak, wife?" Shaarvan asked softly. His hand slipped down to rest on Shaarac, who obligingly gave him a very strong kick. "I will allow it, my bold one, but speak softly. What is this *surf the waves*? "

I explained as best I could, and then he laughed, not quietly at all.

"The *Croota* would love to have some tasty feet and legs dangling down in the water. They are smart, quick, and deadly, not like your fish at all, and they are numerous. No one sports in the oceans of Altar."

Shaarvan's eyes, as he talked, were smiling down at me. There was a closeness, a sharing that made me feel warm. I felt Shaarac moving happily inside me. He, too, responded to Shaarvan's friendly words.

"The oceans of Altar are perilous at all times. Ships that sail the oceans are rare."

When Shaarvan took the time like that to talk with me, his hand holding mine, his eyes kind, I sometimes had a fleeting thought that maybe I loved him. Could it be possible to love someone who claimed they owned you?

Shaarvan kept his hand on Shaarac. It amused him to feel his son's vigor. He didn't have to wait long. Shaarac was delighted to share the moment's closeness. Shaarvan's eyes met mine, and he smiled. My heart skipped a beat, and I melted. Yes, I loved him. How could I question it? I loved Shaarvan. I lived for his smiles and his gentle moments.

We passed under the moons, and I could see the moon domes where people lived. They reminded me of the tunnels pet mice and hamsters ran in.

"The moon colonies are where older citizens prefer to live because the enclosed environment screens out the sun and plant pollens. The lesser gravity and the constant, unvaried temperature kept warmer there than on Altar is not as hard on their bones."

"I wouldn't like to live in a rat cage, no matter what my age," I said.

For some reason, my words made Shaarvan angry. He turned and glared at me. "You will live where I decide, wife. The choice is not yours," he said, and all the warmth between us shattered.

I will never understand Shaarvan. How could I ever predict what would irritate him when I never understood why he got angry? Why couldn't I keep my mouth shut? Why did I have to say everything I was thinking?

Shaarvan was silent as he led me back to our room. I didn't feel any more anger from him, but I stayed quiet. I sat down in the computer chair and waited. I half-expected a lecture, but Shaarvan only went to the clothes machine and programmed it for appropriate Altarian clothing.

I was pleased when the machine spit out a long, dark, forest-green dress. It was a lovely, soft velvet. I quickly disrobed and put it on. If only Shaarac weren't so far along, it would have been beautiful. As it was, the bulge in my middle kind of destroyed the dress' free fall to the ground.

Shaarvan's eyes, though, glowed when he turned and saw the dress on me. He walked over to me slowly, his eyes holding mine. His arms encircled me, and he bent to kiss my neck. I thought for sure when his hands slid up my legs, he'd make me get dressed twice. He kissed me long and deep, but then he stepped back with a sigh.

"Come," he said. The regret was strong in his voice. I felt the same way, too. Shaarvan had only to touch me with his lips or fingers to make me ache.

My eyes appraised Shaarvan as we returned to the control room. He was wearing the same velvet green of my dress in his shirt. His pants were cut tight against his legs and thighs. He was very handsome. Again, I felt the pang of wanting him.

Shaarvan knew my thoughts. His hand caught mine, and he lifted my palm to his lips. His tongue drew a pattern on the inside of my hand. He watched me breathe in sharply. He smiled his knowing smile.

"When I take you next, we will be on Altar, Shaara. You will like it there, and our son will join us soon."

Shaarvan's left hand moved down to touch my belly, then he tucked my hand in his, and we walked on. I wished that Shaarvan didn't tease me with his patterns. Now, I was more on edge, alive to his touch, and linked to his inner tension.

Landing on Shaarvan's planet was almost frightening. Altar was not a sleepy spaceport. There were ships in every direction, above us, on our right, landing and rising. Many of them were the mushroom and pyramid ships that Shaarvan said belonged to the Westlan Shapechanger. The port was buoyantly awake, swarming with life and excitement. Already, I felt an affinity with it. It was, after all, Shaarvan's home.

As we landed, I was suddenly so nervous I could barely stand still. I reached out for Shaarvan's hand. He seemed surprised and directed a strangely inquisitive look at me. I rarely initiated touch. I was always too afraid of his reaction, but I was petrified about meeting his parents. Shaarvan's hand was the only support I had.

For a moment, Shaarvan reeled me towards him like a dance partner. His other arm circled my shoulder, and he hugged me close. "Do not be frightened, Shaara. You are my wife. They will accept you." He touched his lips briefly to mine and turned me around to face the door.

It's a good thing I didn't know how horrible my first meeting with his parents would be. I'd have begged to return to our shipboard room. If only I could have.

To continue this tale, please read:

Book 2 of the Shaarvan Series

Shaara of Altar

www.ingramcontent.com/pod-product-compliance
Lightning Source LLC
Chambersburg PA
CBHW070840250626
47159CB00003B/860